Praise for *Shades of Milk and Honey*

"*Shades of Milk and Honey* could easily fit into Austen's canon, except of course for the inclusion of magic. Kowal has captured both the style and content of an Austen novel, adding her own speculative fiction twist. . . . Hits all the high points of Austen's dialogue and plotting while still having its own identity." —The Jane Austen Centre

"Readers will be disappointed only when they finish this enchanting story, which is suffused with genteel charm. The author's judicious and effective changes to aspects of daily life clearly communicate how similar but different this world is from ours. With the grace of *Sense and Sensibility*, a touch of classic fairy-tale magic, and an action-packed ending, this debut novel by an award-winning short story writer will appeal to fans of Jane Austen, Jane Yolen, Patricia Wrede, Susanna Clarke, and even Jasper Fforde." —*Library Journal*

"Kowal's first novel is a beautifully told story of being true: true to love, true to family, and true to art, even when it seems that one of them must give. It's a marvelous and promising debut, and hints at more wonders to come." —Cory Doctorow, *BoingBoing.net*

"*Shades of Milk and Honey* is a lovely, smart, strange novel with everything on earth (and elsewhere) to recommend it. Smoothly crafted with a flair for romance and mystery, this story is one part meticulous manners and one part wild magic—composing a whole that's utterly irresistible." —Cherie Priest

"Simply enchanting, and another great advance in an already impressive literary career. You're going to love this." —John Scalzi

TOR BOOKS BY MARY ROBINETTE KOWAL

Shades of Milk and Honey

Shades *of* Milk *and* Honey

Mary Robinette Kowal

A Tom Doherty Associates Book

New York

This is a work of fiction. All of the characters, organizations, and events portrayed in this novel are either products of the author's imagination or are used fictitiously.

SHADES OF MILK AND HONEY

A Tor Book
Published by Tom Doherty Associates, LLC
175 Fifth Avenue
New York, NY 10010

www.tor-forge.com

The Library of Congress has cataloged the hardcover edition as follows:

Kowal, Mary Robinette, 1969–
Shades of milk and honey / Mary Robinette Kowal.—1st ed.
p. cm.
"A Tom Doherty Associates book."
ISBN 978-0-7653-2556-3
1. Women—Conduct of life—Fiction. 2. Mate selection—Fiction. 3. Sisters—Fiction. 4. Magic—Fiction. 5. England—Social life and customs—19th century—Fiction. I. Title.
PS3611.O74948S53 2010
813'.6—dc22 2010032725

ISBN 978-0-7653-2560-0 (trade paperback)

Printed in the United States of America

10 9 8 7 6

To my grandmothers, Mary Elois Jackson and Robinette Harrison, who taught me the importance of family and storytelling

One

Jasmine and Honeysuckle

The Ellsworths of Long Parkmead had the regard of their neighbours in every respect. The Honourable Charles Ellsworth, though a second son, through the generosity of his father had been entrusted with an estate in the neighbourhood of Dorchester. It was well appointed and used only enough glamour to enhance its natural grace, without overlaying so much illusion as to be tasteless. His only regret, for the estate was a fine one, was that it was entailed, and as he had only two daughters, his elder brother's son stood next in line to inherit it. Knowing that, he took pains to set aside some of his income each annum for the provision of his daughters.

The sum was not so large as he wished it might be, but he hoped it would prove enough to attract appropriate husbands for his daughters. Of his younger daughter, Melody, he had no concerns, for she had a face made for fortune. His older daughter, Jane, made up for her deficit of beauty with rare taste and talent in the womanly arts. Her skill with glamour, music, and painting was surpassed by none in their neighbourhood and together lent their home the appearance of wealth far beyond their means. But he knew well how fickle young men's hearts were. His own wife, while young, had seemed all that was desirable, but as her beauty faded she had become a fretting invalid. He still cherished her from habit, but often he wished that she had somewhat more sense.

And so, Jane was his chief concern, and he was determined to see her settled before his passing. Surely some young man would see past her sallow complexion and flat hair of unappealing mousey brown. Her nose was overlong, though he fancied that in certain lights it served as an outward sign of her strength of character. Mr. Ellsworth fingered his own nose, wishing that he had something more to bequeath to Jane than such an appendage.

He slashed at the grass with his walking stick and turned to his elder daughter as they walked through the maze comprising the heart of the shrubbery on the south side of the house. "Had you heard that Lady FitzCameron's nephew is to be stationed in our town?"

"No." Jane adjusted the shawl about her shoulders. "They must be pleased to see him."

"Indeed, I believe that Lady FitzCameron will extend her stay rather than returning to London as she had planned." He tugged at his waistcoat and attempted to speak idly. "Young Livingston has been made a captain, I understand."

"So young? He must have acquitted himself ably in His Majesty's navy, then." Jane knelt by a rosebush and sniffed the glory of the soft pink petals. The sunlight reflected off of the plant, bringing a brief bloom to her cheeks.

"I thought perhaps to invite the family for a strawberry-picking Thursday next."

Jane threw her head back and laughed. It was a lovely laugh, at odds with her severe countenance. "Oh, Papa. Are you matchmaking again? I thought Lady FitzCameron had it set in her mind that the captain was to marry Miss FitzCameron."

He stabbed the ground with his walking stick. "No. I am merely trying to be a good neighbour. If you have so little regard for the FitzCamerons as to shun their relations, then I have misjudged your character."

Jane's eyes twinkled and she pecked him on the cheek. "I think a strawberry-picking party sounds delightful. I am certain that the FitzCamerons will thank you for your courtesy to them."

The tall yew hedges hugged the path on either side of

them, shielding them from view of the house. Overhead, the sky arched in a gentle shell of blue. Mr. Ellsworth walked in companionable silence beside his daughter, plotting ways to bring her together with Captain Livingston. They turned the last corner of the maze and went up the Long Walk to the house. On the steps, he paused. "You know I only want the best for you, my dear."

Jane looked down. "Of course, Papa."

"Good." He squeezed her arm. "I shall see to the strawberries, then, to make certain they will be suitably ripe for next week." He left her on the steps and went to the hill on the east side of the house, making plans for the party as he walked.

Jane folded her shawl over her arm, still thinking of her father's thinly veiled plans. He meant well, but would surely tip his hand to Captain Livingston, who was, after all, several years her junior. She had first met Henry Livingston before the war broke out when he wintered with Lady FitzCameron while his parents were away on the continent. He had been an attractive boy, with large dark eyes and a thick crop of unruly black hair. Though a favourite of Lady FitzCameron, he had not been back to the estate since, and it was hard to imagine him as a grown man. She shook her head, settled the folds of her muslin frock, and entered the drawing room.

The smell of jasmine nearly overpowered her, burning

her nose and making her eyes water. Her younger sister, Melody, who wove folds of glamour in the corner, was evidently the source of the overwhelming aroma.

"Melody, what in heaven's name are you doing?"

Melody jumped and dropped the folds of glamour in her hands; they dissolved back into the ether from whence she had pulled them. "Oh, Jane. When I visited Lady FitzCameron with Mama, she conjured the loveliest hint of jasmine in the air. It was so elegant and . . . I cannot understand how she managed such a subtle touch."

Jane shook her head and went to open the window so the jasmine fragrance could dissipate with more speed. "My dear, Lady FitzCameron had the best tutors as a girl, including, I believe, the renowned German glamourist Herr Scholes. It is hardly surprising that she can manage such delicate folds." When Jane let her vision shift to the ether, so that the physical room faded from her view, the lingering remnants of glamour were far too bulky for the effect that Melody had been trying to attain. Jane took the folds between her fingers and thinned them to a gossamer weight which she could barely feel. When she stretched them out, they spanned the corner in a fine web. Once she anchored the folds to the corner, the glamour settled into the room, vanishing from view. The gentle scent of honeysuckle filled the air, as if from a sprig of flowers. It took so little effort that she barely felt light-headed.

Melody squinted at the corner where Jane had left the web, as if trying to see the invisible folds.

"Please do not squint, dear. It is unbecoming." She ignored Melody's scowl and turned back to the web. Not for the first time, she wondered if Melody were near-sighted. She could never handle fine work, even with needlepoint, and her glamour seemed limited to only the broadest strokes.

"What does it matter?" Melody threw herself on the sofa. "I have no hope of catching a husband. I am so abysmally poor at all of the arts."

Jane could not help herself. She laughed at her sister. "You have nothing to fear. Had I half your beauty I would have more beaus than the largest dowry could settle upon me." She turned to straighten one of her watercolours on the north wall.

"Mr. Dunkirk sends his regards."

Jane was thankful that her back was to her sister, for the sudden flush she felt would have given her away. She tried to hide the growing attachment she felt towards Mr. Dunkirk, particularly since he seemed to have a higher regard for Melody, but his gentle manner drew her to him. "I hope he is well." She was pleased with the steadiness in her voice.

"He asked if he could call this afternoon." Melody sighed. "That is why I wanted to freshen the drawing room."

The wistfulness in Melody's voice would only be appropriate if she had reached an understanding with him. Jane turned to her sister, scrutinizing her countenance.

A gentle glow suffused Melody's delicate features. She

stared into the middle distance as if her cornflower blue eyes were blinded by a radiant image. Jane had seen the same expression on her own plainer face in unguarded moments. She could only hope that Melody had been more cautious in company. She smiled gently at her sister. "Shall I help you set the drawing room to rights, then?"

"Would you?"

"Of course."

The drawing room already had a simple theme of palm trees and egrets designed to complement its Egyptian revival furniture. For the better part of an hour, Jane and Melody twisted and pulled folds of glamour out of the ether. Some of the older threads of glamour in the palm trees had become frayed, making the images lose their resolution. In other places, Jane added more depth to the illusion by creating a breeze to ruffle the fronds of the glamour. Though her breath came quickly and she felt light-headed with the effort of placing so many folds, the effect was well worth such a trifling strain.

Placed in pairs in the corners of the room, the trees seemed to brush the coffered ceiling, accenting its height with their graceful forms. Between each tree, an egret posed in a pool of glamour, waiting an eternity for the copper fish hinted at below its reflection. Simpler folds brought the warm glow of an Egyptian sunset to the room, and the subtle scent of honeysuckle kissed the breeze.

When all was settled, Jane seated herself at the pianoforte and pulled a fold of glamour close about her. She played a simple rondo, catching the notes in the loose fold; when she reached the point where the song repeated, she stopped playing and tied the glamour off. Captured by the glamour, the music continued to play, wrapping around to the beginning of the song with only a tiny pause at the end of the fold. With care, she clipped the small silence at the end of the music and tied it more firmly to the beginning, so the piece repeated seamlessly. Then she stretched the fold of glamour to gossamer thinness until the rondo sounded as if it played in the far distance.

The door to the drawing room opened. Melody leapt to her feet with a naked expression of welcome on her face. Jane rose slowly, trying to attain a more seemly display. She placed her hand on the pianoforte as the room spun about her with the lingering effects of working glamour.

But only their father entered the room. "Hullo, my dears." The plum brocade of his waistcoat strained across his ample middle. He looked around the drawing room in evident pleasure. "Are we expecting company?"

Melody said, "Mr. Dunkirk said he would honour us with a visit this afternoon."

"Did he?" Her father looked befuddled. "But I saw him not fifteen minutes ago passing through our fields with the FitzCamerons. They looked for all the world as if they were going hunting. Are you certain you did not mistake his meaning?"

Melody's face soured. "His meaning was clear. But perhaps he preferred to spend the afternoon in the company of a lady than a farmer's daughter."

Jane winced as Melody flew from the room.

"Good heavens. What has gotten into the child?" Mr. Ellsworth turned to Jane with his eyebrows high. "Does she think that the whole neighbourhood must dance attendance to her whims?"

"She is young, and . . ." Jane hesitated to commit her sister's potential indiscretion to words, but as her sister had not taken her into confidence, and as Jane feared for Melody's state of mind, she continued on. "I fear she may be developing an attachment to Mr. Dunkirk."

"Does he return it?"

"I do not know." Jane plucked at the waist of her frock. "Certainly his behaviour has been above reproach in every instance of which I am aware."

Mr. Ellsworth nodded, evidently satisfied with that reassurance. "Then we must hope that Melody will not embarrass herself while we wait for this fancy to pass."

The front door slammed.

Jane hurried to the window and peered out. Melody strode across their lawn, heading for the fields between their home and Banbree Manor. Jane caught her breath. "I fear that is what she has set out to do."

Her father looked over Jane's shoulder. "I will go fetch her before she can damage our neighbour's good opinion of her."

Jane nodded, though she wanted to tell her father to let Melody do as she would. Let the headstrong girl make a fool of herself. The rational part of Jane knew that Melody was not her obstacle to Mr. Dunkirk's affection. Jane was too plain and too quiet to engender any interest in him or any other gentleman.

Jane turned from the window and sat at the pianoforte. She loosened the fold around it, silencing the distant song. Quietly, she began to play, losing herself in the music.

Her fingers played across the keys and stroked thin folds of glamour on the ebony and ivory surfaces. Colours swirled around her in answer to the sound. She welcomed the lightheadness, which came with too much glamour, as a distraction from her cares.

When the front door opened, Jane kept her attention on the pianoforte; she did not want to speak with Melody and have to comfort her. But that was unjust; Melody could not know how her actions affected Jane.

Bringing the song to a close, she looked up as the colours around her faded.

Mr. Dunkirk stood in the door to the drawing room. His face was alight with wonder. "Forgive me, Miss Ellsworth. I had told your sister I would call, and am later than I intended."

Jane's heart pounded with more than the effort of glamour, and a flush of warmth flooded her face. "Mr. Dunkirk. You have just missed her; she has gone for a walk with my father." Jane rose with care, pretending that gray blobs did not swarm in her sight. She would not swoon in front of him. "But please be welcome. May I offer you tea or a brandy?"

"Thank you." He accepted the brandy she offered and raised the glass to her. "I had no idea you were such an accomplished musician and glamourist."

Jane looked away. "It is an idle amusement, sir."

"Nonsense. Music and the other womanly arts are what brings comfort to a home." He looked at the palm trees and egrets adorning the drawing room. "I hope to have a home such as this one day."

Jane put her hand on the piano to steady herself, keenly aware that she was alone with him. "Indeed," she murmured. "Though I would venture to say that Robinsford Abbey is most gracious."

"But it lacks that comfort which a wife with the gift of glamour might bring." He inhaled the scent of honeysuckle and exhaled it in a sigh. "Other men might seek a lovely face, but I should think that they would consider exquisite taste the higher treasure. Beauty will fade, but not a gift such as this."

"Do you not think that glamour might be learned, whereas beauty is innate?"

"Glamour, yes. But not taste, I think." He smiled and inclined his head. "It was a conversation close to this topic which prompted my tardy arrival here. Have you had occasion to meet Mr. Vincent?"

"I'm afraid you have the better of me."

"Ah. I thought Miss Melody might have mentioned him.

Lady FitzCameron has retained his services to create a glamural for her dining hall. He is a fascinating fellow, who studied with Herr Scholes and has taken commissions from the Prince Regent. Stunning talent, really."

"Did Melody meet him, then?" It seemed odd that her sister would fail to mention it. Visitors to their neighbourhood were rare enough to be newsworthy, but to have such an accomplished glamourist in the vicinity was a significant event.

"I thought they met, but perhaps I am mistaken. In any case, Mr. Vincent had much to say on the subject of glamour, which I think you might find to be compelling arguments in my favour."

The front door opened again, and Melody flung the door to the drawing room wide. Her face was red and stained with tears. When she saw Mr. Dunkirk, she uttered a cry of dismay and fled the room.

Jane closed her eyes. Poor Melody. What must she think? To see Jane quite alone with a man for whom Melody so clearly had an attachment must seem as a betrayal. When Jane opened her eyes, he had set his glass down to greet Mr. Ellsworth.

Excusing herself, Jane said, "I feel that I must look in on Melody."

"I hope she has not suffered an accident," Mr. Dunkirk said.

Jane's father harrumphed and mumbled that Melody had twisted her ankle while walking, to which Mr. Dunkirk replied, "Then I will leave you to tend to her." He took his leave, only pausing at the door to say, "May I call again?"

"Of course!" Mr. Ellsworth beamed. "Come whenever you like."

"Then I will see you soon." Mr. Dunkirk bowed. "Your daughter is a credit to you, sir."

When the front door closed, Mr. Ellsworth said, "Well. Melody needn't have worried after all. 'A credit.' "

Jane smiled. "Indeed."

Still glowing with the words of Mr. Dunkirk's praise, Jane went abovestairs and knocked on the door of Melody's room. Such a small thing, those words, but it was the first time she could recall coming to his special notice. He had always been courtesy itself when in her company, but her attachment to him grew more from how he treated others than from any sense of his having regard for her.

She leaned her head against the door, listening for sounds within the chamber. "Melody?"

"Go away."

Jane sighed. "Dear. Let me come in."

The silence stretched out, during which Jane had time to examine the wood grain on the door and the age worn in the softened edges of its panels. "Melody?"

Cloth rustled within, and the key turned in the lock, unlatching the door. As Jane opened the door, she was in time to see Melody fling herself artlessly upon the bed, where the rumpled spread shewed how she had spent the time since Mr. Dunkirk's visit. Her golden curls lay across the bed in an intricate lacework, and tears glittered on the ends of her lashes like diamonds.

Jane closed the door behind her and leaned against it, regarding her sister. "Mr. Dunkirk sends his apologies for his tardiness."

Melody sat up with alarming speed. Her face flushed. "Is he still here?"

"No. Papa let him understand that you had twisted your ankle while out walking." Jane sat next to her sister.

Placing her hands over her eyes, Melody groaned and fell back on the bed. "Now he thinks me clumsy as well as overexcited."

"I am certain he does not." Jane wiped her sister's brow, which was hot with the force of her excitement. Reaching into the ether, Jane conjured a cooling breeze to soothe her.

Melody pulled her hands away from her eyes, though she kept her lids shut and turned her face toward the breeze. "But he does. I stammer and blush when he is present. La! Do not tell me you have failed to notice." She opened her eyes and glared up at Jane.

"Until today, I had not the faintest notion that you had any affection for Mr. Dunkirk beyond that of a neighbour. Indeed, I had thought you were no more fond of him than of one of our uncles." Jane smoothed the folds of her skirt, praying that her own countenance was not as transparent to feeling as Melody's. "Have you an understanding with Mr. Dunkirk?"

Melody burst into laughter. "An understanding? My

dear Jane, Mr. Dunkirk is gentleness embodied. He is grace and elegance and all that is good in a man, but he is also too conscious of propriety to betray anything beyond courtesy. This is why I had such hopes when he said he would come to call today. I had hoped that perhaps he might have begun to pay notice to me as myself instead of as simply the daughter of his neighbour." She groaned and rolled over, burying her face in her arms. "What did you speak of while I was out acting the fool?"

"Very little. Music. Glamour. Lady FitzCameron's glamourist." Jane waited to see if Melody would speak of meeting Mr. Vincent, but her sister charged ahead with her litany of woes.

"You see! I could not speak with him of any of those. I am talentless." She clenched her fingers in her hair, and for a moment Jane feared that Melody would pull her own hair out by the roots.

Such were Melody's torments that Jane gave away the comfort that she had taken for herself. "Not true. Ask Papa what he said about you."

In an instant, Melody turned over, her eyes a vivid, sparkling blue. "What did he say? Do not teaze me, dear sister."

"He said, 'Your daughter is a credit to you.' "

Melody's face lit with an inner glow of pleasure, but it faded quickly. "He was surely speaking of you."

"I was there, Melody. Why would he speak of me as if I were not present?" And as Jane spoke, she realized that it was true. She had taken Mr. Dunkirk's words to her heart as if he had spoken of her, but he surely had not. Who else could he have meant but Melody? Had his compliment been intended for Jane, he would have said, "*You* are a credit to your father." There could be no doubt that he had meant Melody. Jane reached out and tousled Melody's hair to mask the wet disappointment that seeped through her. "You see?"

Melody sat and flung her arms around Jane. "Oh, thank you. Thank you for telling me."

"Of course. We must find these small comforts where we may." Jane held her sister and wondered where she would find her own small comfort. She reached for a new topic, to push away the pain of this one. "And now, should I chide you for not telling me of Lady FitzCameron's glamourist?"

Melody pulled back, her eyes wide with guilt. "Oh, Jane! I am so sorry. When Mr. Dunkirk said he would call, all else slipped my mind. Though, truly, there is little to tell."

"Well. What sort of man is he?"

"More bear than man, really. La! He said barely two words the whole visit. Lady FitzCameron says that he is frightfully clever, but I did not see any signs of it."

"Fortunately, one does not need to speak to weave glamour." Jane sighed. "I should like to have had the training that he has had."

Melody leaned against Jane, wrinkling her nose. "See! You chide me, but you already know more of him than I do."

"You were too distracted by Mr. Dunkirk, I daresay."

When Melody blushed, her infatuation was writ large on her cheeks. "Oh, Jane. Is Mr. Dunkirk not the most handsome, most admirable man you have ever met?"

"Yes." Jane hugged her sister, so that her own telling countenance was hidden. "Yes, he is."

Two

Doves and Roses

As the family sat in the drawing room after their nuncheon, the maid brought in the afternoon's mail on a silver tray and handed the letters to Jane's father. He looked over them and harrumphed before passing one heavy letter to Jane's mother.

Jane tried not to stare when Mrs. Ellsworth exclaimed at the address. Out of the corner of her eye, she could see the weight of the paper, and the thick wax seal on the back. As Mrs. Ellsworth slid her penknife under the sealing wax, Jane kept her focus on the watercolour before her.

"The FitzCamerons are hosting a ball!" Mrs. Ellsworth nearly dropped her penknife.

Her hands trembled, making the invitation rattle like a miniature thunderstorm.

Though the FitzCamerons were their closest neighbours, Lady FitzCameron was rarely in residence at Banbree Manor since her husband's death, preferring to spend her time in London with the ton. There had not been a ball at Banbree Manor since before Melody's coming out.

Melody dropped the fringe she had been crocheting, and ran across the drawing room with a squeal of delight.

Mr. Ellsworth shook his head. "I suppose young Livingston has arrived?"

Mrs. Ellsworth studied the letter without responding. "Oh! She barely gives us time enough for the modiste to make us new gowns."

Jane glanced at her father. Though she coveted a bolt of dove silk at Madame Beaulieu's Haberdashery, Mr. Ellsworth was constantly worried about funds. His face softened as he looked at Melody. "Well. I want my girls to shew well against young Miss FitzCameron."

"Charles, do not be silly." Mrs. Ellsworth put the letter down and glared at Jane's father. "Everyone knows that Miss FitzCameron uses glamour to enhance her appearance, though with the dowry she carries, most overlook it."

"Does she?" Like most men, Jane's father was nearly blind to glamour folds. Jane rather thought it was from lack of training than lack of a native ability, for he could do rudimentary warming spells when hunting.

"Yes," Mrs. Ellsworth said. "Heavens, do you not recall how her teeth stuck out like a horse?"

"Oh. Yes. I thought perhaps she had outgrown it."

Melody snorted. "La! If she had, then she wouldn't faint all the time. If you watch at the ball, I am certain that she will faint. When she awakens, she will cover her mouth with her hand until she has the charm in place again."

"But why does her mother allow it?" Mr. Ellsworth asked.

Jane put down her paintbrush. "I imagine that she turns a blind eye because she hopes her daughter will make a better match for it."

"Neither of you do that, I hope."

Jane picked up her paintbrush again, painfully aware that he looked at her, not at Melody. "I trust that it is apparent that I do not."

As she laid brush to paint, dabbing at the blue with which she hoped to capture yesterday's sky, her father blustered with a poor attempt at apology. "No, of course. Both of my girls are too sensible for such nonsense."

"Sensible." Jane guided the brush across the page, letting the paint bleed across the water. "Yes. We are sensible girls. Are we not, Melody?" Such was her bitterness that she could not contain that small jab at her sister's moment of weakness from the day prior. At the paling in Melody's cheeks, Jane instantly regretted her pettiness and tried to turn her words. "And so we should have no trouble in using our sensibility to convince you of the importance of new gowns for the ball."

"Oh yes, Charles. They must have new gowns." Mrs. Ellsworth rapped the table as if she could summon the modiste instantly.

Mr. Ellsworth laughed, belly quivering under his waistcoat, and the moment passed. "New gowns and a new thing for your hair." He gestured loosely at his own thinning pate. "Whatever it is the young ladies are using to look becoming these days."

"May we go now?" Melody danced on the carpet of the drawing room as if she were already at the ball dancing a cotillion with Mr. Dunkirk.

Jane shook her head to clear it of such thoughts and returned her attention to her watercolours. It was unjust of her to have so much petty bitterness toward Melody. Jane knew well that she was past what small bloom youth had provided her. She had resigned herself to life as a spinster; there were certainly less honourable ways to spend one's declining years than attending to the comforts of one's parents. Her best hope was to see Melody happily wed. Indeed, her own welfare could be said to depend on such a happening, for if Melody gained the sort of husband which she deserved, then after their parents' passing he would welcome the spinster sister into the household like a good and true gentleman. Then Jane might have the pleasure of helping raise Melody's children and they need not trouble with a governess. Indeed, that seemed her best and only course.

She washed her brush in the glass of water she kept on the side table for this purpose and smiled at Melody. "I should like to go as well. I have been eying a bolt of silk at Madame Beaulieu's for some time now."

"Then you shall go and you shall take the carriage." Mr. Ellsworth leaned back in his chair, and Jane felt the weight of his love for them warming her.

Melody dashed across and wrapped her arms about his neck, kissing the bald spot on the top of his head. "Thank you, Papa." She danced out of the room, followed quickly by Mrs. Ellsworth, who rattled opinions about fashion and cut as if she were getting a new gown herself.

Rising more decorously, Jane took a moment to set her paints in order before following her mother and sister out of the room. When she turned, her father was regarding her with a curious tenderness. He held out his hand to her.

She crossed the room and took it, wondering at the softness in his gaze.

"Jane, will you humour an old man?"

"Of course, Papa."

"I should like to see you in something with roses." He squeezed her hand. "Will you do that for me?"

Her beloved dove silk vanished from her mind. How could she deny him such a simple request? "I will speak to Madame Beaulieu. I am certain sure she will have just the thing."

Roses. What made him think of that?

Always when Jane went into Dorchester she found herself instantly wearied by the bustle of people and carriages as they went about their business. She could not help but wonder where they were all going, and what business pulled them out of their homes with such urgency.

There, she saw two boys who must be on their way to someone's home with a delivery. One carried a greengrocers box, full of lettuce, turnips, and early strawberries. The other, a cold-monger, worked folds to keep a chill over the box.

And there, the girl walking with the young man in a captain's uniform: was he her brother returned from the seas or a suitor hoping to win her heart? Indeed, the town seemed quite full of young men in uniform, their epaulets and decorations adding a brilliant sparkle to the streets. Jane scanned the crowd, wondering if any of the young men were Henry Livingston and if she would recognize him should she see him. Indeed, he might be the young captain she had seen walking with the girl; the man's hair had been dark enough.

The carriage pulled to a halt in front of Madame Beaulieu's Haberdashery, and Jane alighted from the carriage with her mother and sister. Though Mrs. Ellsworth had no need of a new gown, she had contrived to convince Mr. Ellsworth that it was in their best interests for her to have one as well. After all, she said, would not their neighbours recognize the shabbiness of her own dress as an indication of their income? And to imply that their income was lower than it was would surely harm the chances of the girls at wedding. Almost, Jane had declined to accompany them at that point, knowing that her own dress would be but a masquerade to delay the confirmation of her spinster status a while longer, but for all that, she was still a girl at heart and loved pretty things.

Madame Beaulieu's establishment was crowded with girls. From the chatter it seemed that Lady FitzCameron had invited every eligible maid from the surrounding countryside.

True to her promise to her father, Jane looked through the bolts of cloth for one with roses figured upon it and found but one, which seemed too garish for her features. The roses, worked in yellows and peaches, would only make her skin more sallow.

Jane's mother and sister finished their business with the modiste and excused themselves from the overcrowded shop while Jane, who had yet to reconcile herself to the yellow roses, continued to look at cloth in hope of finding a fabric which suited her.

In despair, she was about to chuse the yellow cloth when the modiste approached. "I thank you for your patience, Miss Ellsworth. How may I help you?"

Jane sighed and fingered the bolt of yellow roses. "My father has made a special request that I be dressed in roses. I throw myself on your mercy, for this is the only cloth with roses, and I fear I lack the complexion that it requires."

Madame Beaulieu stepped back and narrowed her eyes, raking them over Jane and seeming to take the measure of her soul as well as her figure. "The figured cloth won't do, but we may suggest roses by other means."

She led Jane across the shop to a bolt of palest pink. Picking up the cloth, she continued to the bolt of dove grey which Jane had so coveted. Laying the two cloths together to assess the colours, she nodded in satisfaction and then turned to Jane. "Something like this, I think."

Her fingers danced in the air, pulling folds together in a small simulacrum of Jane. This tiny manikin wore Jane's beloved dove silk, but with an open pelisse of the pink. A high waist with a sash of that same pale pink gave the illusion of height and slenderness to her figure. Softening Jane's face, Madame Beaulieu had added a turban *à la Oriental* which cupped her hair with cunningly wrought silk roses. A simple shawl completed the picture with elegant grace. She caused the image to execute a graceful pirouette so that Jane could see how the garment moved. Jane breathed in wonder. She hardly dared hope that her own true form would look half so fetching. "I believe you have it, Madame Beaulieu."

The modiste smiled and beckoned one of the shop girls. The girl trotted over and took over the folds from the modiste, moving the image to the back of the shop and leaving her mistress free to spend her energies in other designs. Although Madame Beaulieu could tie off the image and have it remain in place without effort, if she did, the shop would soon become crowded with manikins. A shop girl could be trusted to maintain the integrity of the folds while moving them to the back of the shop, where they could be tied off until it was time to make the dress. As the curtain to the back parted, Jane caught a glimpse of other tiny manikins, as if the ball had already begun in miniature.

After she spoke with Madame Beaulieu briefly of the price and time of delivery, Jane moved to the door, only to find her way blocked as a gentleman entered the shop. For a moment, the light from the street rendered his identity a mystery, leaving only a man-shaped silhouette. Then he stepped fully into the shop and Jane saw that it was Mr. Dunkirk. He swept his hat off at once upon seeing her. His face brightened, unexpectedly. "Miss Ellsworth, this is good fortune."

"How do you do, Mr. Dunkirk?"

"Very well, thank you, the more so because my sister has come for a visit." Here he turned and beckoned a girl, surely no more than sixteen, with the same dark eyes and noble brow as her brother. "May I present Miss Elizabeth Dunkirk?"

As the girl bobbed a curtsy, Mr. Dunkirk continued, "Miss Ellsworth is our neighbour, Beth. She is a woman of uncommon taste." He twisted his hat in his hand and looked deeply apologetic. "I do hope I might impose on you for some advice. Beth arrived only yesterday, and as we were not expecting the FitzCamerons to be so generous with their hospitality, I find myself tasked with the duty of outfitting my sister for the ball. Were we in Downsferry, my mother would handle this, but I do not feel equal to the task. Could you . . . ?" His voice trailed off, and most unaccountably, he flushed, as if embarrassed. "I am quite hopeless in such things. I may recognize a gown of exquisite taste, but do not know the necessaries of a young woman's toilet."

"I would be delighted to help, Mr. Dunkirk." The shop grew almost unbearably warm. "Though, I must assure you that Madame Beaulieu is a modiste of excellent merit. Miss Dunkirk is in safe hands, you may be certain."

He nodded and looked somehow disappointed, so Jane continued, "But of course I shall be happy to share my own feeble opinions as well."

"Thank you." He gave a short bow. "I do not like to impose, but I would like for Beth's first ball to be all that it may."

"Her first ball?" Jane felt the enormity of the task all the more. "Is she not out yet?"

Mr. Dunkirk looked so grave for a moment that Jane quailed, wondering at her trespass. "No, Miss Ellsworth. This is to be her coming out. My mother has—" Here he broke off. "I beg your pardon. I do not wish to tire you with my family history."

"No. The apology is mine. I should not have been so indelicate in my question. It hardly matters if a girl is out or not. I abhor the custom myself, but . . . well, let us consider what dress might suit her, shall we?"

During all of this conversation, Miss Elizabeth Dunkirk stood behind her brother, listening with silent attention. Her dark eyes were serious beyond her years, sharing some of the reserve of her brother. On her, the high forehead, which seemed so representative of nobility in Mr. Dunkirk, ended in the same glossy black mane, but curved in a more delicate manner, as if her thoughts were tempered by her femininity. Her bones were delicate and her skin as fair as the moon, with blue veins beating at her temples. There was about her an air of sadness, which left Jane most curious. And to be "not out" in a family of such consequence as the Dunkirks! It was most odd, but Jane would not pry for all the world by word or deed.

She offered Miss Dunkirk her arm and led her to a bolt of white lawn, the fabric most appropriate to a debutante. Then Jane suggested a deep green velvet which she thought might set off Miss Dunkirk's hair to advantage. Jane tried to affect the graceful, easy carriage of her sister, but could scarcely be at ease, so conscious was she of Mr. Dunkirk's presence. How had he come to have a good opinion of her taste? In the two years since Mr. Dunkirk had settled in the estate at Robinsford Abbey, she had never felt his notice of her to be beyond that of a neighbour, save for that one afternoon when she had been alone with him in their drawing room.

Jane held her breath as Miss Dunkirk fingered the rich cloth. When the girl agreed that it was very fine, some of the tension left Jane's body. Between the two of them, they selected a lace which complemented the cloth as well. Jane found it much easier to imagine a dress for someone else than for herself. By the time Madame Beaulieu disengaged from her other customers to see to Miss Dunkirk, Jane had sketched out a plan for a gown which pleased the girl greatly.

Madame Beaulieu admired the ideas which Jane wove in

the air for her, and added her own touches to bring the whole together. Miss Dunkirk turned to her brother, her eyes asking the question to see if he approved.

At this tacit invitation, he stepped closer and bent to examine the design. He smiled. "I was quite right that meeting you was a stroke of good fortune, Miss Ellsworth. This is everything I had hoped."

His approbation brought a flush to Jane's cheeks, and she turned to his sister to hide her disconcertion. "I do hope, Miss Dunkirk, that you are pleased as well."

"Thank you, I am." The girl kept her eyes downturned, but a hint of a smile curved her cheek.

Before they parted company, Jane sought and received the Dunkirks' assurance that they would call at Long Parkmead so that they might have an opportunity to converse in more agreeable circumstances.

Three

Nymphs at the Ball

Banbree Manor was lit with thousands of candles and hung with streaming folds of glamour, which filled the halls with light and colour. Jane adjusted the shawl draped over her dress, which was all that Madame Beaulieu had promised, and patted her turban *á la Oriental* to make certain it was poised to best advantage.

"You look charming, Miss Ellsworth." Mr. Dunkirk appeared behind her as though drawn out of the ether himself.

"Thank you, Mr. Dunkirk." Oh, that he had not caught her preening like a vain idiot. She cursed her ill-placed vanity and vowed to keep her hands at her side.

He bowed to her before turning to Melody.

"And Miss Melody Ellsworth illuminates the hall with her presence, as always."

His bow to Jane's sister was precisely as deep as it had been to her, but Jane could not help noticing that Melody was luminous while she was merely *charming*.

"But where is Miss Dunkirk?" Jane asked.

"My sister is within. Lady FitzCameron would hear of nothing less than having her maid do Beth's hair. I expect that I shall not recognize her when she descends." He looked self-conscious for a moment and then said, "I cannot thank you enough for your kindness to my sister."

"It has been my very great pleasure to make her acquaintance."

The smile on Melody's face seemed set in plaster. "I look forward to making Miss Dunkirk's acquaintance as well."

"Thank you. You are both very kind." Then, as if in an effort to cast off the mood and embrace the festivities in Banbree Manor, he said, "Have you seen Mr. Vincent's glamural yet?"

"No, indeed, I have not." Melody's eyes, wide and cornflower blue, fixed on Mr. Dunkirk as if he were the only person in the crowded hall.

"But you must." He held Jane with his gaze. "I would very much like to shew it to you."

Her heart danced to a faster tempo than the music in the hall. "I should like to see it."

"He has an exquisite command of glamour, which I think will appeal to you." Then Mr. Dunkirk turned back to Melody and the room grew dimmer. "May I detain you from dancing for a trifle longer?"

"Of course." Melody followed him artlessly, so that it seemed he led only her to the dining hall, with Jane an unwanted straggler.

There, a combination of glamour and paint contrived to turn the hall into a nymph's grove. Though yet incomplete, the illusion teazed the spectators with scents of wildflowers and the spicy fragrance of ferns. Just out of sight, a brook babbled. Jane looked for the folds which evoked it, and gasped with wonder at their intricacy. Her perception of the physical room faded as she traced each fold in an effort to understand it.

Mr. Dunkirk and Melody whispered behind her. Of course, they could not see the effort which went into the art, and would consequently become bored with it more quickly. She shook herself, focusing once more on her surroundings.

A broad-chested man stood in front of her, watching her too intently. As soon as Jane focused on him, he broke his gaze, acting as if he had not been staring at her. Then a swirl of guests streamed between them and he vanished into the crowd.

Puzzled, Jane turned back to Mr. Dunkirk and Melody. "Did you see the gentleman standing there?"

"No." Melody shook her head, curls bobbing around her cheeks. "What did he look like?"

Jane resisted the urge to pat her own hair, forced into

curls with an iron. "Tall, and very broad of chest. His hair was chestnut and curled about his head like Gérard's portrait of Jean-Baptiste Isabey." She stopped speaking as Mr. Dunkirk gave a start of recognition.

"Why, Miss Ellsworth, you have seen the artist himself."

"I wish Mr. Vincent had stayed so that I might compliment his work."

"I am certain that the regard with which you viewed the glamural was ample compensation." Mr. Dunkirk gestured to the other guests around them. "You see how few stop to pay heed."

"That is because it is a ball, not a museum." Melody wrinkled her nose and looked wistfully toward the ballroom.

Mr. Dunkirk bowed. "Then may I ask for a dance?"

"Of course." Melody took his offered arm.

Before he led her away, he turned to Jane. "Miss Ellsworth, I trust you will also honour me this evening."

Melody stiffened beside him, very slightly. Her eyes seemed to beg Jane not to dance. And how could she? How could she compete with her beautiful, charming sister? "Thank you, Mr. Dunkirk. I feel that I would like to remain here and admire the glamural for a while. I do not quite understand how he is reproducing the brook sound. It has not repeated yet."

Mr. Dunkirk and Melody made their apologies for leaving her unaccompanied, but upon her assurances that she wished to study the folds and twists of glamour, they retreated to the ballroom. Jane moved slowly about the perimeter of the room, lost in her own thoughts. She paused again where the sound of the brook was loudest and began to look deeper, trying to understand how the glamourist had managed to make the sound continue without repetition. The fold was not tremendously long, as one might expect, but was rather thick and wound back on itself after a very short distance, surely no larger than a dinner platter. Jane put her hand on the sideboard to steady herself and looked deeper still. As she did she perceived that the sound of the brook was made not of one fold, but of several braided together. Each carried a part of the brook's babble and each was of a slightly different length so that the various sounds changed their relation to one another as they spun through the cycle, thus creating the illusion of variation. Jane smiled at the artfulness of the technique and pulled her vision back to the room at large.

The man, Mr. Vincent, stood opposite her once again. Jane started when she saw him and then smiled, resolving to address him and compliment him on his work. She took two steps toward him, no more, before he abruptly turned and walked away. She knew that he had seen her—indeed, he had been staring at her when she emerged from her study of his work—and yet he had walked away as if she were not there. No: he had walked away with a clear desire to avoid her company.

Jane hoped she had not offended him by her curiosity

into his methods, but he truly was the most accomplished glamourist she had yet encountered. He made her own not inconsiderable skills seem paltry and mean. Among the questions that Jane wished to ask Mr. Vincent, she was most curious about how long it had taken him to do the work in this room. While he did use physical paint as a foundation for his glamour, the amount of illusion piled and layered upon the room would have taken Jane weeks to create.

Satisfied with her viewing of the dining hall, and not anxious to chance further offense to Mr. Vincent, Jane followed the sounds of the music to the ballroom. There she found the company engaged in a quadrille.

Jane looked around for faces she knew. Mr. Dunkirk was dancing with Miss FitzCameron, who was smiling as if she wanted all the world to see the glamour masking her teeth. Such vanity, and yet she fooled no one save for Jane's father. At the other end of the set, Melody danced with a young officer with a fine head of dark hair. He laughed, spinning her in the next step of the quadrille. The laugh gave Jane a jolt of recognition as she remembered seeing him in town walking with a young woman the day she went to Madame Beaulieu's.

Jane watched her sister, who seemed to be enjoying herself enormously, and then caught sight of Miss Dunkirk. She was being escorted by Mr. McIntosh, an elderly Scotsman who still had a fine love of the dance. Miss Dunkirk did not seem cowed by his enthusiasm, which somewhat surprized Jane. The girl's green velvet mantle shewed off her slender figure to advantage. Ringlets of hair escaped from under a bandeau of matching green and lay against her neck like a necklace of jet.

Working her way through the press of people, Jane made her way to where her mother and father stood on the sidelines. Mrs. Ellsworth leaned close and said, "Don't they look fine! I daresay that Melody will capture the officer's heart before the evening is out."

"Melody could not fail to capture anyone's heart." Jane said and shifted her gaze to Mr. Dunkirk, wondering that he had given up the dance with her sister rather than retaining her hand for the next set. Or had Jane stayed in the dining hall longer than she intended?

"But this would be such a fine match, don't you think?" Mrs. Ellsworth insisted.

"He dances well, but more than that I am not willing to say without any acquaintance with his character."

"But Jane, you know him well. That is Henry Livingston, Lady FitzCameron's nephew."

Shocked, Jane returned her attention to the young captain. As he turned, she saw something of the boy he had been when he last visited Lady FitzCameron at Banbree Manor. He retained the same arch of the brow and flashing eyes, but the soft roundness of youth was gone from his cheeks, leaving more rugged features in their place.

Mr. Ellsworth took Jane by the other arm. "Perhaps you would like to dance with him next, Jane."

"If he asks me to dance, Papa, I shall be happy to oblige, but I am otherwise content to watch."

"If he asks, you would be a fool girl not to be pleased," Mrs. Ellsworth said, rapping Jane's hand with her fan. "Any man that would have you should be encouraged."

Jane set her jaw and did not respond to her mother's provocation. Seeing this, Mr. Ellsworth patted her hand and drew her a little away from her mother. "Do not fret, dear. She is ill-tempered because she wishes that Captain Livingston would ask *her* to dance."

Laughing, Jane said, "Then you should dance with her, Papa."

"Ah. I am not so nimble as I was."

The song ended and the dancers left the floor, milling about to seek new partners while the musicians began the next set. Mr. Dunkirk appeared rather suddenly in front of her. "How did you find the rest of the glamural, Miss Ellsworth?"

"Very well, Mr. Dunkirk. Although the mysterious Mr. Vincent once again put in an appearance and vanished before I could pay my respects. I begin to think that my attention offends him."

"I am certain you mistake him. It is more likely, is it not, that he did not wish to disrupt your enjoyment of his work?"

"No. For I had met his gaze and clearly started toward him with the intention of speaking. He turned and left quite abruptly."

"Odd," said Mr. Dunkirk. "I've run across him once or

twice out on the grounds, and he has always seemed most amiable. I shall introduce you at the next opportunity. I venture a guess that like many artists he is shy about his work"—he glanced at her—"and, as this piece is yet undone, perhaps he does not wish to hear compliments of it."

"Ah. I think you have the right of it. I had not thought of how it must be for him to have people tramping through and looking at his half-finished glamural."

The musicians finished the next dance, and again the guests began shifting about, exchanging partners. Jane noticed that Melody was still partnered with Captain Livingston. Both their faces were bright with merriment.

Beside them, Miss Dunkirk now danced with a young man closer to her age. Jane smiled to see her so happy.

Mr. Dunkirk turned to follow her gaze. "Would you care to join me on the dance floor, Miss Ellsworth?"

Jane looked again at Melody, laughing with Captain Livingston. "Yes, thank you. I would be delighted."

Though it was not her custom to dance, as it made her limbs appear more gangly and awkward than graceful, Jane enjoyed the dance with Mr. Dunkirk. He was attentive and graceful as a partner. She felt her own steps gradually flowing with more ease as the dance progressed. When it ended and he excused himself to dance with his sister, Jane was prepared to retreat to her father's side, only to find her hand requested by Mr. McIntosh. The old gentleman was so jolly that she could find no excuse for putting him off, and so joined in the dance with a will to enjoy it. The only burr in her enjoyment was that Melody was still dancing with Captain Livingston. Jane was certain that her mother was pleased at his solitary attention to Melody, but for propriety's sake, it would be best if he asked another young woman to dance. It was true that Melody far outshone every other woman at the ball—with that perfect composition of form, grace, and youthful spirits—but a true gentleman would not be so presumptuous as to hold a partner through so many sets.

Once the dance began, Jane had little time for reflection before Mr. McIntosh whirled her about as if she were a bundle of hay. She was quite as breathless at the end of the dance as if she had tried to unfurl a house-sized fold. As soon as she could, she thanked Mr. McIntosh and then escaped to her father's side, carefully keeping him between her and Mrs. Ellsworth.

"You looked well on the dance floor," Mr. Ellsworth said.

She thanked him and then said, "I wonder if you might ask Melody to dance."

"What?" her mother demanded. "Why?"

"For propriety's sake, would it not be better if Captain Livingston danced with some of the other ladies? I am certain that Lady FitzCameron cannot be pleased that her favourite nephew is ignoring the rest of her guests."

At this, Mrs. Ellsworth started and looked around, craning her neck for Lady FitzCameron. "Do you think? I had not thought of it, but of course you are right, dear. It would not do at all to offend Lady FitzCameron. Charles, go and dance with her. Go and dance with Melody at once."

Mr. Ellsworth pushed through the dance floor until he arrived at Melody's side. Though she was clearly not happy, she had no choice but to acquiesce to her father's wishes. Captain Livingston, thus relieved of his favoured dance partner, turned to find the nearest substitute, and lighted upon Miss Dunkirk. She was standing next to her brother and had a becoming flush of exertion upon her cheeks. When Captain Livingston bowed and requested the dance, she looked to her brother for permission before accepting gravely.

Jane hoped that Mr. Dunkirk would come back to ask her to dance again, but he turned to the young woman closest to him and engaged her for the next set. Jane passed the whole of that set trying to steer her mother to a conversational topic other than Melody and how well she looked.

"Oh look! Miss FitzCameron has fainted. I told your father she would. Didn't I tell him?" Mrs. Ellsworth scurried forward, adding to the press of people surrounding the poor girl, no doubt anxious to see how much the glamour had been masking. Jane stayed where she was, unwilling to participate in the shew of vulgarity in which her neighbours indulged by acting as if Miss FitzCameron were a curiosity on display. Jane could hardly believe that Lady FitzCameron would tolerate such a thing, knowing the toll that extended glamour use must surely take on her daughter's health.

Though she did not intend to watch, Jane could hardly fail to notice the effect of Miss FitzCameron's faint. Lady FitzCameron rushed forward, crying, "Livia!" and then directed the two closest gentlemen to help carry her ailing daughter to the side of the floor. By coincidence, Miss FitzCameron had been overcome when the figures of the dance carried her between Captain Livingston and Mr. Dunkirk, surely two of the most eligible bachelors in the room.

So neatly did she remove these gentlemen from the ladies on which they were attendant that Jane began to wonder if, in fact, it were not deliberate. Had anyone save her noticed, or was it a mere accident of timing? Miss Dunkirk looked lost on the dance floor without a partner, so Jane slipped through the crowd to her father, and suggested that he escort the young woman.

He happily acquiesced, leaving Jane with Melody.

"Did you see him, Jane?"

"Who?" Jane said, as she drew Melody to the side of the floor, though she knew well who Melody meant.

"Captain Livingston! If there is a more handsome, graceful man, I know not where to find him. He is all that is courtesy. And wit! La! Such wit he has, and his tales of his work with the navy are fascinating. He has made a fortune for himself with his captures, and at so young an age."

"I am certain you did not think so highly of him when he left a frog in your sewing kit."

Melody laughed. "Indeed. He reminded me of that as we

were dancing. So droll. He said that had he known what a beauty I would become, he would have left roses for me instead."

"I am certain he would have still left frogs. Boys of that age do not think of girls and roses in the same thought."

"You are cruel, Jane. He is so noble and gracious."

"Were he truly gracious, he would not keep your hand through three sets of dance. Truly Melody, I thought you knew better."

Melody stopped and tossed her head, eyes sparkling. "And I thought better of *you*. Jealousy is unbecoming on you, dear sister. It is not my fault he finds *me* beautiful."

Even in the crush of the ball, with the noise of the people and the singing of the instruments, Melody's words were a thunderclap to Jane's ears. Never had her sister attacked her in this manner. Never had she thrown her appearance out like a badge of honour. Jane opened her mouth to reply, but no words came. Her cheeks flushed with anger, and she turned, deciding to leave rather than say something she would regret later.

But she found her path blocked by the very Captain Livingston of whom her sister thought so highly. He smiled and sketched her a very pretty bow.

"Miss Ellsworth! I had hoped to see you this evening. Your sister has spoken so highly of you, and I have such fond memories of you from my time here in our youth."

Jane arched an eyebrow, unable to resist needling Melody.

"Fond memories, Captain Livingston? Would those be the memories of the frogs or of the snails?"

He threw his head back and laughed so heartily that Jane could not keep her hard feelings, for he clearly appreciated a joke upon him. "By my word, Miss Ellsworth. Your wit is as quick as I remember." He offered his arm, eyes twinkling. "Would you give me the honour of this dance?"

With a bare glance at Melody as she accepted his proffered arm, Jane said, "Thank you, yes." She glided onto the floor, leaving Melody standing on the side.

Her minor victory soon soured, as it became clear that Captain Livingston danced with her only to find out more about Melody. His every question was about her taste and character. What amused her; what did she find of interest? The musicians seemed to slow their tempo, stretching the half hour of the dance out into an eternity. As they danced, the small grace which had slowly come to her movements while dancing with Mr. Dunkirk vanished, leaving her with all the elegance of an animated stick figure. When Melody passed them, already partnered with another gentleman, Jane saw how every man turned to watch her sister dance, how she moved as if the music were part of her.

Jane left the floor after the dance with Captain Livingston and retreated to the dining hall, where she would not have the danger of being asked to dance again. She spent the remainder of the ball there, trying to lose herself in admiration of Mr. Vincent's glamural. Its creator remained elusive, and twice she thought she saw him but when she turned the corners were empty. Jane could not shake the feeling of being watched. Finally she realized that she was so hungry for companionship that she was inventing phantasms.

The ball crept until the wee hours of the morning, when all the girls spilled out of Banbree Manor and into their waiting carriages, like flowers spilled from a bridal bouquet. Jane followed them, her dress gray as ashes, the roses on her habit a failed camouflage.

Four

Neighbours and Salts

The morning after the ball, Jane sat in the drawing room, painting, while her mother and sister dissected the joys of the night before. Their pleasure in disparaging other young women's gowns was interrupted by the unmistakable sound of horses in front of the house.

Melody dashed to the window to peer out. "It is the Dunkirks!"

Mrs. Ellsworth exclaimed, "Melody! Do not gawk. What will Mr. Dunkirk think of you staring out the window like a girl not yet out of the schoolroom? Sit down at once."

"Will not my eagerness please him more, that I am so anxious to see him?"

Any comment was forestalled when the maid

knocked upon the door to announce Mr. Dunkirk and Miss Dunkirk.

Miss Dunkirk hung behind her brother, much as she had at the shop, so that Jane could easily imagine that she had not been out in society much at all. The Ellsworths welcomed the Dunkirks warmly and began the conversation with such simple forms as the weather, both how it had been and how they thought it would be. Then they turned to discussing how it had been the year previous and comparing that to the current weather for Miss Dunkirk's benefit so that she might understand what luck she had with the fairness of the weather for her visit.

This led naturally to an inquiry as to how she found the country for riding.

"I have not seen much yet, but what I have is very nice," Miss Dunkirk said. "I adore riding. You cannot think how much I do."

"Indeed, Beth rides a fairer mare than any horse in my stables. I am hard pressed to keep up with her."

"Oh, Edmund, if you would rid yourself of that old gelding then we could go much farther afield." She laughed at her brother, shewing the first real warmth Jane had yet seen in her, and turned back to the company. "I plan to have Edmund shew me everything there is to see in the neighbourhood."

Mr. Dunkirk laughed. "I shall hardly have time to attend to my business while you are here, I see. I will know the landscape better after your visit than I do now."

"You must ask Jane where to take your rambles. She is always going about out-of-doors with her paintings," Mrs. Ellsworth said.

"Do you paint, Miss Ellsworth? Edmund told me about your music and skill with glamour, but he did not tell me you painted as well."

"I did not know," her brother said.

Gesturing at the walls, which had several of Jane's better pieces hanging upon them, Mrs. Ellsworth said, "All of these are her work."

Miss Dunkirk sprang from her seat and ran to the nearest; it was a small watercolour of Melody at Lyme Regis. The light on that day had been exactly suited to shewing off the coils of her golden hair. Picked out in the golds of late-afternoon light, her hair seemed to dance on the breeze; an effect that Jane had enhanced with subtle glamour when Mr. Ellsworth had hung the picture in the drawing room. If the watercolour were ever moved, the glamour would remain tied to the spot, leaving a ghost of waves and golden hair drifting against the wall until the folds gradually frayed and unraveled back to the ether. Jane had seen such things in an aging cathedral her family had visited on holiday. For now, though, the painting and glamour intertwined to give the hint of life to the portrait.

Miss Dunkirk clapped her hands together as she looked at it and then the next. "Oh! Dear, how beautiful these are! Do but look, Edmund, how sweet! I adore art, but I have not the slightest skill in it myself."

"That is because you do not apply yourself, Beth. It is but a matter of practice, truly."

An odd expression crossed Miss Dunkirk's face and she lowered her head as though she had been reprimanded.

"Your efforts are well worth the time which you have spent upon them." Mr. Dunkirk strolled across the room, studying each painting with an attention that surprized Jane. "These accomplishments are what make a home comfortable."

Melody said, "I thought that a home was made comfortable by those who live in it and their regard for one another."

"This is true, Miss Melody, but if one presumes the affection which should be in all homes, then those homes which are most comfortable are also those which possess an understanding and appreciation for the arts."

Melody flushed as though she had received a rebuke. Mr. Dunkirk was still studying a painting and did not see the red spots appear on Melody's cheeks, though if he had, he would undoubtedly have thought her all the more beautiful. Jane kept silent, not wanting to add to her sister's discomfort, but neither did she want to end it. Though she knew it was unjust, Jane could not help resenting her sister for her very presence.

Their mother had no such compunctions about holding her tongue. "Jane's painting is nothing compared to her glamour. She is so terribly clever at weaving music and glamour together. Why don't you play something for us, Jane?"

Horrified at her mother's proposal, Jane demurred. "I am certain that Mr. Dunkirk and his sister do not want to spend their leisure time listening to me."

"Oh, but I do, Miss Ellsworth." Miss Dunkirk spun. "Truly I do. Edmund has said so much about your skills, and I very much want to experience them for myself. Just the small hint I see from your efforts here has made me hungry for more."

Jane attempted to demur again, though her attention was caught by the fact that Miss Dunkirk had said that Mr. Dunkirk had spoken of her. But surely it was not unusual for a brother to give an accounting of his neighbours. And as glamour could be said to be the only distinction which Jane possessed, of course it is what he would have mentioned to his sister.

Such was Miss Dunkirk's insistence, soon joined by her brother's, that Jane found herself seated at the pianoforte. Jane began to play a simple gavotte. As the music poured from the pianoforte, she stroked folds of glamour into being, suggesting a forest clearing with a faun gamboling in the afternoon sun. It was no large matter to add a few birds flitting over his head with the high notes of the tune.

When that song ended, Miss Dunkirk burst into rapturous applause, begging for another. So great was the girl's approbation that Jane began a rondo and suggested figures of nymphs dancing around them in time with the music. These were not as fully rendered as the glamour that adorned their walls, since it required much effort to produce a moving image extemporaneously while she played, but the effect was nonetheless pleasing.

At the song's end, Jane could not help but notice Mr. Dunkirk's steady gaze. He stood behind his sister's chair and seemed still lost in the spell of the music. A greater compliment was not possible.

The room spun somewhat, and Jane decided that the wisest course would be to refuse another song, or at least an embellished one, lest she faint at its conclusion. But when Miss Dunkirk asked Jane to explain how she caused the nymphs to surround them, a particularly tricky piece of glamour, Jane could not resist re-creating it, which in turn led to another piece of glamour. Jane found herself shewing the girl how to create folds until they were both breathless and overwarm with their efforts.

Perceiving the strain on Miss Dunkirk's delicate frame, but glad that some of the melancholy had left her features, Jane said, "You are welcome to return at any time, my dear, and I would be happy to shew you what little I know."

"We should take our leave, Beth," Mr. Dunkirk said, "and let the Misses Ellsworth return to their afternoon's engagement." He stopped and turned. "But where is Miss Melody?"

Jane suddenly realized that Melody had slipped out of the room without any of them noticing. She sprang to her feet, forgetting the effort she had just expended on glamour. The room spun around her, darkened, and she tumbled to the floor.

A sharp burning odor penetrated Jane's nostrils, making her sneeze. She opened her eyes. Miss Dunkirk sat on the sofa next to her, passing a small glass vial of smelling salts under her nose. Nancy, the housekeeper, stood behind her, twisting her hands together and bobbing convulsively in a series of curtsies. Across the room, Mr. Dunkirk attended to Jane's mother, who had collapsed in her chair, as though *she* had been the one to overextend herself.

Miss Dunkirk said, "She is awake!"

At this, Mrs. Ellsworth roused from her swoon. "Oh, Mr. Dunkirk. What should we have done? What should we have done if you had not been here?"

Jane flushed with sudden understanding. It seemed that Mr. Dunkirk had lifted her to the sofa. She eased herself into a sitting position, careful lest she faint again. "I beg your pardon, Mr. Dunkirk. I am sorry to have troubled you."

"Not at all, Miss Ellsworth. It is I who should apologize. I fear we took unpardonable advantage of your hospitality."

Miss Dunkirk's eyes were wide with upset. "Yes, please forgive us, Miss Ellsworth. I oughtn't have asked you to play another song, but your playing was so very pretty."

"No need for forgiveness. I had worked a number of

other bits of glamour this morning and quite forgot the amount of strain I had undergone. I should know better than to spring up after a song, so I am far more vexed at myself than at anyone else."

"Oh, yes," Mrs. Ellsworth exclaimed, pressing Mr. Dunkirk's hand. "The fault is entirely Jane's. You mustn't give it a moment's more thought. Truly, you mustn't."

Mr. Dunkirk compressed his lips and looked to Jane, his gaze seeming to carry a suppressed laugh. "Well, Mrs. Ellsworth, regardless of where the fault lies, I believe it is clear that Beth and I should end our call."

Miss Dunkirk rose reluctantly from the sofa. "You will be all right?"

Jane smiled. "Of course. Have you never fainted from too much glamour?"

"Oh, I do not know how to work glamour." The girl shook her head, and some of the darkness of her mood came back to her features.

"What?" Mrs. Ellsworth cried. "But how could your mother allow it? What were your governesses doing to earn their keep if not teaching you such necessaries?"

Jane interjected, "Mama, you might as well ask why everyone does not play the piano. Glamour is no more a necessary than that. I am certain that Miss Dunkirk is accomplished in other regards."

Despite Jane's efforts at glossing over her mother's callous remarks, Miss Dunkirk retreated into her shy silence once again. Mr. Dunkirk placed a hand on her shoulder to guide her out, and Jane was reminded of the girl's youth.

They parted, with Jane promising to return their call on the morrow. Only when they had departed did Jane realize that in the flurry over her swoon, all had forgotten Melody. She almost went upstairs to look in on her sister, and then, upon reflection, decided that Melody needed to learn to govern her passions.

She would have to do that without Jane.

Five

Art and Glamour

Tapping her fingers on the brim of her straw bonnet, Jane tried to evaluate the effect of the Venetian glass cherries against a green silk ribbon. She had hoped that the ribbon would serve as leaves, but it was too pallid. She switched to a velvet ribbon in a deeper Pomona green, pinned the cherries in place over it, and nodded in satisfaction. Though it was silly to take so much care with her appearance, she had never before called at Robinsford Abbey by herself. If not for the excuse of returning Miss Dunkirk's call, she would not have dared to go now, but there was no harm in looking her best in case she happened to see Mr. Dunkirk.

"That looks very nice." Melody stood in the door of the drawing room.

"Thank you." Jane considered the drape of the ribbon, pretending that it held all her attention. Melody had not spoken to her beyond the barest monosyllable since the Dunkirks' visit the day prior. Desire to mend the breach between them warred in Jane's breast with simple pride. She had done nothing wrong to make Melody deal her such petty slights, but she knew it would be fruitless to wait for Melody to apologize. "Are you feeling better?"

"Pardon?"

"You were cross yesterday, so I thought you must be unwell."

"Oh." Melody twisted her fingers together. "Yes. I had a headache."

Jane took up her needle and thread. "I see. It was a pity you had to leave without saying good-bye. Mr. Dunkirk remarked on your absence."

"Did he?" Melody crossed the room to sit next to Jane. "I only left because I had nothing to add. No wit or art, which seem to be the only things anyone appreciates. I am just a pretty face." As she said this, her voice went beyond self-pity and into genuine despair.

Jane bit the inside of her cheek. She truly *had* monopolized the Dunkirks' visit. "You are more than that. You are charming and good-hearted."

"When I am not cross, you mean."

Jane set down her hat, laughing. "Yes, but I have yet to meet the person who remains charming and good-hearted while cross."

"But Mr. Dunkirk was right when he said that beauty fades. Except for artificial beauty." Melody reached out and touched the delicate glass skin of a cherry. "I was hoping that you might teach me about glamour."

Startled by the request, Jane could not disguise her pleasure at being asked. She took Melody's hand in hers. "Of course. Whenever you like."

"Oh, thank you, Jane." Melody squeezed Jane's hands with both of hers. "I mean to start at once so that . . ." She loosened her grip on Jane's hand. "What is the matter?"

Without thought, Jane's gaze had dropped to the hat on her lap. "Oh. I had promised to call on Miss Dunkirk today." She kept her eyes lowered rather than watching the disappointment cross Melody's face. "May we postpone until this evening?"

The room was quite still for a moment, and then Melody lifted the hat off Jane's lap. "Of course. I would not want to interfere with your duty to our neighbours." She set the bonnet on her head and crossed the room to a mirror. Adjusting her ringlets under the hat, she bared her teeth in some semblance of a smile. "Are you wearing this to the Dunkirks'?"

"I had thought to, yes. Melody, dear, you are welcome to come with me. I am certain that they did not intend the invitation for me alone."

"Are you?" Melody spun in front of the mirror, admiring her reflection from all angles. Even unfinished, the hat looked fetching on her. "And yet you did not think to mention it to me until now. La! Jane, I rather believe that you did not intend for me to ever know. Well. I am certain that I do not want to intrude where I am not wanted." She took off the hat carelessly and set it on the table under the mirror.

Despite the overly dramatic nature of Melody's words, they stung because they bore some truth. She did *not* want to disappear into the background of her sister's charm. To stop the guilt she felt, she said, "But I do want you to come. I did not see a time to mention it because you have been so cross with me. Do say you will come. We can work on glamour tonight."

Melody studied her for a long moment before nodding. "I—I would like that. Thank you."

Though she still felt the tension between them, Jane was determined to give Melody no further cause to doubt her affection.

When Melody had changed into a gown suitable for morning calls—primrose calico, trimmed with crisp white ribbons—and Jane had finished her millinery endeavors, they set out to Robinsford Abbey. They spoke of nothing consequential on the walk, merely the weather and whatever in the landscape caught their eye.

Chief among these was Robinsford Abbey itself. The long drive wound through the orchard that the monks who had originally built the abbey had planted. Ancient gnarled trees gave way to a broad expanse of lawn, which rose gently to the Gothic splendor of the abbey. Each facet of the leaded glass in the high arched windows reflected different aspects of the view. Though its age was obvious, the abbey was so well-maintained that it gave every appearance of being as comfortable as a modern structure.

Still, as they entered the vestibule and presented their cards to the butler, Jane could not help but feel dwarfed by the grandeur of Robinsford Abbey. Melody did not seem to be affected by the echoing stone halls, as though her beauty made her immune.

Once in the drawing room, Jane at once felt more at ease. Miss Dunkirk stood, waiting to receive them, and crossed the room with evident pleasure. "Oh! How glad I am to see you. Edmund has gone on an errand, and I find myself quite at loose ends."

"Such a shame!" Melody took Miss Dunkirk's hand and tucked it under her arm in a shew of solicitude. She led her to the sofa, away from Jane. "That he should leave you here without amusement. La! I am quite shocked, I must tell you, that a man of your brother's intelligence should display such an uncaring sensibility to his own sister."

"Oh, he is not like that at all. Whenever he has been away, Edmund always brings me a present to make up for my time alone."

Jane trailed behind them and settled on a mahogany Sheraton chair next to the sofa. The drawing room might better be called a library, for one wall was almost entirely given over to books. The mahogany furniture reflected strong masculine tastes, even down to a pair of crossed sabres on one wall and a set of dueling pistols in a rosewood box on the mantel. A neatly rendered glamour created the illusion of fire in the fireplace, lending the room a coziness it might have otherwise lacked. For all his professed admiration of glamour, Mr. Dunkirk indulged in little other display of it. Not even the prints on the walls, which tended to hunting scenes or architectural studies, shewed any enhancement.

Small talk followed, detailing the weather, then the quality of the tea which the butler brought as well as praises of the china it was served in, which was an exquisite example of Delft bone china. During all of it, Melody held Miss Dunkirk's attention with ease while Jane resigned herself to the background. Only two years separated Melody and Miss Dunkirk's ages, while Jane, at eight and twenty, was a good ten years older than her sister. It was small wonder that the two young women found so much to discuss.

Jane occupied herself by gazing out the window at the expanse of lawn and the woodlands beyond, not paying full attention to their discussions of fashion and novels, only nodding or laughing occasionally as the subject warranted.

Then a man stepped out of the woods. Though he wore the garments of a laborer, the easel on his back clearly marked him as Mr. Vincent. For a moment, he seemed to stare directly at Jane. She stiffened in her chair at the challenge on his face, then relaxed as she remembered the way the light had reflected off the leaded glass; he could not see her. Indeed, when he set his easel down and placed a canvas upon it, his intent became clear.

Jane turned her attention back to Miss Dunkirk and Melody and cleared her throat. "It appears that we have an admirer."

Both girls exclaimed and turned to follow her gaze. "Who? Where? Well, I never! Is that Mr. Vincent?"

They fairly flew off the sofa, running to the window to look out at him. Melody leaned against the casement. "Is he painting us?"

His easel angled slightly away from them, and to Jane's eye, their window was not the subject of his attention. "I do not believe so."

Miss Dunkirk said, "I wonder if Edmund has asked him for a study of Robinsford Abbey?"

"Perhaps that is his present to you." Melody squinted. "I do wish I knew what he was painting."

"The abbey, surely," Jane said, though she too wanted to see the canvas.

Melody spun, her face glowing with delight and mischief. "Shall we go out to see?"

Jane recalled Mr. Vincent's forbidding expression when she had studied his work at Banbree Manor. "Oh, no. I do not wish to disturb him. Were I him, I should hate to have someone watch me."

"La! Jane, you are too nice in your sensibilities. You

spent an afternoon with the Dunkirks watching you play piano and work glamour. How can you think that Mr. Vincent would object to us calling on him when he is on Miss Dunkirk's lawn?"

Miss Dunkirk bit her lower lip. "Did we trouble you, Miss Ellsworth?"

"Not in the slightest," Jane said, "but those were pieces which I had practiced and were intended for performance. Mr. Vincent has barely laid brush to canvas, so to come upon him now would be the same as coming upon me while I am practicing a new piece. No matter his talent, he cannot enjoy having someone look upon an unfinished piece."

Melody wrinkled her nose. "You always think you know how other people feel, but really, Jane, we saw an unfinished piece at Lady FitzCameron's ball, and he did not seem to mind then."

Miss Dunkirk took Jane's side. "I am afraid I think Miss Ellsworth has the right of it."

"Poo. Let us ask him rather than guessing." Melody unlatched the casement, threw it wide open, and leaned out. "Mr. Vincent!"

He turned his head sharply, and a deep frown creased his face. Jane backed away from the window and stepped into the shadows, praying that all he saw was the two young women leaning out toward him, not her.

He nodded once, then returned his attention to his canvas.

"What are you painting?" Melody called.

The glamourist did not respond. Jane put her hand on her sister's arm. "Let him alone, Melody."

Miss Dunkirk looked from one sister to the other, concern drawing a line between her brows. Moving away from the window, she said, "Seeing Mr. Vincent reminds me of a question about glamour, Miss Ellsworth. Might I impose on you?"

Grateful for the distraction, Jane followed her, leaving Melody at the window. "Of course."

"I want to surprize Edmund and add some of the enhancements that you have in your home—you can't think of how often he speaks of it. But I am having some trouble with the folds you showed me, simple though they were."

Mr. Dunkirk had spoken of her work? Jane flushed so that she might have blamed the fire if it had not been glamourous in nature. "I would be delighted to help, if I may."

Without turning from the window, Melody said, "To be sure, Jane is frightfully clever with glamour." Her voice was all that was sweetness, but Jane knew well that she was irked.

"What sort of effect did you have in mind?" Jane looked about the room, evaluating possibilities.

"I hardly know. My parents—that is, I have had little opportunity for study, so I am not certain what is possible." Miss Dunkirk straightened a picture on the wall. She seemed to be overly conscious of her lack of schooling in glamour. It was hardly her fault, though. A young woman had little control over whom her parents selected as a tutor.

"Perhaps if you told me what folds you were having difficulty with?"

Miss Dunkirk flushed and gestured at the painting—an oil of a stag in a forest clearing. "I wanted to start with something small, so I thought to make the trees move in the wind, as you did with Miss Melody's hair. My brother was most taken with that effect."

Looking at Melody, framed in the window as if she were art, Jane thought that it was rather as likely that Mr. Dunkirk was taken with the subject matter as with the technique. "I am afraid that effect is more complicated than it appears. Though it is small, one must stitch together many tiny folds to create the illusion of movement."

"Oh." Miss Dunkirk looked crestfallen.

Jane thought back to her first lessons. "Perhaps a simple enhancement of light would serve? Near the books, shall we say? I think it might add some warmth and play well off the gilt on the binding." It was also a simple glamour that did not require very subtle manipulation. Melody's attention was still held by the scene outside. To draw her back in, Jane said, "Melody, perhaps you could help me demonstrate?"

Her sister turned around, clearly startled to be addressed.

"Oh, Miss Melody!" Miss Dunkirk clapped her hands together in delight. "I did not realize that you were also a glamourist."

"I do not claim the accomplishments of my sister, but we did have the benefit of the same tutor." Melody glided toward the bookcase with a poise and voice that suggested more comfort with the art of glamour than Jane had yet seen her demonstrate.

"Here, I think." Pulling a fold of glamour from the ether, Melody stitched it across the bookcase with large, awkward threads. The fold was bulky and wrinkled; light careened across the gilt titles. "You see how simple it can be."

"Indeed." Jane came to stand by Melody, suppressing a wince at the clumsy effect. "And with only a little effort you may adjust the folds to the brightness or shade you desire." She plucked Melody's stitches free and shook the folds out so that the wrinkles dropped away. "You see how I can stretch the fold to change the degree of brightness? Thinning any fold in this manner will mute its effect."

"You make it look so simple." Miss Dunkirk studied the air with the abstracted gaze so indicative of an absorption of glamour.

"Here." Jane plucked the fold from the shelf and held it out to Miss Dunkirk, the light dripping in strands of gold that would have made Rumpelstiltskin proud. "Hold it so that you can feel its weight, and then I will show you how to thin it."

Eyes widening, Miss Dunkirk accepted the sheer fabric of light from her. At first it wrinkled in her hands, sending rainbows of color at odd angles across the surface. But with gentle prompting, she was eventually able to straighten the fold so it gleamed evenly.

Laughing together, they pulled and twisted the fold,

exploring the many possibilities inherent in a single fold of glamour. Miss Dunkirk displayed a greater aptitude than Jane had expected. In the end, she was able to create the effect of sunlight glancing across the books, and if it were not as subtle as Jane might have managed, neither was it as inept as one might expect from someone who had never studied glamour.

Breathing rapidly and somewhat flushed, Miss Dunkirk stepped back from her last carefully placed stitch.

Jane nodded in approval. "Very nicely done."

Turning from the bookcase, Miss Dunkirk said, "Miss Melody, what do . . . Oh."

From Miss Dunkirk's tone, Jane fully expected her sister to have slipped the room again, and in this she was correct.

Somewhat more unexpected was the view through the window, wherein Melody conversed amicably with Mr. Vincent. Or, rather, she conversed. He drew.

He had turned aside from his easel and picked up a leather notebook. Judging from the angle of his gaze, he was probably sketching Melody.

They were quite alone. Jane compressed her lips. Would Melody never learn the bounds of propriety?

"Miss Dunkirk, will you excuse me? Melody and I should return home for dinner."

"Of course." The girl's face was paler than Jane would like, but they had not done so much glamour that she felt cause to worry. "I have kept you too long."

With a minimum of farewells and a promise to see each

other soon, Jane left Robinsford Abbey and went round to the side of the house where Mr. Vincent painted and Melody watched.

As Jane walked across the neatly trimmed lawn, a breeze carried Melody's voice to her. "Ah, you see. My sister comes to be my nursemaid and chaperon, as I told you she would." She waved and raised her voice. "Jane! Do look at what Mr. Vincent is drawing."

Noting that her sister made no move to perform introductions, and was unlikely to do so, Jane halted in front of the pair. "I am afraid that we need to return home for dinner."

Mr. Vincent shut his slim, leather notebook and stood waiting for Melody to introduce them. His eyes were a warm brown, but they studied Jane without a hint of emotion—no compassion, disdain, or condescension marred his visage. Indeed, Jane had detected more interest in his expression when he was painting Robinsford Abbey than when he looked at her.

Melody wrinkled her nose. "Oh, do be reasonable, Jane, or you'll have Mr. Vincent thinking that we dine unfashionably early."

"I trust that Mr. Vincent, whom I have yet to meet, will understand."

"La! He is standing right here. Don't pretend you don't know him." She leaned toward Mr. Vincent and lowered her voice. "Jane spotted you out here first and was quite mad with curiosity about what you were painting. Don't mind her concerns with propriety. She can sometimes be over-nice."

Jane burned with a mixture of anger and embarrassment. She had to hold herself quite still to control the urge to turn and march away, leaving Melody alone with this man.

"Miss Ellsworth, I am afraid that is all the introduction we are likely to receive." His voice, which Jane only just realized she had never before heard, rumbled in his chest at the lower end of baritone. "What about my work made you curious?"

"Nothing, I assure you. My sister has confused my remarking on your presence with an interest beyond the commonplace. By the angle of your easel and the direction of your gaze, I surmized that you were painting Robinsford Abbey. I will defer any further interest until the piece is ready for showing."

"And yet you had no compunctions about looking at my glamural at Banbree Manor."

"I was invited to view it. I had no way of knowing it was in progress when I agreed."

"And when you returned?"

Jane compressed her lips and raised her chin. "Clearly, I was in error to do so. If you will excuse us, Melody and I must be going."

"I have no wish to detain you." Mr. Vincent inclined his head in the briefest of bows, then returned his attention to his canvas as if they had already departed.

Without waiting to see if Melody was following, Jane

gathered her skirts and crossed the lawn in the direction of Long Parkmead. She heard a few more words behind her; then Melody was by her side, breathless and laughing.

"I do not know that I have ever seen such a pair as the two of you."

Jane kept her gaze fixed on the path, letting her bonnet hide her expression. Had she lifted her head, the fury on her face would have been enough to make Medusa envious. "I am glad I could amuse you."

Melody's renewed laughter did nothing to improve Jane's spirits.

Six

Strawberries and Bonnets

The strawberry-picking party was delayed once because of weather and again because Captain Livingston had an engagement in town, but at last all the elements co-operated and the party gathered at Long Parkmead in anticipation of their outing.

Miss Dunkirk arrived on horseback, quite alone. As she alighted, her face was rosy and aglow with delight.

"Oh, Miss Ellsworth, you would not believe how beautiful it is this morning. I woke before the sun and thought I should never see such a morning. I begged Edmund to take me riding."

"But where is Mr. Dunkirk?"

"Oh, his gelding is so slow." She waved a

hand languidly behind her as Mr. Dunkirk appeared on the road. "There. See? He is only now coming. He would have stayed in Robinsford Abbey all day, but I made him go out. The sky was so glorious with colours. You would not believe such colors."

"Then you must tell me all about them so that I may imagine them for myself." Jane smiled and took her young friend by the hands. They had spent a great deal of time together of late. The girl had come to call at every opportunity, sometimes riding over without her brother to spend the afternoon learning some of the finer points of glamour from Jane. Other days they spent the afternoon rambling through the estate and talking of nothing and everything, for though their ages were separated by more than ten years, Miss Dunkirk had about her a combination of youthful exuberance and steadiness of manner which Jane found appealing. Too, Jane had to admit, she was often out of sorts with Melody these days, and Miss Dunkirk provided a welcome distraction.

In short order they heard the unmistakable sound of Lady FitzCameron's coach-and-four arriving. Jane was not at all surprized to see Captain Livingston accompanying Lady FitzCameron and her daughter, but she was quite surprized to see the other gentleman who arrived with them.

"I do hope you do not mind extending your invitation to Mr. Vincent." Lady FitzCameron indicated by her smile that of course they could not possibly mind her taking the liberty. "He has expressed an interest in the view from your hill for quite some time."

"But, Lady FitzCameron," exclaimed Mrs. Ellsworth, "you had only to tell us. Mr. Vincent would have been welcome at any time. You only need let your wishes be known. We are too, too happy to oblige."

"So kind," Lady FitzCameron murmured, already losing interest in the conversation.

Mr. Vincent made a short bow and took up a station by the wall of the drawing room, looking as stiff and uncomfortable as it was possible for a man to be. Jane occupied herself on the far side of the room, leaving Mrs. Ellsworth to sweep over to him and try to engage him in conversation. His answers were short, almost to the point of rudeness, so much so that Jane almost mustered some empathy for her mother from where she conversed with Miss FitzCameron and Miss Dunkirk. Mrs. Ellsworth had attempted to ascertain something of Mr. Vincent's family—specifically, which of the Vincents he was associated with—by asking where he was from, and only received the most cursory of answers: that he was from London.

As Mrs. Ellsworth remarked later to Mr. Ellsworth, there was no way to tell if he was related to Vincent the haberdasher or Vincent the M.P. She was quite vexed, and resolved to appeal to Lady FitzCameron for more intelligence at the first opportunity.

She next turned to the subject of art. "Have you seen our landscapes? Our eldest daughter did these."

Jane wanted to sink through the floor. Instead, she kept her attention outwardly fixed on Miss Dunkirk, who was describing the delicate pearls of clouds she had seen on her ride.

Mr. Vincent turned to the nearest, raised an eyebrow, and said, "Indeed."

Neither compliment nor condemnation, but simply a recognition of fact. Jane supposed she should be grateful for that.

Failing in her attempts to draw him out, Mrs. Ellsworth was relieved beyond expression when her especial friends Mr. and Mrs. Marchand arrived, sparing her the necessity of further conversation with Mr. Vincent. Jane was, if possible, more relieved than her mother.

With the party thus assembled, bonnets were donned and baskets picked up so that a sizable collection of wicker paraded through the drawing room and out to the shrubbery. Mr. Ellsworth was justly proud of the shrubbery on the south side of Long Parkmead and so led the party through there, though it was not the fastest route to the strawberry patch. Jane walked with Miss Dunkirk, which of necessity meant conversation with Mr. Dunkirk, an effect that Jane did not in the least regret. Melody walked with Captain Livingston and Miss FitzCameron, the three of them laughing and trying to outdo one another with wit.

Ahead of them strode Mr. Vincent, with his folding easel slung over his back. He soon left the party, disappearing around the bend of the shrubbery. By the time the larger party rounded the bend at their more sedate pace, he was halfway across the lawn between the shrubbery and a copse of trees, on the opposite side of which stood the strawberry patch, in a spot best situated to take advantage of the sun. His carriage was easy, and the stiffness which he had displayed in the drawing room had relaxed into the long stride of a man most comfortable out-of-doors.

"Mr. Vincent seems anxious to reach the strawberries," Jane remarked.

"He is often ill at ease in the drawing rooms, which is not a surprize considering his history," Mr. Dunkirk said.

"Oh. Do you know his history then? Do not let my mother know, or she will be quizzing you for half an hour or more. She is overcome with curiosity about him."

"Thank you for the warning." He affected a grave countenance, but his lips twitched with the hint of a smile. "I do. I researched his history before engaging him."

"Edmund! You said you wouldn't tell."

He arched an eyebrow at his sister. "Nor have I, Beth. Though you are very nearly compelling me to do so, since it is rude to Miss Ellsworth to have a conversation from which she is excluded."

Abashed, Miss Dunkirk looked down. Jane tugged at her bonnet and looked at Mr. Dunkirk with an overly innocent expression. "I am sorry. I heard my name, but I am afraid my bonnet kept me from hearing anything else. Did you address me?"

He laughed, a clean, pure laugh that came up from his

belly. Jane wanted above all else to make him laugh again, and to look at her always with such delight. Miss Dunkirk laughed with him, and for a moment, Jane felt a part of their family.

"Miss Ellsworth, I had asked Edmund not to tell you because I wanted it to be a surprize, but I will confess. He has engaged Mr. Vincent to tutor me in glamour. Is that not the most exciting thing you have ever heard?" Miss Dunkirk slipped her arm through Jane's and leaned close to confide. "Edmund has such an admiration of your skills, and I envied them, so I pestered him for lessons until he agreed."

Jane glanced at Mr. Dunkirk, but he was studying the landscape around them, having already lost interest in the conversation. Surely he could not admire her skills overmuch if he had engaged Mr. Vincent rather than letting Jane continue to help Miss Dunkirk discover her talents. Though, truly, to be tutored by a man of Mr. Vincent's skills was enviable, and surely the best for the girl no matter what her feelings about the man's manners might be. "Mr. Vincent is supremely talented."

Miss Dunkirk wrinkled her nose. "He is so odd, though. You wouldn't believe how droll he can be. He seems to love the visual arts to the exclusion of language. Outside of lessons, I do not think he has said more than five words at a time to me. Though when he is speaking of art and glamour, he can wax poetic." She shook her head, laughing. "Really, he is very droll."

They passed beneath the dappled shade that the copse

of trees provided before they came upon the strawberry mounds. The sudden cool was such a relief that conversation ceased for a moment, only to begin again when they emerged from the trees. Each group exclaimed as they saw the strawberry patches, which even from a distance shewed the heavy red berries nestled among the glossy leaves.

When Mr. Ellsworth had had the strawberries planted, he had instructed his gardener to make them seem a natural part of the landscape. They meandered along low hills and a cunningly contrived stone wall that seemed to be a picturesque ruin, yet raised the strawberry plants so that one did not have to stoop to pluck them.

On the hill above them, Mr. Vincent was unpacking his easel and his paints under the shelter of an ancient arching laurel.

Mr. Ellsworth stopped short and turned in some astonishment. "Where are the servants? I expressly told them to set the nuncheon under the laurel tree. Virginia"—he turned to Mrs. Ellsworth—"did you tell them to go elsewhere?"

"No, Charles, I did not." She peered up the hill, and her brow furrowed. "I do not see them on the hill. They must be somewhere else."

"Clearly they are somewhere else, if they are not here. The question is where."

Mr. Dunkirk said, "Perhaps they are on the other side of the hill?"

"Ah. An excellent thought. I will see about just that.

Meanwhile, I urge you all to avail yourself of the strawberries." Mr. Ellsworth started up the hill while the rest of the company fell to the strawberries with a will.

The conversations were simple and inconsequential, as all were distracted by the sweet succulent berries. It seemed that Lady FitzCameron had spoken with her nephew about his conduct at the ball, for Captain Livingston paid all the ladies equal attention, even going so far as to compliment Mrs. Ellsworth's parasol. Without the monopoly on Captain Livingston's attentions that she had no doubt expected after the ball, Melody turned to Mr. Dunkirk, and soon had him carrying her basket for her as she plucked strawberries from the mounds.

Mrs. Marchand was quite taken with the strawberries. She kept exclaiming over each one she found as if it were the largest she had ever seen—"Never have I seen the like!"—then devoured the berry before anyone else could ascertain the veracity of her claims. Her husband joked, "I declare, I wonder if you are even touching them, or if you are eating them straight from the plant."

Mrs. Marchand laughed at that, and colored prettily, but her husband's comment did not slow her enthusiasm for the strawberries.

In short order, Mr. Ellsworth returned, face as red as a strawberry from his climb up the hill and back down. He was laughing, his eyes wrinkled small with merriment. "You would not believe what clever Mr. Vincent has done."

Jane looked up the hill, but Mr. Vincent was not there. "Has he finished his painting so soon?"

Mr. Ellsworth chuckled and shook his head. "He is still painting, I daresay. Shall I tell you, or shall you guess?"

Captain Livingston said, "He has received an appointment to the King."

"No. Nor the Prince." Mr. Ellsworth placed his hands on his waistcoat. "He made the servants and himself disappear, because they marred the view."

"What?" "Did he?" "How clever!" The crowd quite forgot the berries. Each stared up the hill, declaring that they could see this sign or that of the servants' location. Jane studied the hill, stunned both that he could have created such a complex and large fold of glamour in so short a time and that the folds themselves could be invisible, even with her vision attuned to the ether. Of course, many great halls used glamour folds to mask musicians at a ball, but they required constant attention, and were enormously detailed to create an exact duplicate of the room as it would have appeared were it empty. Mr. Ellsworth shook his head, laughing. "Not a one of you is looking in the right place. Come, I will shew you."

As a group, they trooped up the hill, the strawberries quite forgotten, exclaiming all the while about the cleverness of Mr. Vincent and his faculty with glamour. As they neared the top of the hill with still no manifest sign of either Mr. Vincent or the servants, Captain Livingston remarked, "The Admiralty could use skills such as these."

"Not at sea," a rough voice proclaimed, and suddenly Mr. Vincent was before them, with easel and the first faint sketches of the scene below. His jacket was off and the top of his shirt was undone, but he gave no notice of the impropriety of either as he continued to paint, all but ignoring the gathered party. His countenance was easy and confident, with no trace of the strain upon it which one would expect from working so large an illusion. Jane turned away from his canvas, involuntarily looking for signs of the glamour that he had dropped in order to ascertain what folds he had used.

"But why not use this to hide our fleets from Napoleon?" Captain Livingston said. "It cannot take so much energy, or you would not be able to keep it up while painting."

Mr. Vincent's face shewed no expression, but he briefly glanced at Miss Dunkirk. Jane sensed that he was challenging her to remember her lessons.

Jane kept silent, watching the girl as she pieced the answer together. "It cannot be done because he tied the fold off. A fold tied off is stationary, but the sea is in motion."

"Correct." Mr. Vincent turned back to the easel and lifted his brush again.

Melody said, "But where are the servants?"

He pointed with the tip of the brush and gave no other answer.

Jane looked, but still did not see the folds masking the servants. Exasperated, she walked past Mr. Vincent, and then gasped as the servants appeared.

"Jane!" Melody cried, behind her.

The servants looked up, as startled by her sudden appearance, and yet, she could see the landscape around them clearly though she had expected it to be obscured by the glamour with which Mr. Vincent had hidden them. Certainly, all her prior experience with masking glamours indicated that the illusion would be visible even from the center. Jane turned to look back, but Mr. Vincent and the rest of the party had vanished again. It was most perplexing, for she could hear them exclaiming in wonder, but could not see them.

And then Miss Dunkirk was there, without even a ripple in the landscape; she simply appeared between one moment and the next. She, too, gasped in astonishment. The illusion was so seamless that Miss Dunkirk's passage made no disruption in the ether. She had thought that Mr. Vincent had dropped the glamour when they saw him, but the truth seemed to be more interesting than that.

"Do you know how he is doing this, Miss Dunkirk?"

The girl shook her head. "I am afraid that we are still working on basic colours and shapes. I had hoped you could tell me."

"I do not know either. Every vanishing charm I know is more cumbersome than this, and leaves traces in the ether. I am most curious." Jane sank onto the nearest blanket and studied the place where Miss Dunkirk had appeared. She let her view of the physical world dissipate and concentrated on the glamour. At first, she saw nothing, and then, as Miss

FitzCameron and Captain Livingston stepped through, she saw a slight shimmer. Focusing on that, she let her vision go deeper as the rest of the party entered. Each entrance gave her a clue about the nature of the glamour, but the fold was so thin that it was almost invisible.

The last to appear was Mr. Vincent.

He instantly saw what she was doing and smirked, as if certain that she could not discern his craft. Jane would not tolerate that and, in a rare moment of pride, was determined to prove herself the equal of this haughty, silent man. She saw now the fold; a single gossamer cloth of glamour creating a canopy that stretched to the ground, covering the group.

He was manipulating light itself.

Jane began to work backwards to understand how it had begun. It twisted just so. When she thought that she understood Mr. Vincent's methodology, Jane cupped her hand around a glamour of pure light, tied off a fold of it, and attempted to create a tiny bauble which sunbeams skittered around. Then, working carefully, she stretched the light out to a fine thin weave until it enveloped her. Most remarkably, by tying the fold off before she began stretching it, it took no more effort than working with a minuscule fold. The sunbeam continued on its happy journey, detouring around her so that no one observing her would be able to discern that it had veered from its course. It was a monstrously clever illusion.

"Oh, well done, Miss Ellsworth, well done!" Miss

Dunkirk clapped. "I knew you could understand it. I was certain you could."

In the protection of her bubble, Jane allowed herself the luxury of a smile of pride. That man thought she was incapable of following his trick, did he? But as her vision returned to the physical world, and she saw the others clapping for her, and the look of illness on Mr. Vincent's face, she lost some of her pleasure in her accomplishment. What purpose had assaying to match his feat in front of the others served beyond stroking her own vanity? It would have been better if she had let him have his triumph, rather than making it seem as if anyone could do this pattern by simply sitting down and copying him. She had played a churlish trick.

Jane released the ties on her bubble and feigned breathlessness as though it took more effort than it had. "I do not think I have the right of it, Mr. Vincent."

If anything, her subterfuge made his sneer deepen. "You did." Without a word more, he strode out of the group and into his own bubble, vanishing back to his paints. As the others continued their exclamations, Jane stared after him, perplexed beyond all measure.

When she returned her attention to the group, she found Mr. Dunkirk staring at her. For a brief moment his face was unguarded, but Jane hardly knew how to read what she saw there before it vanished. He had already turned away and begun a conversation with Miss FitzCameron before Jane could be certain that she had seen anything at all.

Then her attention was taken by Miss Dunkirk, who wanted to know all of the particulars of how the disappearance had worked. The rest of the afternoon passed in a blur of simple pleasures as they enjoyed the meal set out for them by the servants. Mr. Vincent appeared only once more, quite suddenly, as he released the ties on the folds masking them. He had donned his coat and packed his box of paints and his easel.

"Oh, Mr. Vincent, you are not leaving us, are you?" Lady FitzCameron said from her place on the blankets. "I had hoped you would join us."

He hesitated. Some of the tension came back into his shoulders as his patroness made claims upon his attention. "Of course, Lady FitzCameron."

"Oh, good." She smiled, well aware of her power. "What I should like most to complete this enchanting afternoon is a *tableau vivant*."

Mrs. Marchand looked up from her strawberries. "What a marvelous idea, Lady FitzCameron."

Mr. Ellsworth said to Captain Livingston, as if they were discussing a horse and how well it trotted, "Jane is uncommonly good at *tableaux vivants*."

"I do remember that, and can only imagine that her talents have improved with the passage of time."

From where she was sitting, between Captain Livingston and Mr. Ellsworth, Melody said, "Oh! They should do a *tableau vivant* together."

Caught by the words of her family and neighbours, Jane

tried to find a way to politely refuse. Her every interaction with the man had only angered him. She was certain that only the desire to avoid being paired in *tableaux vivant*s united them. "I would only hamper Mr. Vincent's efforts."

"Nonsense." Mr. Vincent bowed to Melody. To Jane's deep astonishment, he said, "I think your sister has hit upon a splendid plan."

Seven

Nymph on the Hill

Trying to mask her dismay and astonishment, Jane rose and went to where Mr. Vincent stood by his paints. So quickly that she could not see him do it, he raised and thinned a fold of glamour. She was at first uncertain as to what he had done because she could still see the party, but it became apparent from their actions that they could not see her. Then he cast another fold around them and the sounds of the party vanished. Both tricks were astounding enough in themselves, but the speed and ease with which he did them was more so. Even if Jane could understand how he had quieted the world around them, she could never match his speed.

"My apologies, Mr. Vincent, I—"

"They cannot hear us, Miss Ellsworth." He shrugged, rolling his shoulders under his coat. "You need not be civil to me."

Stunned, Jane stopped speaking and stared at him. "I do not understand your meaning."

His jaw clenched and he seemed about to say something, but the moment passed and his anger subsided. "What *tableau vivant* shall we do?"

"No. No, you may not start such a conversation and pretend that you did not. Tell me my offense so that I might apologize." Even as she said this, Jane remembered her brusque conversation with him on the lawn at Robinsford Abbey. "I am sorry that I did not take the time to view your painting when we last saw one another."

He snorted and shook his head. "I was grateful that you did not, but your behaviour today shows that is not your usual wont."

"My behaviour!"

"I am a glamourist, Miss Ellsworth. I create illusions in an effort to transport my viewers to another place. So I do not like it when people expose how my illusions work. Each person who looks at what I do takes my work away from me."

"But you are teaching Miss Dunkirk. How can you complain about others knowing your secrets if you are teaching them?"

To her surprize, he lifted his hand and pressed it to the bridge of his nose, squeezing his eyes shut. "You mistake my meaning. I should learn to keep my thoughts to myself, as I rarely express what I mean." He sighed. "It is not the knowledge of glamour which I guard; it is the art created by it. Illusions should be entrancing without someone looking behind the scenes to see how they are made. Would you enjoy a play where you saw the mechanicals exposed? For me, it is much the same. I want the illusion to remain whole. If someone thinks about how it is done, then I have failed in my art."

At last Jane apprehended his meaning and how she had transgressed at the ball and then again here, but her own principles were different. "I have always thought that an educated audience could more fully appreciate the effort which went into creating a piece of art."

"The effort, yes, but I want to transport the audience to another place; I do not want them to think of effort or technique."

Jane was silent. She did not agree with him, but knowing now his feelings on the matter, she resolved to avoid offending him in the future. "I can enjoy both, Mr. Vincent. I assure you, your art is compelling. I nonetheless apologize for looking behind the curtain, as it were."

He regarded her for a moment, then looked away, his face expressionless. Without accepting her apology, he said, "They must wonder why we are taking so long to prepare the *tableau vivant*."

Jane started, having forgotten entirely why she stood, seemingly alone, with this man. She looked at the silent party, who had begun gesturing animatedly in their direction. "Have you one prepared? I can pretend to lend my support, or—"

He smirked. "You are quite good, Miss Ellsworth; I have no doubt that you have a *tableau vivant* of your own prepared."

"And you are a faster glamourist than I, so can follow my lead." She took his meaning. "Could you create an Apollo to my Daphne?"

He glanced at the laurel tree arcing over them and said, "An apt choice."

Quickly they sketched out the play. Then, working faster than she knew she could, Jane tugged folds over her to create a mask of Daphne, and the delicate garments such an ephemeral nymph would wear as she fled the sun god. She also worked one set of folds into a slipknot, intending to create a surprize at the end of this *tableau vivant*. Mr. Vincent might be faster than she, but Jane would prove her worth as a glamourist.

She sensed the ether trembling beside her as Mr. Vincent worked Apollo into being. When all was ready, he untied the folds that masked them from view.

As soon as Daphne was brought into view, the spectators gasped in delight. It was only when her friends began to glance at Melody did Jane realize that, in her haste, she had modeled the figure on her sister. Daphne's golden hair tumbled in the same ringlets, and although her cornflower blue eyes were wide with apprehension and each element was purified for the glamour, they undeniably had their base in Melody's form.

Appearing taller than he was, and glowing with the light of the sun, Mr. Vincent embodied Apollo, his hands outstretched to reach for the frightened nymph. As their guests studied the *tableau vivant* with exquisite fascination, Jane released the slipknot she held, and hidden folds slid around her into a laurel tree. She was gratified by the gasps of surprize and pleasure from their viewers. It was no small thing to change a detailed glamour so smoothly.

Then, to her surprize, Apollo dropped to his knees and embraced the laurel tree, weeping with such conviction that Jane very nearly released the folds masking her within the laurel tree; but to have done so would have made the unbidden intimacy more apparent, so she bore it until the party's applause indicated it was time to end the *tableau vivant*.

Mr. Vincent stood and became himself, his broad chest heaving from the effort of maintaining the folds while he was moving. As Jane dropped the folds masking her in the laurel tree, she strove to pretend that the trembling in her hands and the shortness of her breath was from the glamour. Nothing could explain away the flush on her cheeks, though.

Mr. Vincent excused himself as soon as he could, saying that he must clean his brushes, despite all begging him to stay and telling him the afternoon would be lost without his company. Lady FitzCameron did not join in these pleas, seeming to know exactly how far she could command his loyalties, and waved her acquiescence when he expressed his earnest wish to return to Banbree Manor. Bowing shortly to Mrs. Ellsworth and Lady FitzCameron, he took his leave and walked down the hill.

The party remained under the shade of the laurel until the sun began to set; then they wandered back to the house, each carrying a basket of strawberries.

Jane walked beside Captain Livingston and Miss Dunkirk, feeling more like a chaperon than a maid herself. The good captain reached for both of the ladies' baskets, refusing to let either one keep hers, despite the fact that both had carried them while picking the fruit. As Jane released hers, she said, "I recall that we were safest when your hands were full."

He laughed and said, "And I recall that I was safest when you did not have your thimble."

"My thimble? What can you mean by that?"

"I mean that you thumped me soundly on the head whenever I came in reach. I still have a lump from one of your beatings." He bent his head to Miss Dunkirk. "See if I don't."

"I am certain that if Miss Ellsworth thumped you upon the head, you deserved it."

"Oh! I am wronged. What have I done to provoke such mistrust?"

"It is not that I mistrust you, but Miss Ellsworth is so trustworthy and elegant that I am certain she would never do something that was not proper. Therefore, it must have been proper to thump you on the head with a thimble."

"I was the sweetest boy imaginable, I assure you. I have it on the greatest authority; you need only ask Aunt Elise how kind and gentle I was." He spun, looking for Lady FitzCameron, but they had entered a copse of trees and were shielded from the rest of the party. "Well, when we emerge, she will tell you. See if she doesn't."

Jane laughed. "Captain Livingston, I would say you are as much of a rogue now as you were then, but your methods have altered."

"Wronged! Oh, the ignominy. The wretched—" His words were cut off by a sudden pained cry behind them.

Recognizing her sister's voice, Jane's heart leaped to her throat, lodging there with sudden fear. She hurried back from whence they had come, moving as quickly as she could over the twisting path, but was soon passed by Captain Livingston.

Beyond the copse, her mother called, "What is it?" and other members of the party cried their queries. Jane rounded a tree in time to see Captain Livingston and Mr. Dunkirk lift Melody off the ground between them. Their arms were clasped together, creating a makeshift sedan chair. Melody leaned, pale as death between them.

Her slipper lay on the ground.

Miss Dunkirk came up behind Jane and grasped her arm. "What has happened?"

Her brother replied, "Miss Melody has stumbled on a root. I fear she has twisted her ankle badly. Run along, Beth, and tell Mr. Ellsworth."

Jane stayed by their side as they picked their way through the copse of trees. Even with care, Melody's foot bumped against odd branches, eliciting moans from her lips. When they were out of the trees, Jane led them across the field to the back of the house, knowing that they could get Melody to comfort soonest by entering through the breakfast room and avoiding the shrubbery, whose twisting paths would be sure to pain her sister further.

They were halfway across the field when Mr. Ellsworth joined them, puffing from exertion. After a hurried conference, he preceded them to the house to help set things to rights for Melody.

Once inside, they carried her through the hall to the drawing room, and laid her upon a sofa. A whimper escaped as they set her down, and her eyelashes fluttered upon her cheeks.

Seeing her daughter's state, Mrs. Ellsworth immediately sank into a chair, needing smelling salts and air in order to retain her senses. Jane urged her mother to take to her bed so she would not have two invalids to care for.

Mr. Dunkirk offered to ride for a doctor, but as there was little swelling, Mr. Ellsworth declined. The party disbanded, each member promising to call the next day to see how Melody fared.

Eight

Flowers and Novels

Good to his word, the following day Captain Livingston called as early as decency would allow. He brought with him a bundle of peonies gathered from Lady FitzCameron's garden by the very hand of the Viscountess, who sent her concerns and her fond wishes for Melody's full recovery.

Melody lay propped on the sofa in the drawing room, her hair unbound and tumbling about her shoulders, with her ankle wrapped in bandages and propped on a pillow. Fortunately, there had been little swelling. Melody only stayed on the couch at the repeated insistence of their mother; otherwise she would have hobbled to the breakfast table with the rest of the family.

While she said there was no pain, she gasped at the slightest touch upon her injured extremity.

Jane had been reading to her from Cowper when Captain Livingston arrived with a bundle of posies. Jane set the book on the side table to greet him. While he was courtesy itself to Jane, it was clear that his attention lay solely with Melody.

"How is the invalid this morning?" he said, seating himself in a chair opposite them.

"I am quite well, thank you; only mortified to have caused so much trouble yesterday." She colored becomingly and looked down at the flowers in her lap. "It was so kind of the Viscountess to think of me and to send you with such beautiful flowers. Jane, dear, may I trouble you to put these into water for me? I would hate to have them wilt."

"Of course." Jane took the flowers from Melody. She tried not to look at the bell which had been placed within Melody's easy grasp so she could summon Nancy if she needed anything.

It was clear that Melody wanted a moment alone with Captain Livingston, and Jane was willing to grant her that. He was not as cultured a man as Mr. Dunkirk, but his youth and lively humor seemed more suited to Melody. Jane carried the flowers out of the room and found a vase, taking time to arrange them before returning to the drawing room. She made certain to generate adequate noise to announce her imminent arrival. Captain Livingston was seated in his chair still, but Melody's cheeks were a trifle rosier than when Jane had left the room.

"Where shall I put them?"

Melody gestured to the small occasional table at the end of the sofa and said, "There, so that I may gaze at them without effort and think fondly on the kind nature which brought them to me."

Jane set the flowers down and returned to her chair, taking up the volume of Cowper once more. They talked idly of the day before, hashing over the events and doubling their enjoyment by examining each happy moment in minute detail. A rap sounded at the door, and Nancy shewed Mr. Dunkirk into the room shortly after.

Upon seeing Captain Livingston, he said, "I see that we came on similar errands." Thereupon he drew forth from his pocket the three slim volumes of *The Italian* by Mrs. Radcliffe. "My sister thought you might wish something to read while you recovered."

Melody's face blossomed in delight. "Radcliffe! I adore Mrs. Radcliffe's work beyond all measure!"

"I am afraid, then, that I have not brought you anything new with which to amuse yourself."

"But you have, for I do not have *The Italian*. I have only read *The Mysteries of Udolpho*, which I thought so compelling, so very interesting. Do you not think so, Captain Livingston?"

"You have the better of me. I have not read any of Mrs. Radcliffe's works. There's precious little time for reading aboard ship, especially when facing the Monster's navy." He straightened as he said this and looked the slightest bit down his nose at Mr. Dunkirk, who raised an eyebrow as if he understood what Captain Livingston was suggesting and was not in the least perturbed by it.

"That is unfortunate. I find that reading greatly improves one's mind." He smiled, very civilly, and Jane was hard-pressed not to laugh as he turned back to Melody, effectively cutting Captain Livingston out of the conversation. "And how is your ankle, if I might inquire?"

"Much better, thank you. I am only lying here because Mama makes such a fuss when I try to stand."

"That is understandable, having hurt the same ankle twice so close together. You must take care that it is fully mended this time," Mr. Dunkirk said.

Melody's eyes flashed to Jane with a silent plea, then back to Mr. Dunkirk. She assured him that she would take care, but Jane had seen that moment, and it was more than a simple entreaty. The look alone might have simply indicated that Melody did not want Jane to reveal that she had not sprained her ankle when she had chased Mr. Dunkirk, but the manner in which her face went pale and then red said more.

Jane recalled that Melody's ankle had not swollen last night.

A horrible conviction seized her that the injury was a sham, that Melody had not injured herself last night at all. As these thoughts went through her head, she was thankful that neither gentleman was looking at her, for she felt unable to govern her countenance in the slightest. Melody saw her unguarded expression and paled further.

Jane longed for the gentlemen to leave so that she could confront Melody directly. It was not possible; it could not be possible that her sister had lied to secure the attentions of Mr. Dunkirk. How much of the injury had been a sham? Had Melody truly stumbled, or had even that been part of her *tableau vivant* to draw Mr. Dunkirk in? For surely he, and not Captain Livingston, was the target of her play, else she would have enacted it while with Captain Livingston.

The morning passed in a torment for Jane as she struggled to conceal her suspicions from the men, and Melody strove to detain them.

Jane could scarce believe the preening and strutting that they performed for the benefit of Melody.

If Mr. Dunkirk mentioned his hunter, then Captain Livingston had to tell of his, and of how high a fence the horse could leap, which then caused Mr. Dunkirk to relate an anecdote about a previous hunt.

They went on in weary circles, Jane pretending to listen, while Melody seemed positively enraptured by their efforts, though Jane knew she loathed hunting. It was clear that Melody did not want to be alone with her sister, and so she encouraged the men to stay as long as they would.

Once, when Captain Livingston remarked on how fine the day was, Melody remarked, "Ah. I wish I could go outside, but I shall hope that it is as fine tomorrow."

Then, nothing would do but for each man to offer to help her outside. Placing her in a chair, they each took an arm of it and carried her out onto the lawn. Jane followed in her role of chaperon, wishing that her mother or father would emerge so that she could retire and be done.

Though she knew that she should aid her sister in making a match, Jane could not stomach the games that Melody played. When at last Nancy came out to let Jane know that their tea was laid, the gentlemen carried Melody back inside and excused themselves. Mr. Dunkirk had promised Beth that he would be home to take her riding, and Captain Livingston had business to attend to for Lady FitzCameron.

As soon as the front door had shut and the men were safely away, Jane turned to Melody, having spent the afternoon deciding on the best course to take in questioning her sister. If she were wrong about Melody, the damage of her suspicion would not be borne, but she did not have an opportunity to exercise her plans, for as soon as she turned, she saw that Melody was sitting up with both feet upon the ground and tears in her eyes.

"Oh, Jane, forgive me." Melody put her head on her hands and gave way to her feelings in a manner that shocked Jane. "I did not mean to—I do not know why I did it—but once done, I did not know how to undo it. It's wretched, I know, but don't tell." She raised her head, eyes red with anguish. "Please do not tell."

To give herself time to think, Jane crossed the room and sat opposite Melody. "Am I to understand that you did not hurt your ankle yesterday?"

"I hurt it exactly as much as I hurt it a fortnight ago.

Only my jealousy injured me." Melody flung herself back on the sofa.

"Jealousy? What or who are you so jealous of that you would pretend to be injured?"

"Of you! How am I to compare with you and your great talents? I saw how everyone admired your *tableau vivant* and how they looked at me as if wondering what I could do, and the answer is nothing. I can do nothing that a man such as Mr. Dunkirk would esteem. And so when I stumbled and lost my shoe and Mr. Dunkirk—" Here she sighed and covered her face again. "He was by my side, so suddenly and so quickly helping me up. I wanted it to last longer, so I pretended that I needed more aid than I did, and then when Captain Livingston came to my aid as well . . . ! It was wrong. I know it was wrong. But you must understand that I could not then admit that I had not hurt myself."

Jane shook her head, bewildered by her sister's jealousy toward her. Her! Who had not the slightest hope of marrying, were it not for the sum that Mr. Ellsworth had put away for her dowry. But more than the bewilderment, she was dismayed by what her sister had confessed. "You could certainly have explained that the injury was not so great as it first appeared; that shock had given it more weight than it merited. Oh, Melody, what were you thinking?"

"I was not thinking! I was feeling! And is it so terrible a thing? I have hurt no one save myself, and he came today, did he not?" She twisted her hands together in supplication. "Please. You cannot tell anyone. I should die if he knew."

It was not clear whether "he" were Mr. Dunkirk or Captain Livingston, but Jane felt that it hardly mattered. She could not censure Melody strongly enough. To be entreated to keep this a secret between them, when all her common sense cried out to tell her father, was almost too great a burden. Though the greater part of her knew that it would do no good, Jane tried to impress upon her younger sister the seriousness of what she had done. "Yes, he came. In response to a lie. Melody, you must understand that lies are not confined to words; deeds, too, may be—"

"I do not need to be lectured by you, dear sister, to know what I have done." Melody stood abruptly, without any sign of the injury she had claimed. "I confided in you, hoping that you would understand the very real torment in my breast, but you have thrown my confidence back in my face. I trusted you with my peace of mind and you have taken that from me. Now who will I turn to, if I cannot trust you?" Without waiting for a response, she strode across the drawing room. At the door, she paused and then limped cautiously out, giving lie to her protestations of torment as she made her slow way out of the drawing room, prolonging her falsehood in the sight of any who saw her.

Jane sat in silence, struggling to compose herself. If she had any hope of taming her sister's notions of propriety, then she would have to find a way to mend this breach between them.

Nine

A Tonic in the Maze

It seemed as if Jane's words to Melody had some effect, for Melody assayed a rapid recovery from her false injury. The next day she was declaring that she felt quite fit and that the injury had not been as severe as she initially thought. Jane heard her own words parroted back when Mr. Dunkirk and his sister came to call: "The shock of the fall made me think that the injury was greater than it was."

His doubt was so apparent that Melody suggested they walk among the shrubbery to prove that she was quite steady on her feet. He ventured to question whether that would be wise, which only made Melody the more determined to go out. "The paths in the shrubbery are quite flat and well paved. There is not the slightest danger of injury, I assure you."

Mr. Dunkirk appealed to Jane. "Do you think it is quite safe?"

Beside him, Melody's face was a mute mask of appeal.

"If my sister says she is well, then I am quite certain she is able to walk," Jane replied.

They set out to explore the expanse of the shrubbery, as Miss Dunkirk had only previously been on the Long Walk. The tall yew hedges provided ample opportunity for the parties to become separated from one another. Jane, perceiving that the surest way to shew her sister that she had no cause to be jealous was by withdrawing and allowing her to walk alone with Mr. Dunkirk, contrived to draw Miss Dunkirk deeper into the twisting passages of the shrubbery and then into the maze carved into its center.

Miss Dunkirk exclaimed in delight upon learning of the maze and at once wanted to find the middle of it. They set off, leaving Mr. Dunkirk and Melody promenading down the Long Walk. Jane followed a few paces behind Miss Dunkirk, hiding a smile as they rounded one corner and then the next, knowing full well that it would lead to a dead end. Though she had long since memorized the maze, she remembered the satisfaction of learning the paths as a child. Now, she never led anyone straight to the heart of the maze, but rather let them find it on their own so that they might enjoy the same pleasure of solving a puzzle.

This same satisfaction came to her when she was trying

to understand a particularly complicated bit of glamour or piece together the answer to a charade; puzzles in all their forms fascinated her.

After a happy wander, they came to the rose beds in the middle of the maze. Heavy blossoms still bobbed on their canes in a dwindling palette of pinks, reds, and whites.

"Oh! How beautiful!" Miss Dunkirk dashed to the nearest rosebush and inhaled the subtle perfume. "One imagines lovers from one of Mrs. Radcliffe's novels walking through these flowers and declaring their love and undying passion."

"It is hard for me to imagine that! My memories are of hiding from our governess here."

"Did you truly hide? I would have imagined that you were a dutiful pupil."

"I was, for the most part, but for a period of several months our governess was quite taken with dosing us with the vilest tonic you can imagine. I hid whenever it was time for the tonic, hoping that this time, I would get away, but she always found me in the end. So now, every turn makes me think of the secret passages and running from tonics."

Miss Dunkirk's face lit with delight. "Are there secret passages?"

"Not formally, but there were places where a shrub is missing and tree branches were trained to cover the gap." Jane laughed as old memories came trooping back. "I had quite forgotten how I used to frustrate Henry—Captain Livingston, now—when he stayed with his aunt. Lady

FitzCameron would let him come to play with us, but his idea of playing involved chasing us with snakes or toads."

"Did he! I cannot imagine him being so awful." Miss Dunkirk clapped her hands and leaned closer, her face shining with merriment. "Oh, do tell me. What was he like as a boy?"

"A scoundrel. I suppose all little boys are, but he was the only one close to our age at the time. Nothing delighted him more than making us shriek. So I would run into the maze and hide while he looked everywhere for me. It was easy, for a small girl could slip through the gaps. The hardest thing was controlling my laughter as he ran past me. I have not thought to cut through the hedge in years, and it is likely that I am no longer small enough to do so." She touched the petals of a rose, thinking of her father's request that she wear roses, and then of the ball, where she would gladly have slipped through the walls. "I think I prefer your imaginings to my memories. This should be a place for lovers."

"Mr. Vincent would like it, I think. It is so hard to tell what he likes and does not like, but I think that he is fond of seclusion, so a hidden garden would appeal to him. Do you not think so?"

"Perhaps. I know very little of him." Jane winced, remembering the *tableau vivant* on the hill. "I am afraid that he does not care for me."

"Oh, but that's not true! He likes you very much."

Surprized, Jane said, "Does he? It does not seem so to me. What has he said to make you think that he does?"

"*I* said that you were very talented, and he didn't say that you *weren't*—which might not seem like much to you, but to one who knows him, it is clear that he agreed, or he would have said otherwise. Oh, he is very droll like that. A look or a glance will be all he will allow of his thoughts, but to one who knows him, it is as if he had said a volume."

Jane wondered that Miss Dunkirk would boast so of knowing him, almost as if they had the intimacy of family. "I must bow to your judgment, since I know so little of the man and you study with him."

"He is such a wonderful teacher. Truly he is. Though I wish I had half the talent that you do." Miss Dunkirk sighed and sat on the bench in the middle of the roses. "He is like my brother: They both think that the arts are the highest accomplishments and think little of people without those skills."

A small hope flared in Jane's breast that Mr. Dunkirk might learn of Melody's deficiency in the matter of the arts, but she quashed it as ruthlessly as she could. Though she felt she would have been justified in exposing Melody after her trick the day before, Jane would not—she could not—bring herself to be anything less than virtuous with regards to Mr. Dunkirk if she had any hope of gaining his—

Jane reined in her thought there. No. She had no hope of that. She must remember herself and not be tempted by the idle thoughts of Mr. Dunkirk's sister, who was, after all, very young and given to fancies.

"Now, I know you have spoken falsely, for your brother holds you in high regard."

"Well, he is bound to! Mr. Vincent is not, but I begin to think that he likes me a little, because he is not so cross as when he first came. I have seen him once or twice almost smile at me when I did something right."

"Ah. 'Almost smiles' are indeed something worth working for."

"You may teaze me, but Mr. Vincent's praise is more valuable for being rare." Miss Dunkirk's gaze turned inward, and her countenance darkened. "Teachers with quick praise are not to be trusted."

Jane regarded her, wondering again what her history was that gave her periods of such darkness. These moods had become rarer as she and Miss Dunkirk had gotten to know each other, but some chance word or turn of phrase would still cast her spirits down from time to time. Jane wanted to bring her back to her former laughing self, so she said, "I have always thought that the least trustworthy teachers were the ones with tonics."

A laugh broke out of Miss Dunkirk, restoring gaiety to her face. "I thank the heavens I have never had a tutor with tonics."

At that point, Mr. Dunkirk and Melody finally reached the center of the maze. "There you are. We have been hearing your laughter, but could not find you. At least, I could not. I am certain that Miss Melody knew her way through the maze precisely."

"It does not do to go too quickly to the heart, Mr. Dunkirk," Melody said, her gaze cast downward, looking out from under her eyelashes at him. "I knew you would find your way sooner or later."

Oblivious to Melody's flirtation, Miss Dunkirk hurried at once to her brother's side. "Oh, Edmund. You must build a shrubbery at Robinsford Abbey with a maze in it. I can think of nothing more charming. Say you will. Do, say you will."

He ruffled Miss Dunkirk's hair fondly, as if she were still a little child. "And where does this desire come from? I cannot think of hearing you express a preference for mazes before now."

"It is only that it is so charming and romantic. Well, Miss Ellsworth doesn't think it is, but I do. Say you will build one."

"Oh?" He ignored her renewed entreaty and arched an eyebrow at Jane, who had remained at the bench when they entered. "And what is your opinion of mazes?"

Between Jane and Miss Dunkirk they related the tale of the governess with the tonic. Melody joined in the recital with details which Jane had quite forgotten. As the group made their way out of the maze, Jane gradually faded to the back of the conversation. Melody sparkled and laughed, holding the attention of the Dunkirks with her charm. So Jane, who had not the heart to listen, was the first to see the man exiting their house.

To her surprize, Mr. Vincent had come to call.

Ten

The Broken Bridge

Upon seeing them, Mr. Vincent looked as though he would like to vanish, either into the house or under one of his charms, but after a moment he greeted Miss Dunkirk with more cordiality than Jane would have suspected him capable, and offered only slightly less to the rest of the party.

Miss Dunkirk wanted to shew him the maze at once, but her brother suggested that perhaps Mr. Vincent had come for some purpose and that they should let him communicate that first. At that, Mr. Vincent stammered and rubbed at the ground with his boot and looked so ill at ease that Jane suggested that they retire to the drawing room, thinking that it might give him some time to gather his wits. It seemed apparent that her judgment was entirely correct in that by the time they reached the drawing room, he had returned to his usual taciturn self.

Once they had seated themselves and Jane had rung for some refreshments, Mr. Vincent seemed to gather his strength. He said, "Lady FitzCameron sent me. She thought I might amuse Miss Melody in her convalescence." He left unsaid the rest of his thought, that Melody seemed uninjured and that his trip was to no purpose.

"How kind, Mr. Vincent! I am quite well, as you see, but I do appreciate Lady FitzCameron's generous attention." Melody's warmth was too much for Jane to bear, knowing how much of the attention was due to a deliberate falsehood.

"If you will excuse me," Jane said, "I should see to our mother. She was not well this morning and I have been too long away." As she let herself out of the room, she reflected that her own words, while strictly true, were at their heart as much a falsehood as Melody's. Though Mrs. Ellsworth had been unwell that morning, Jane had no real concern for her well-being. She simply needed to be away so that she did not have to bear witness to the fruits of her sister's behaviour.

She went upstairs to her mother's rooms and spent a quarter hour helping Mrs. Ellsworth with the arrangement of her pillows—which were not fluffed enough and then were lofted too high, and with the blankets, which were too hot and then too cold—when she heard the front door close.

"Who do you suppose that is?" Mrs. Ellsworth queried.

"I am sure I do not know. It might be the Dunkirks departing, or Mr. Vincent."

"Well, go at once and look. My nerves cannot abide not knowing."

Jane went to the window and, seeing the figures on horseback ride down the front sweep said, "It was Mr. and Miss Dunkirk on their way to Robinsford Abbey." Which meant that Melody was now alone with Mr. Vincent. Well, Jane need not rescue Melody from that quarter: he may torture her with silence and his brusque nature, but he would not do anything to inspire any real danger of impropriety from Melody. So Jane stayed by her mother's side adjusting all the small comforts needed to ease her fretting. She had just begun to read to her from William Meinhold's *Sidonia the Sorceress: The Supposed Destroyer of the Whole Reigning Ducal House of Pomerania* when the distant sound of the front door opening and shutting interrupted her recital.

"Who is that?" Mrs. Ellsworth demanded.

"Mr. Vincent departing, I should expect," Jane said.

Her mother plucked at the blanket fretfully and craned her neck toward the window as though by artful twisting of her head she might see out it. Jane put aside the book without waiting for her mother to ask a second time. She looked out the window, fully expecting that Mr. Vincent would be striding across the lawn, but saw no one.

"Well?" her mother demanded querulously from the bed. "Who is it? Was it Mr. Vincent?"

"No. Someone must have arrived, but I do not know who it could be." Jane returned to her book, intent on resuming where she had left off, with Sidonia in danger from a bear, but her mother was not willing to let the matter rest.

"Oh, I do hope it is not Lady FitzCameron. Perhaps I should prepare myself in case it is. It would not do to receive her in bed. Now, if it were Mrs. Marchand, it would be quite a different story because Joy is always so generous and so understanding of my neuralgia. She would be quite, quite willing to see me in the state that I am in, especially after the fright over poor Melody."

"First, Mother, I am certain that it is not Lady FitzCameron, for her carriage is not at the door. Second, you have no reason to be still afraid for poor Melody, as we went for a walk in the shrubbery this morning and she gave every sign of having affected a full recovery."

"Oh! I do wish I had been consulted. I would have told her not to go walking under any circumstances. A fall such as hers can have grave consequences later, without any warning. Mark my words, she will be plagued with health troubles for the rest of her life."

Jane feared that was true, though not for the reasons put forward by her mother. She had a vision of Melody becoming an invalid like Mrs. Ellsworth, for the purpose of the attention it brought to her. She wondered if that was how her mother's case had begun, and if Mrs. Ellsworth knew any longer what her real aches were and which were imagined. Melody's moans of pain had seemed genuine enough. Still, Jane reassured her mother on Melody's general good health as best she could and then asked if she should continue reading *Sidonia the Sorceress*.

"Oh no! I should not be able to concentrate without knowing who is belowstairs. Pray, do go and see who has come. If it is a person of consequence, I should pay my respects."

Jane could have told her mother that if it had been a person of consequence, Nancy would have brought his or her card up straightaway, but she knew that to argue would only prolong the moment when she went to quiet her mother's unease. "Of course. I will be happy to ascertain that for you."

Setting the book aside once more, Jane made her way downstairs. She paused by the parlour door, struck by the bouts of laughter within. Jane cracked the door, peering in at a scene which astounded her.

Melody was seated on the couch by Captain Livingston, who must have been the recent arrival. They faced Mr. Vincent, who was conjuring small vignettes on the tea table before them. Jane could barely make out the illusion from where she was, so she crept farther into the room in order to see better. Mindful of Mr. Vincent's feelings, she endeavored not to watch the folds he manipulated, but to focus on the small manikins. Even so, she marveled at his skill in managing the minuscule folds needed to create the illusion. The scenery, he had tied off; but beyond that, she was unwilling to look. She would try to enjoy the scene for what it was.

He had conjured a setting of trees which served as a sort of proscenium arch. Their jeweled leaves glowed in the air with the idealized beauty of stained glass. The figures were cunning silhouettes, without color, like living shadows made from the fabric of glamour. A traveller, after a number of obstacles, approached a bridge, which was in the process of being destroyed by a workman with a pickax. Jane at once recognized it as the French shadow-play *The Broken Bridge*. The traveller tried to get the workman to tell him how to cross the river, and after receiving a series of increasingly rude answers, he found a boat and crossed the river.

Though it was a crude story and she knew how it ended, when the traveller approached the workman from behind and kicked him into the river, Jane laughed as heartily as the others.

Mr. Vincent dropped the folds he was holding and, with his breath still somewhat quickened from the shadow-play, rose to his feet. Captain Livingston sprang to his feet an instant after, ever the gallant, but Melody stayed seated, her face subsiding into a mask of bland pleasure.

Sketching a quick bow, Captain Livingston said, "Miss Ellsworth, I had hoped you would make an appearance. Mr. Vincent is being most gracious and amusing us with his talents. Do join us."

"Forgive me, I did not mean to interrupt, I only came because our mother wished to know who had arrived. I must go reassure her; she is not well today."

"Of course. Please give her my regards and my hopes that she is soon recovered," Captain Livingston said. Though he was perfect courtesy, Jane felt as if she were already out of the room in his mind.

"I enjoyed watching your shadow-play, Mr. Vincent," Jane said.

"Did you?" His flushed countenance seemed to doubt her words.

"*The Broken Bridge* has but rarely amused me, while your rendition made me laugh aloud. Though he was but silhouette, I could quite imagine the face of the workman as he fell into the river."

"La! Jane, you will strip enjoyment from everything with your endless examinations." Melody picked her fan up from the side table and flicked it open; the sharp rattle as the fan opened expressed her irritation far beyond the sweet tone of her voice.

"I would not want to diminish your enjoyment." Jane forced a smile to her face. "Good day, gentlemen."

Escaping the drawing room, she could not stand to return to her mother. Finding Nancy in the hall, Jane asked her to tell Mrs. Ellsworth who the visitor was and that Jane would attend to her later.

Jane headed out of the house to lose herself in the maze, which she hoped would hold a measure of peace in its heart.

* * *

As the weeks passed, Captain Livingston came to the house on an increasingly regular basis, until it seemed he was quite a regular fixture. Jane wondered if Lady FitzCameron were well pleased with this devotion of Captain Livingston's to a family which was not his own. Jane needed more frequent reasons to be out of the house, so she was particularly grateful to have found a friend in young Miss Dunkirk. Though years separated them, she felt that she and the young woman were kindred spirits. As she and Miss Dunkirk spent more time in each other's company, it was only natural that they began to call one another by their Christian names as a sign of their mutual affection for each other.

Though it too often put her in contact with Mr. Dunkirk, Jane was frequently in Beth's company at Robinsford Abbey. It was all too easy to see that Beth was lonely for feminine companionship. For her part, Jane endeavored not to shew by word or deed or look that seed of feeling which had taken hold of her heart. This task was much the easier on days when he was away on business, and so Jane found herself timing her visits to coincide with his absences.

On one such afternoon Jane stitched while Beth read aloud. After a particularly emotional passage, Beth stopped and said, "Oh, Jane, have you ever been in love?"

Jane twitched in surprize and drove the needle into her finger, wondering if she had given herself away by some sigh. Looking up, she saw that Beth was staring out the window with a gaze both melancholy and with the same tenderness which Jane had seen on her sister's face, and in unguarded moments, on her own. "Every girl does, I think, but the feeling soon passes."

"Not if it is real love, it doesn't." Beth seemed to recollect herself. She returned her gaze to the book, stammering, "At least, that's what all the books say."

"One must not put trust in novelists, Beth; they create worlds to fit their own needs and drive their characters mad in doing it." Jane returned her gaze to her sewing, but continued to watch Beth from the corners of her eyes. "What has made you think of such a thing? Is it only the book we are enjoying?"

"Well, that, and something that Mr. Vincent said the other day when he was talking of art. He said that it was his one true love, and that he had no room in his life for anyone other than his muse. And I said, 'What, really?' because I had always thought that artists were passionate, but he was always so cold."

"What did he say to that?"

"He said that he wasn't cold, merely focused. That he could not trust himself to speak because his passion made him uncivil."

Jane laughed, remembering her encounter with him at the strawberry party. "He can be at that."

"I don't think he means to be, though." Beth was silent for a long moment, still staring out the window toward,

Jane realized, the spot where Mr. Vincent had stood painting. "I think his muse is a real person who he cannot be with due to his circumstances. Did you know . . . ?" She leaned forward and said in a hushed voice, "Did you know that Vincent is not his real name? I do not know what it is, but I know that he has some secret in his past, because I overheard my brother talking about it with the investigator before he hired Mr. Vincent to tutor me. Is that not the most romantic thing? I think *that* is why he is so brooding all the time, because of his muse."

"I think he is brooding because he enjoys being disagreeable." Jane waited for Beth to laugh, but she did not. Jane suddenly had the uncomfortable sensation that Beth had other reasons for wondering about love and muses. Carefully, so that it might seem like playful teasing, Jane tried to draw her out by saying, "And why do you brood? Do you have a muse?"

At this, Beth did laugh, blushing, and turned her face away. "It is not Mr. Vincent, if that is what you think."

A silence reigned between them for some moments, until Beth picked up the book and resumed her reading, as if nothing had occurred. Too distracted to follow the plight of the heroine of Beth's book, Jane continued working on her needlepoint, willing to pretend that the conversation had not happened, but conscious that Beth held a secret in her heart.

The door to the drawing room opened and Mr. Dunkirk stood, framed in the opening, windswept and breathless.

"Miss Ellsworth. I am glad to see you; it seems too long since our paths have crossed."

Jane put her sewing aside and rose to greet him. "Mr. Dunkirk, you are so often away on business that I wondered if you were still in residence."

"I am not away so often as that." He pulled off his riding gloves and strode into the room. "One might begin to think that the two of you conspire to exclude me."

Jane flushed and stammered that he was incorrect, painfully aware how inadequate a rebuttal she made.

"Edmund! You know she speaks nothing but the truth. You are forever away," Beth said. "Jane, you simply don't know how often I wish Edmund would be home, but he is instead away to London. And he will never take me with him."

"London would not suit you, Beth." He beckoned to her. "But perhaps you might like what I have brought for you. It is a gift that I have had in mind for some time, and I suspect will inspire you to forgive me for being gone today."

"Do you see! Do you see how he bribes me so I will forgive him for inviting me here and then ignoring me?" Beth turned in her chair, as if to shun her brother, but it was clear by the curve of her cheek that she enjoyed teazing him.

"Then humor me, and come see it."

Beth's looks spoke loudly of a curiosity about what he might have brought, and it did not take much more coaxing to draw her into the hall. Jane followed them, wondering what it would be like to have Mr. Dunkirk dote upon her as he doted upon his sister.

The front door of the abbey stood open, letting the sunlight stream in and gild the dust motes. Outside the door, framed in the perfect pastoral setting, stood a roan mare. Even to Jane's unpracticed eye, she seemed the most graceful of beasts. Her mane blew in the gentle breeze, showing off her long, fine neck.

By chance, Beth was looking around the foyer instead of out the front door, and so did not see this elegant creature. Mr. Dunkirk stopped her in the hall. "Beth, stay a moment. Do you see nothing that you like?"

Jane held her breath, watching, waiting for the moment when Beth saw the mare. With a puzzled frown, Beth turned slowly, looking about the foyer for a parcel or some other small gift. Only when she had completed nearly a full circle did she face the door.

"Oh." Deep in her eyes, a glow kindled. She turned to her brother, slowly, eyes still caught by the mare. "Is she . . . ?"

"Yours." He put his hand over hers, squeezing with that careful tenderness which belongs to a loving family.

Jane stood outside the tableau, content to not be within the circle of excitement which went round the mare and the Dunkirks, and yet longing for someone in her own family who understood her as thoroughly as Mr. Dunkirk understood his sister. As one, Beth and her brother started forward; Mr. Dunkirk was full of particulars of the mare's heritage and training. He talked of her height and her gaits, but Jane heard only his fondness for his sister.

At the threshold, Beth turned to look back. "Jane, aren't you coming?"

"Yes! Please do. I saw your card when I returned, so I had another mare saddled for you." Mr. Dunkirk kept possession of his sister's arm, but turned his body toward Jane. "It would give me great pleasure if you would join us."

"I—I am not a horsewoman. I would only hold you back from your pleasure in the ride." On horseback, her stiff carriage showed itself even more clearly than on the dance floor.

"But, really, you must come. I do not doubt that I shall only want to go slowly." Beth loosed her hand from her brother's arm and reached imploringly to Jane. "I shall not want to go unless you come with us."

"In that case, I would be delighted to accompany you." Her dress did not suit, but neither was it one which she feared to injure; indeed, for the Dunkirks, Jane would have shredded her favourite gown with only a small pang of regret.

She followed them out onto the front steps. Another groom stood with two other horses to the side of the door. Mr. Dunkirk saw his sister safely onto the new mare and then walked with Jane to a placid gray beast. She knew that it was placid, and yet she could only see its size, and remember the exhilarating fear she experienced every time she was on horseback. Before that memory of fear could overwhelm her, Mr. Dunkirk was handing her up to the horse and helping her settle in the saddle. His hands were strong; his movements sure.

He handed her the reins, seeming to sense the fear in the line of her back. "Her name is Daisy. She will follow my horse, and I will be certain to keep the pace slow. Beth may forget her promise and want to run her new mare, but I will stay back with you."

"No, you must not. You must stay with her."

He shook his head and looked down, resting his hand on Daisy's neck. "Do not protest, unless it is to truly and honestly declare that you love to gallop. I rely on your honour, Miss Ellsworth."

Closing her mouth, Jane sighed. "No, I will be happiest at a walk. It is true."

"Then we understand each other." Mr. Dunkirk swung into the saddle of his tall black gelding. "Shall we?"

As Mr. Dunkirk predicted, Beth enjoyed the walk for about a quarter of an hour before she succumbed to the need to gallop her new mare. "I cannot name her until I do. It is quite impossible, and she must have a name which suits her." Beth wrinkled her nose. "Bacon? Who would name a dainty mare that?"

"I think it is the pattern in her sock. The area where the roan blends down to the white does look very much like the marbling in bacon."

"Well. My horse will not be called Bacon. It is utterly ridiculous. She is grace and elegance itself, but I must know how she runs to know her name. I must know if she yearns for it or is a more timid creature."

Mr. Dunkirk glanced sideways at Jane with understanding before suggesting that Beth ride to the fencerow ahead of them, and then come back to join their more sedate pace. She agreed at once.

Without waiting a moment, she urged her mare forward and widened the distance between them so suddenly that it seemed to Jane as if her own mount had begun to move backwards.

Mr. Dunkirk sighed. "I am glad to see her in such high spirits about the mare. I worry that she suffers in my absence. I cannot thank you enough for the kindnesses you have shown her."

"You must believe that spending time with Beth is my pleasure."

"She is a good girl." He sighed again and watched the distant figure of his sister. "She has friends in the city whom I could invite to visit. Do you think that would be a good course?"

"Perhaps . . . or perhaps you might take Beth up to town with you on some trip."

Beth turned back, her horse quickly depleting the distance and time in which Jane could have private conversation with Mr. Dunkirk.

"That is a thought. The families of some of Beth's friends must be in town. Although our mother will have a fit if she is not allowed to bring Beth out in grand London style. I think Beth is too fragile for that."

Though Jane longed to know why he thought Beth was fragile, she merely said, "Being in town does not mean she must be out. Numerous good people do not count such things as important."

"Really?" Mr. Dunkirk said. "I am not certain I have met a young lady who is not vitally concerned with the minutiae of 'out' and 'not out.' I thought it was all that women talked of."

"Oh yes, certainly. Of a certainty. Just as all men are only concerned with their pointers. Indeed, Mr. Dunkirk, I am surprized that you have been able to restrain yourself from giving me the distinguishing features of your pointers for so long as you have."

He laughed, a deep and glorious laugh. "Ah, Miss Ellsworth. It is no wonder that you have done Beth so much good."

And in the space where Jane's answer would have been spoken, Beth thundered up to them, reining in her horse with enviable ease. "Llamrei! Her name is Llamrei, after King Arthur's mare! And she is the most wonderful horse ever. We reached the hedgerow and I could feel that she wanted to jump, but we did not, though *I* wanted to as well. Oh, Edmund. She is glorious. I could not ask for a finer horse."

Mr. Dunkirk affected a frown. "Beth, you will hurt poor Daisy's feelings."

"Poo! She is a nursemaid, not a horse." Beth clasped her hand over her mouth. "Oh, Jane, I did not mean to suggest . . ."

Jane laughed and forced herself to remove one hand from the reins so she could pat Daisy on the neck. "A nursemaid is precisely the horse for me. I am not the horsewoman that you are."

"Should we go back?" Newly aware of her friend's unease on horseback, Beth was anxious to guard her comfort.

"No, the day is pleasant yet. And though it surprizes me to admit this, I am enjoying the ride. My nursemaid is taking splendid care of me."

"Are you certain?

Jane said that she was. Mr. Dunkirk turned his horse's head to ride along the side of the hedgerow. For a time, the three of them ambled together, talking idly of the sorts of easy topics which a pleasant day inspires.

As the hedgerow turned, they spied Mr. Vincent sketching under a shaded patch on the far side. A quicksilver of unease flourished through Jane's joints. They had come upon him while he was engaged in the very activity in which he least appreciated company.

Mr. Dunkirk hailed the glamourist, who, much to Jane's surprize, smiled upon spying him. By the word "smile," make no mistake that Mr. Vincent bared his teeth or in any other way effused, but the slight upturn of his lips warmed his face and gave ample evidence of a sincere pleasure at their presence.

Or, rather, at the Dunkirks' presence, for Jane detected a slight compression in his jaw when he spied her. No doubt he had wished to see her sister. Nonetheless, he bowed correctly and shewed no other sign of displeasure.

Beth said, "What a fine day for drawing. You must be in

raptures about the light. Truly I can think of nothing that mars the day."

"If you discount the bugs and the heat, then yes, it is a fine day." He returned his attention to his sketchbook and continued drawing, as if expecting them to leave shortly.

Laughing, Beth said, "You would find something to complain about in Paradise."

"I do not complain about flaws; I merely note them." His gaze lifted from the page for a moment to look at Jane. "I believe this is a trait belonging to all artists. Do you agree, Miss Ellsworth?"

Her heart sped unaccountably at the challenge in his gaze. "In part, which I suspect proves your point. I think it is difficult for an artist to view something without an eye to improving it."

Mr. Dunkirk said, "So would you then also find the flaws in Paradise?"

"I do not know. One would think that by its very nature, Paradise must embody perfection. Thus if one were to find flaws, it must not be Paradise. But I have often thought that the juxtaposition of the perfect with the flawed is the only thing which allows us to appreciate perfection."

Mr. Vincent nodded but said nothing; his pencil continued to move across the page. Jane cast about, looking for the thing which held his interest so completely. Beyond them, a gnarled apple tree twisted in a most picturesque manner, the branches seeming to have been pruned by a heavenly gardener into a pleasing shape.

Beth wrinkled her nose. "Mr. Vincent, I do not notice you enjoying the day any more because of the bugs and heat."

He snorted in response. "The heat allows me to enjoy a cooling breeze more than I would were the temperature merely pleasant."

"Then do you introduce imperfections deliberately in your own work?" Mr. Dunkirk sidled his horse next to the hedgerow, leaning over as if to see what Mr. Vincent drew.

"No."

"No? You surprize me." Mr. Dunkirk turned to Jane. "And you, Miss Ellsworth?"

"I do not. Were I ever to achieve perfection, my opinion might differ from Mr. Vincent's, but it is a theory I am unlikely to have the opportunity to test."

"Oh, but Jane, your portrait of Miss Melody is a perfect likeness. You have captured her in every way imaginable; even the glamour that you placed on the portrait makes her hair move in just the right way. Oh, Mr. Vincent, have you seen this portrait? Do you not agree with me?"

Mr. Vincent stopped with his pencil held over the page for a long moment. His tongue wet his lips. "Perfection is different to every viewer. I will agree that the portrait is a remarkable likeness."

"But not perfect?"

Jane could stand no more of this. "You flatter me, Beth,

but it is not perfect. Do not press Mr. Vincent any further. I assure you that I know of several answers that he could make to explain how it is lacking, and we have kept him from his drawing quite long enough."

Mr. Vincent closed his sketchbook. "Not at all. This has been a stimulating conversation."

In response, Mr. Dunkirk bowed his head. "It has indeed. If you are finished here, then perhaps you would care to join us at Robinsford Abbey to continue it?"

"Thank you. I accept."

Jane twisted the reins in her hands as Mr. Vincent clambered over the fencerow. "Alas, I am afraid that I must decline. I am expected at home and have left my mother alone too long."

Though the Dunkirks protested, Jane felt that spending another minute as a subject of comparison to the talented Mr. Vincent was intolerable. She kept her face placid, though, and focused on her concern for her mother. Mr. Vincent agreed to meet the Dunkirks later, after they saw Jane back to Long Parkmead.

Leaving Mr. Vincent at the fence, they turned the horses to Long Parkmead, impressing Jane with the speed by which they were able to cover the distance between their two estates. It felt as if no time had elapsed between her stated interest in returning home and when they arrived at the sweep.

Mr. Dunkirk dismounted to hand Jane down from Daisy. She felt as light as an infant as he almost lifted her from the saddle and set her on the ground. Standing on her own, she felt heavy and stiff.

"I trust we did not discomfit you." Mr. Dunkirk pressed her hand, his voice low. "My sister is too forthright at times."

"You need have no concern." The sound of her heartbeat rang in her ears. Jane turned to Beth, lest she be overcome by his closeness. "May I call tomorrow?"

Receiving assurances from them both that she was always welcome in their home, Jane said her good-byes and went inside.

Eleven

A Dinner Invitation

Some weeks later, Jane returned from a walk and found the house in a frenzy of activity. The Ellsworths had received an invitation from Lady FitzCameron to a dinner celebrating the completion of Mr. Vincent's glamural in the dining room.

Mrs. Ellsworth was trying to persuade Mr. Ellsworth that they must go at once to order new gowns for the occasion, to which her husband replied, "If our friends and neighbours do not understand and value our daughters' talent and beauty by this point, then a new gown will not increase their estimation."

"But what of Captain Livingston?" Mrs. Ellsworth said. "Surely he has not been in our company long enough to form an opinion. Surely we must impress him." She looked here at Melody. Jane kept the placid expression on her face only by long practice.

Mr. Ellsworth said, "As Captain Livingston has not had time to see the innumerable dresses hanging in your wardrobes, I doubt that he will be more impressed by a new gown than by one which he merely has not seen. Besides, I do not think there is enough time for the modiste to outfit all of you."

Mrs. Ellsworth was forced to concede his point, so she turned the talk to exactly which of the gowns she and Melody would wear. Jane was included in the conversation, but more as a consultant than as a participant, since the chief purpose of Mrs. Ellsworth's enthusiasm was to bring Melody to the forefront of Captain Livingston's attention.

Mr. Ellsworth stood and drew Jane away from the conversation to the side of the room. Looking out the window, he sighed several times before speaking. At last he came forth with, "Will you walk with me, Jane?"

Jane followed her father out of doors, surprized at his request for her company. They proceeded down the Long Walk for some minutes before he ventured to speak. When he did, the topic did not seem one which merited a solitary walk.

"Will you wear the white dress? The one with the pretty"—he waved his hands at his chest in a vain effort to supply the right word—"the pretty green things."

Her white sprigged chemise, with its sash of delicate

green ribbon, which Mr. Dunkirk had once said reminded him of spring. It would be a suitable dress to wear to the FitzCameron dinner. "Of course. I had no idea you took such an interest in my wardrobe, Papa."

He chuckled and tucked his fingers into his vest. "I take an interest in my daughters' welfare." So saying, he was quiet for some time as they continued down the Long Walk, leaving Jane to ponder what it might be that so troubled her father. At last he continued, "I shall trust to your discretion, Jane, but I do worry, as any right-thinking father would. And so I ask what might not be seemly to ask. Does it seem to you that Melody might have shifted her affections? To be precise, have you observed a growing attachment between her and Captain Livingston?"

Jane was so taken aback by this query that they walked on for some feet before she felt herself equal to answering. "I hardly know what answer to give, sir. My sister has not confessed her heart to me, and if she did, I would feel obligated to preserve her trust."

He nodded. "But you told me when you thought she had developed an attachment for Mr. Dunkirk, did you not? Does this query represent any less of a concern for your sister's well-being? I will not require you to answer, only think: does keeping your silence help your sister, or will it ultimately harm her?"

"I cannot think that you believe Captain Livingston capable of harming my sister." But Jane wondered if her own motive in exposing her sister's regard for Mr. Dunkirk had been less a concern for her sister's reputation and more from a wish to separate and halt a relationship which she had no reason to desire. "Is there some reason you ask me this?"

"Only that I notice that he calls more frequently and that in their excitement to be ready for the dinner, Melody and your mother spoke only of Captain Livingston." He paused in his walk and fingered the branch of a shrubbery as if it were an aid to his thoughts. "*You* do not speak of Captain Livingston."

His emphasis left little doubt of his meaning, and his next words removed all uncertainty. "Is there one of whom you do speak, or wish to speak?"

Jane thought of Mr. Dunkirk and of the happy hours in Beth's company, which had afforded Jane time to closely judge his character and to find it in every way as good and honest as it had appeared from a distance. She had not hitherto allowed herself to hope, but if Melody's affections had truly transferred to Captain Livingston, that would remove the most immediate obstacle to Mr. Dunkirk. It left her plainness and her awkward carriage, but to a man such as him, might these things be overlooked in favour of her talent?

But these were idle fancies, not suitable for voicing even to herself, much less to her father, howsoever much she honoured him for his concern on her behalf. Jane said merely, "There is no one to speak of."

Her father broke off his study of the shrubbery and turned to her. Jane kept her composure under his gaze, knowing that she had told nothing but the truth.

The small hope in her heart was nothing of which she could speak.

The night of Lady FitzCameron's dinner party, Mr. Ellsworth presented each of his daughters and his wife with a posy which he had picked with his own hands from the rose garden in the middle of the maze. Though he had needed Nancy's aid in turning them into something other than an odd assortment of flowers which he had wrested from the rosebushes, the final effect was so pleasing that the Misses Ellsworth and Mrs. Ellsworth lost no time adding the corsages to their toilette for the evening.

Jane stood before the mirror in her room, attempting to find the most pleasing arrangement of the pale pink blossoms with which her father had gifted her. Left alone for a moment as her mother and sister fussed over their toilet in the next room, Jane indulged in something which she had never before considered.

She worked a small glamour on herself.

It was a tiny thing, but she was suddenly struck by a curiosity as to what her face would look like if her nose were not quite so long. By twists and turns, she gave her nose an appearance more suited to her face. Her breath quickened only a little as she turned her head to examine the glamour, while keeping tight control over the strings holding the folds in place over her nose. Without its prominence, her eyes seemed softer. Her chin, though still sharp, no longer seemed ready to pinch someone.

The sudden reappearance of Melody made Jane drop the folds hastily.

"Jane! What are you doing?"

She colored and busied herself with the roses. "Merely amusing myself."

"I saw." Melody crossed the room. "Do it again."

"No. I was only playing to pass the time."

It was apparent that Melody did not believe her. "Well. You should consider playing more often."

The casual cruelty of Melody's statement almost undid Jane. She turned her head away to hide the sudden burn of tears, but Melody saw her upset nonetheless. "Oh, Jane, no. Forgive me. I only meant that you are so clever, and, well, if Miss FitzCameron does it, surely there can be no harm. Is it so much different from chusing a dress which is flattering, or a hairstyle which makes one's neck look longer?"

For a moment Jane let herself be lured by Melody's words. Who would it harm, save her own health? But her conscience scratched at the thought. "Imagine if I did attach a man who believed me to have a shorter nose. Imagine then the day when I must let the glamour drop. He would be more appalled by the sudden change in my appearance than if he had become used to me over time." She shook her head to push the temptation away. "I will not do it again. It was only a passing fancy."

Melody watched her with narrowed eyes, measuring what she had said. "I sometimes wish, for your sake, that you were not so nice with your opinions."

Mrs. Ellsworth bustled in before Jane could reply. The chill between Melody and Jane went unnoticed by their mother, who was too concerned with the placement of her roses. Once she was happy with it, they descended to the carriage and thence to Banbree Manor.

Lady FitzCameron was known to pride herself on the elegance of her table, but took no joy from entertaining. On the occasions when the Ellsworths had been invited to sup with her, she had always received them with the utmost grace, yet remained reserved in attitude. She knew her duty to her neighbours and paid attention to them gladly, but it went no deeper than that: she seemed to care only for her own. However, her attentions to Captain Livingston were gracious to the point of being solicitous, which made Jane wonder if Lady FitzCameron might still have thoughts of arranging a match between Miss FitzCameron and the young captain.

Entering the drawing room, Jane was at once greeted by Beth, and after paying her respects to the Marchands, spent the remainder of the time until dinner was called in conversation with her. They both shared a deep fascination and curiosity about the finished state of Mr. Vincent's glamural.

"You know, he was working on it night and day for the last week. He still came to ours for lessons, but he fell asleep as soon as he sat down. I let him, of course, and he said almost nothing upon waking up. I let him think that he had closed his eyes for only a few moments, but I think he was asleep for a good half an hour at the least. Did you know that he snores? It's such a tiny, such a sweet snore as one might imagine a small cat making."

"I cannot imagine a cat snoring," said Jane.

"Oh, indeed. I had a kitten which always slept with his head tucked upside down between its paws. Mr. Vincent snores just like it. It's such a wee sound to be coming out of a great bear of a man like Mr. Vincent that it is quite droll." As she spoke, her eyes darted about the room in the manner of one whose attention was engaged by another. It never rested for long on any one person, but Jane began to think that Beth was watching Captain Livingston. Since he stood with Mr. Dunkirk, it was possible that she had merely a nervous concern as to her brother's presence. Though Beth was at ease with Jane, she often suffered from an excess of nervous energy when in a crowd. That the people present at Lady FitzCameron's were all known to her did not allow her much peace.

As they stood talking, Mr. Vincent, whose appearance betrayed his fatigue, entered the room and was graciously received by his hostess. His cheeks were sunken and his hair wild; the ruddy glow of health had fled his complexion. Jane could not altogether hide her shock at his change in appearance, and she was not alone in that respect. He affected not to notice, and must have been used to such startled looks as Jane bestowed upon him, for he bowed low to Lady FitzCameron and said, "At your pleasure, my lady."

By this, Jane realized that he had been working up until the moment when he walked into the room. She wondered at Lady FitzCameron's composure and nerve in scheduling a dinner party without knowing if the glamural would be finished. Betraying none of this, Lady FitzCameron assigned each gentleman to escort in a lady. Mr. Marchand came to take charge of Beth, nearly frightening the poor girl with his old-fashioned gallantry. And then, before Jane could stand too long alone, Lady FitzCameron had introduced her to Mr. Buffington, a friend of Captain Livingston's, who was to escort her into dinner.

Mr. Buffington was shorter, with the florid expression of one given to pleasure, but graceful when he bowed his head upon greeting Jane. He was charmed; he was delighted to meet her, having heard so much from Captain Livingston about her. Jane could not help but wonder if he had heard about her, or about Melody. Nonetheless, she accepted his arm graciously and followed him to the dining room.

The couple in front of them paused on the threshold with an intake of breath, then proceeded slowly through the door, their heads turning about in constant amazement.

For her part, Jane nearly stumbled with her own astonishment when she entered the dining room, though the wonders of the room seemed to have no impact on Mr. Buffington. When she had seen the unfinished room at the FitzCameron ball, she had marveled at its artistry and elegance, but she had not imagined how complete, how perfect, the illusion would be upon completion.

The room had vanished, its walls replaced entirely by arching trees; the ceiling, a sky overhead which shimmered with the light of stars and the moon. The trees rustled in response to a conjured breeze, which carried with it hints of jasmine and the pleasant, spicy scent of loam. The brook, which had so entranced her at the ball, continued its babbling, but now it was accompanied by birdsong from a nightingale that sat on one of the tree branches, singing its melody at exactly the right volume to be unobtrusive in a gathering.

They walked on a floor of soft grass that seemed to cushion their feet beyond what any glamour should be able to do.

In the midst of this glade, the mahagony clawfoot table, rather than jarring with all the plates and silver necessary for a dinner of forty, seemed as if it were something out of a tale of enchantment. The crystal and silver gleamed in the glamour and its formal lines were juxtaposed against the wild beauty of the trees to create a careful elegance.

Though the sky shewed nighttime, the room did not lack for light, as the table abounded with candles which gleamed against the silver and crystal assembled there. Mr. Buffington led Jane to her seat while chattering about how it was a shame that this was not a real forest, for there was sure to be good hunting in a wood such as this. He no doubt took her hushed reverence as a sign of her interest in his hunters.

Jane now well understood Mr. Vincent's fatigue. She had imagined after seeing the early steps of the glamural at the ball that he had little remaining to do, but she had not understood how complete his vision would be. Already at the table, Mr. Dunkirk stood behind the chair next to hers, waiting for all the ladies to be seated. He had escorted Mrs. Ellsworth, who chattered to him with the same ambivalence to the surroundings as Mr. Buffington. Jane wanted to apologize to Mr. Dunkirk for her mother, but until the table turned, she was bound to pay attention to Mr. Buffington, leaving poor Mr. Dunkirk to the banalities of her mother's conversation.

She admired the room, resisting the temptation to delve beneath the surface of the illusion. The ambiance of the room soothed her, and she let herself relax into it, without worrying about how it had been created. As she took Mr. Vincent's advice to experience the art without struggling to see behind the scenes, she felt the impact of the piece manifest in an unexpected yearning. The vitality of the room extended beyond the mere execution of glamour and into palpable emotion; Jane could not imagine creating so rich an environment.

As Jane took her seat between Mr. Dunkirk and

Mr. Buffington, she glanced across the table at Melody. Her sister had been brought in by the aging vicar who had the living at Banbree, and was seated next to Mr. Marchand. To her credit, she gave the vicar the courtesy of her attention, though her eyes did wander down the table to the head, where Captain Livingston did the honours as the host. His attention was engaged by his dinner partner, yet he somehow contrived to include Miss FitzCameron in the conversation as well. Jane could not see how Miss FitzCameron's partner was taking this monopoly of conversation, but suspected that with Captain Livingston's natural charm he would not feel ill-used.

When all the guests were settled, Lady FitzCameron raised her glass to Mr. Vincent, who had been accorded the seat on her right as the honoured guest this evening. "Dear friends: Mr. Vincent is a glamourist beyond compare, as his work here testifies. Let us raise a toast to his work and to his health."

They all raised their glasses with a will, even Mr. Buffington agreeing that he had never seen the like. Mr. Vincent rose and bowed, and then, before their acclaim could die away, he reached out and twisted his hand once, releasing a flock of doves which flew up and disappeared against the night sky in a rain of stardust.

Everyone applauded at that, and Mr. Vincent sat down again. His hand shook as he reached for his wineglass. Though Jane longed to know how he had accomplished the illusion, she kept her faith with him by not peeking behind the scenes. Resolutely, she turned her attention away from his end of the table, and back to Mr. Buffington.

For the whole of the first three courses, Jane endured his conversation, smiling when she must and giving his unceasing discourse about hunters, pointers, and pheasants such attention that it unfortunately encouraged him to talk all the more. It was fortunate that he did not require much response beyond, "Oh, my," and "Is that so?" for it left Jane free to soak in the ambiance of the glamour which Mr. Vincent had wrought.

The area she studied most lay past Mr. Buffington's shoulder. A grove of delicate laurel trees trembled in the light breeze. Rendered in far greater detail than Mr. Vincent had employed in the scenery for his shadow-play, Jane could still sense his hand in the graceful line of the trunks. It was apparent that they were inspired by the laurel tree above Long Parkmead's strawberry patch, but none of his trees slavishly copied the original.

When the fourth course began and the table was turned, Jane was at last freed from the dinner partner on her left and could address the one on her right. To talk with Mr. Dunkirk would give her much pleasure as she felt certain he would share her enthusiasm for the forest glade around them. Once they had moved past the pleasantries which convention dictated, Mr. Dunkirk asked, with brow raised, "May I ask for your opinion on Mr. Vincent's work?"

"I have never seen such exquisite attention to detail or

sophistication in rendering." Jane bit her lip, aware that she had spoken of the technical rather than the artistic merits of his work. "It quite makes me feel as if I am out-of-doors and at peace. I would not have thought a dinner party could be so restful as this."

With the barest look beyond Jane at her dinner partner, Mr. Dunkirk said, "Some conversations may be more taxing than others."

"Indeed. I wonder how Mr. Vincent is faring with my mother." She glanced past Mr. Dunkirk to the glamourist, who was gazing at her mother with a glazed expression. From the back of Mrs. Ellsworth's head, it seemed clear that she was discussing something with great animation. "What conversation did she favour you with? Was it the weather or the price of silk?"

"Neither. We discussed the art in your home at length and she told me about as many pieces as she could. I believe we had just finished with the south wall of the drawing room when the table turned, so I will have to call to see what the west wall holds. It is a pleasure to which I look forward."

Jane blushed. "I fear that there are no new pictures in the drawing room, so your visit will find only that which you have seen before."

"I expect that I will have a new appreciation for what I find in your home. This is often the way with things which have been seen, but overlooked by circumstance." He took a drink of his wine. "Your mother has been so gracious as to invite my sister and me for tea tomorrow."

"How wonderful." Despite the cooling breeze that Mr. Vincent had generated, the room was suddenly too hot. "But if we are going to discuss art, let us turn to something worthy of discussion. What is *your* opinion of the room?"

"I find it quite astounding. Beth's first tutor was a man of talent, but would never have been capable of something such as this."

"I had understood that Beth had not studied glamour before arriving here."

Mr. Dunkirk's eyes widened. He looked down hurriedly to examine the dish in front of him, stammering the start of three different sentences at once. She had clearly said something that inadvertently opened a subject painful to him. To relieve him of whatever discomfort he felt, Jane changed the subject by affecting to drop her napkin.

He retrieved it, clearly grateful for the reprieve, but she still puzzled over this. Could this mysterious first tutor be the key to Beth's dark moods and all of her pining over a muse? A muse who, according to the girl, was *not* Mr. Vincent, but seemed somehow to bring him to mind?

After they changed topics, Jane and Mr. Dunkirk were able to speak quite amiably of taste and art for the remainder of the meal until it was time for the ladies to withdraw.

Jane regretted not being able to prolong her conversation with Mr. Dunkirk, but comforted herself with the promise of tomorrow's visit. In the drawing room, the women divided into clumps and began to discuss the particulars of the meal; specifically the merits of the bachelors present.

Miss Emily Marchand went to the pianoforte and began to play a simple air, faintly tinting the space above the instrument with colours reminiscent of the dining room. Jane contrived to avoid a rubber of casino, leaving such card games for Mr. Buffington and Lady FitzCameron, and joined Beth by the French doors overlooking Banbree Manor's garden. Though she wanted to find out how the girl had fared during her conversation with Mr. Marchand, Jane recognized in herself another motivation: when Mr. Dunkirk entered the room, he would seek the company of his sister.

Beth was out of sorts, however, and the enthusiasm she had shown before dinner seemed to be smothered under a layer of melancholy.

"Are you well?" Jane asked.

"Yes, thank you." Beth sighed, but seemed unwilling to continue the conversation. Jane stood by her in silence, reminded of her mood at Robinsford Abbey. In this silence, Jane's mind turned to the aborted conversation with Mr. Dunkirk about his sister's mysterious first tutor. Perhaps he had died from too much glamour and Beth was tragically reminded of him by Mr. Vincent. Or, more romantically, perhaps they had had an illicit liaison, but that was a silly thought given Beth's youth.

Jane shook off her fancies by excusing herself from Beth and asking Miss Emily Marchand if she might take a turn at the pianoforte.

By losing herself in song and glamour, Jane was able to put most of these thoughts out of her mind, though they continued to bubble under the surface. She had just begun on the second movement of Beethoven's *Quasi una fantasia* when the door to the drawing room opened and the gentlemen joined them.

As she had expected, Mr. Dunkirk went to his sister's side. Jane played, attempting to do justice to the music without shewing off. The folds which she worked around her were simple things of color and light, which represented the elements of the music, rather than literally interpreting it. After Mr. Vincent's display in the dining room, Jane felt that the farther she stayed from realism, the more successful her chances of satisfying her audience.

At the end of the song she looked up to find Mr. Vincent standing by the pianoforte, staring baldly at her. Jane did not know what to say to him, so she let her fingers drift idly over the keys, waiting for him to say something. He finally said, "What did you think?"

"Your work is beautiful." She winced at the banality of her compliment. "It made me forget where I was."

His eyes narrowed. "Did you see her?"

Jane lifted her hands from the piano. "Her? I do not know what you mean."

"Look again." Before she could ask him to explain, he bowed and left the pianoforte.

Curious now, Jane stood and ceded her place back to Miss Emily Marchand; then she slipped across the hall into the dining room. The servants had already done their duty, clearing the plates, cutlery, and linens from the table, leaving only the massive wood structure in the middle of the apparent glade.

Jane paced around the perimeter of the room, looking for a "her" among the trees and flowers of the glamural. On her second perusal, she suddenly spotted a face in the bark of a tree and understood who "she" was. The tree was a laurel, and the face, nearly obscured by the bark closed around her, was Daphne, as Jane had rendered her during their *tableau vivant*, or viewed another way, Mr. Vincent had rendered Melody in glamoured wood. Jane stopped, transfixed by the tree and its subtle compliment, though she could not say with any certainty if the compliment was intended for her or for her sister. She stared at the face, at the mix of relief and fear which he had captured in the features, and felt as if the nymph might open its eyes and observe her at any moment. The breeze that Mr. Vincent had placed in the room moved the tree, giving the nymph the illusion of breath. Jane watched until she became worried that she would be missed in the drawing room.

At the threshold of the drawing room, she stopped, arrested by the sound of her own name. Mr. Buffington was laughing and said, "Plain Jane? I should judge her fortunate if she were only plain!"

This provoked a round of merriment from his listeners, so near the door that it was impossible for Jane to enter without notice. Her cheeks burned and tears pressed against her eyes. If she had taken Melody's advice and played with glamour, he would not say such things. It did not matter; she knew it did not; and yet, she could not bring herself to cross that threshold and face their attempt to conceal the conversation. Jane stumbled back, her sight dimmed by tears, and retreated to the dining room.

Twelve

Beast and Beauty

Decrying herself as a weak and vain girl, Jane struggled to restrain her emotions. It did not signify that Mr. Buffington found her less than plain. He was not a man whose attentions she wanted, and so his opinion of her did not matter.

However little she thought of Mr. Buffington's opinion, or of his unseemly attitude in mocking her, some part of her insisted that it was true, and that he must not be the only one who held that opinion. Was it not likely that Mr. Dunkirk also thought she would be lucky to be "only plain"? Had not Jane herself indulged in vanity by using glamour to shorten her nose? Miss FitzCameron did so regularly, and it had done her no harm in the eyes of her suitors, but

Jane, plain Jane, in her honesty and integrity, was mocked for an accident of birth over which she had little control.

Footsteps caught her ear as someone approached the dining room. The tears on her cheeks burned their tale of upset on her skin. Spinning in place, Jane sought another exit, but Mr. Vincent's art had hidden the other doors.

Rather than let herself be seen in this state of violent emotion, Jane pressed herself back into a corner, and used the light from the room to blow a bubble of glamour around herself in the manner which Mr. Vincent had shown her.

Trembling lest she be discovered, Jane held herself as still as possible, trying to hold her breath even. Silently, she blessed Mr. Vincent for giving her the ability to hide.

First through the door was Beth, followed by Captain Livingston. He looked behind him as he came through the door and pulled it closed behind him.

And then she nearly lost her ability to keep still, for Captain Livingston placed his arm around Beth in a manner reserved for lovers. "Now, dearest. What troubles you?"

Beth shrugged his embrace off. "How can you pretend to not know? You must know what torment it is to watch you pay such attentions to Miss FitzCameron."

He laughed. "Is that all? She is my cousin. Further, I was seated with her during dinner, and so could hardly fail to attend her."

"But then you all but ignore me!"

Captain Livingston said, "Dearest, you must understand that if we are to keep from under my aunt's notice, I must share my attentions with others. I have no wish to hurt you, but my aunt, though good, is a jealous woman. She expects me to engage myself to Livia."

"Why can you not tell her that you are engaged to me?"

At Beth's words, Jane pressed her hands against her mouth to hold her shock inside.

"Because I am poor. Until I am assured of her good graces, I do not want to risk a breach. So I must broach the subject carefully. Trust me, dearest; let me proceed as I feel I must. If it were within my power . . ."

"I know, truly I do." Beth lowered her gaze. "But it is hard to wait."

"For me as well. But for now, we should rejoin the party so that no one misses us." He patted his jacket pocket and winced. "Buffington expects me to sit in on the next round of rubber. Dearest, I told him I was going to fetch my wallet, but my room is in the east wing. I don't suppose . . ."

"Oh! Of course." Beth opened her reticule and pulled out a handful of bills. "Father just posted my allowance to me, so I feel quite flush." She pressed the bills into his hand. "You go first. I should like a moment to collect myself. Besides, it would not do to be seen alone together." Her back was to Jane, and hid her expression, but her voice was resolute.

Captain Livingston smiled and kissed her on top of her head. "Thank you, dear." Without further word, he slipped from the room.

Jane clung to the wall, at a loss for what to do. She had

not been intended to overhear this conversation, but was it worse to explain her presence, or conceal it? It was clear that Beth and Captain Livingston had an engagement, but what sort of engagement was this that required secrecy and, worse yet, flirtation with others to conceal?

Standing alone in the middle of the forest glade, Beth seemed as fragile as a deer. Jane could not stand the thought of seeing her on the morrow and pretending that she knew nothing of this odd engagement. It was best to reveal herself at once.

Thankful that the girl's back was to her, Jane released the folds which tied her bubble of safety in place. "Beth?"

As if a hunter's shot had resounded, Beth leapt and spun, her eyes wide and staring. "Oh! Jane! I did not hear you enter. Heavens, you gave me such a fright. I have come to look at Mr. Vincent's fine work once again. I find it quite entrancing." Her face slowly changed as she looked around at the trees and grasses in the great room and came to the realization that there were no other doors visible. "But where did you come from?"

Jane faltered, even before she began to speak. Her mouth would not form the words.

Beth frowned. "Are you quite well?"

Swallowing, Jane tried again. If she could make Beth understand that she had not intentionally eavesdropped, then perhaps her intrusion would be more readily forgiven. "I had a small upset earlier and came here to collect myself."

Before she could continue, Beth had crossed the space between them, all solicitousness. "Oh, you poor thing. Do tell me, if you may, what has upset you."

Jane waved her hand to brush that aside; her own embarrassment did not matter in this conversation, save that it caused her to be in place to overhear the lovers. "It does not matter, so much; simply know that I had been somewhat upset, and took refuge in the—"

"No. No. You may not tell me that someone upset you without telling me who and how."

"But it does not matter."

"It matters to me." Beth took Jane's hands in her own. "Dear Jane, what upset you? Tell me that, and then you may continue with your story."

Knowing that she would get no farther with Beth until she satisfied the girl's curiosity, Jane conceded. "I went to look at the glamural again, and as I was returning to the drawing room, I heard a group of men standing together. One of them made a comment which—"

"What did they say?"

Even now, the words were still burned into her mind. " 'Plain Jane? I should judge her fortunate if she were only plain.' " Jane faltered for a moment, angry at herself that the words should still carry any power.

A vein pulsed at Beth's temple. "Who said this?"

"I did not see the speaker." True, though she *had* recognized Mr. Buffington's voice; but she did not want Beth to be distracted by such a small injury. "It is not important now. What is important is that I went to calm myself in the dining room, and—"

"Oh! And then you found me there when you sought solitude."

"One might say that *you* found *me*, and I must beg your forgiveness for that. You see, I was here first, and too distraught to bear company, so when I heard voices I wove one of Mr. Vincent's bubbles around me in a moment of panic. You must believe that I had no intention to overhear any private conversation, but once—"

"Do you mean to say you have been here since—since I entered?" Beth's voice trembled with sudden understanding.

Jane nodded.

"And you heard . . . ?"

"Everything. Yes. Forgive me. When you came into the dining room, I was too startled to say anything, and then there did not seem to be a good moment to stop you. But I thought it best to tell you what I had heard."

Beth left Jane's side and paced the room, her hands twisting in restless agitation so their fine bones stood out in sharp relief. "I hardly know what to say. I am equal parts angry and dismayed and, to some measure, relieved, for I have had no one to whom I could unburden my heart. And then, too, I am frightened. Oh, Miss Ellsworth. I beg you. Do not tell anyone; you do not know what the consequences could be."

"But surely you would not enter into a liaison of which your family would disapprove."

Beth laughed with a bitterness far beyond her years. “They would approve of Henry, but my brother’s sense of honour would not permit him to allow the engagement to continue unannounced, and, if it is to continue, then it needs be kept secret for Henry’s sake. Please. I beg of you. Tell no one. Will you promise me that? Oh, Jane, will you promise? I do not know what I should do if anyone knew.”

Beth’s posture spoke of desperation, and Jane was reminded of the sadness she saw sometimes in the young woman’s eyes. Though it was not a conversation to which Jane should have been privy, she felt uneasy at contributing to the subterfuge of Beth and Captain Livingston’s engagement.

From without the dining room, voices drew closer. Beth turned to the door. “It is my brother. You must promise. Please, Jane, or we are undone.” She gripped Jane’s hand with such impassioned strength that it left Jane little choice but to blurt, “I will not tell.”

At once, an ease swept over Beth’s features, and she was able to greet her brother with admirable aplomb. Jane was not so easy in her manner. Two upsets so close to one another left her nerves frayed to their very centers.

Mr. Dunkirk and Mr. Vincent entered, discussing in animated detail the touches he had placed within the glamural. Mr. Dunkirk alone perceived Jane’s agitation and raised an eyebrow. “Is anything troubling you?”

At his side, Beth’s eyes widened in entreaty, but Jane kept her faith. “No. Thank you.” Still, Jane’s voice shook so much that even Mr. Vincent noticed her state and inquired again.

Jane struggled to master herself. "Truly, I am fine. I only wanted a respite from the crowded drawing room." She turned away to study the trees in an effort to regain her composure. "I find your work so very, very restful, Mr. Vincent."

"Good." He glanced across the room and said, "Did you see her?"

Jane stammered before realizing that he meant only the dryad, which was close at hand, and not Beth. "Oh yes, I did. It is a fine subtlety. You should be proud of your work, though I am not sure that Lady FitzCameron will appreciate having a tribute to my sister in her dining hall."

"What? What tribute is this?" Beth turned on her heels, as if nothing troubled her save for the mystery which Mr. Vincent presented.

He grimaced, which made the gauntness of his face become more severe. "Look carefully. I think you will find my bit of play. As for Lady FitzCameron, I doubt she will notice—it is for more perceptive eyes. In any event, she was impressed with the *tableau vivant* we performed, so I may always pretend that it was in homage to her taste in liking it."

"It is not?"

Mr. Vincent turned to regard the dryad, and his face softened more than Jane thought possible. "It is not."

A less perceptive individual might have missed the softening. Another might have seen it and mistaken it for regard for Jane's talents, but Jane believed that it was to the art itself that his heart belonged. The art that was embodied in her sister.

"Oh! I see her now." Beth ran to the dryad and exclaimed. "Do look, Edmund. It is so clever of Mr. Vincent to include her. Such a wonderful reminder of our strawberry-picking party. So delightful."

As the others admired the dryad, Jane longed to escape their company; to flee to her home, where she might have the luxury of reflection and calm. But that was not a choice she was granted, so she returned to the drawing room, walking behind the others with Beth as a guard against idle words. The Dunkirks at least valued her for something, however small that may be. Lady FitzCameron looked up as they entered and beckoned, at which point Mr. Vincent excused himself, leaving Jane to Mr. Dunkirk's attentions. Though this was something to be desired above all, Jane could not quite give herself to the conversation.

"I wonder if you might—" Mr. Dunkirk's query went unfinished as a shout broke the idle chatter in the room.

Captain Livingston flung down his hand of cards, his face flushed quite red. At his side, Mr. Buffington leaned back in his chair with the beneficent smile of a weasel.

"I did warn you that I wasn't bluffing."

Scowling, Captain Livingston drew forth the bundle of bills so recently given to him by Miss Dunkirk.

At that moment, Mr. Vincent arrived by her side. His face was grave and his lips tight with some repressed emotion. "Lady FitzCameron requests your attendance."

Baffled, Jane followed him to the Viscountess's side and awaited her pleasure. Smiling, as if already in anticipation of Jane's response, Lady FitzCameron said, "Your *tableau vivant* with Mr. Vincent gave us so much pleasure that, considering our cause for celebration, I wonder if we might prevail on you to amuse us again this evening."

If the performance on the hill had been something to be avoided, how much more so was this, where her own small skills would be put into contrast with the genius beside her? Add to that the anxiety she felt from the overheard "plain Jane" comment and the knowledge of Beth's secret engagement, and it is no wonder that she at once began making her excuses.

But Lady FitzCameron would have none of it. "Nonsense. Let us not hear of your false modesty; we all know how talented you are." She turned to the assembly, which had crowded close to hear the conversation. "My friends, do tell Miss Ellsworth that she has the talent to more than adequately fulfill such a small plea."

The gentlemen and ladies, thus entreated, could do nought but praise her talents, but as her distress and confusion continued, Mr. Dunkirk said, "My lady, as Miss Ellsworth has not had time to prepare, it is understandable that she doubts her abilities, great though they be. Perhaps if she and Mr. Vincent might retire to a room to practice, her mind would rest easier?"

Jane saw this press of misplaced compliments as her best chance. "An opportunity to plan would ease my mind considerably. But if we are not both perfectly satisfied with what emerges, may we then offer our apologies to you, Lady FitzCameron? I would rather disappoint you in this manner than disappoint you with a lackluster performance."

Lady FitzCameron agreed to this plan with very little protestation, though—and Jane surely must have imagined this—her manner suggested that she was in fact somewhat eager for one of them to fail. But which one, Jane was uncertain.

They were shewn to the library, with Jane's mother accompanying them as chaperon, and considered their scheme. After discussing several choices as being uninteresting, too cliché, or too low for the company, Mr. Vincent said, "Would you consider Beauty and the Beast?"

Jane understood why he recommended this story, but her pride twisted at the ways in which this would open her to the mockery of Mr. Buffington and his friends. She could already imagine them saying that it was a pity that she had to release the glamour which created Beauty, but then a delightful thought occurred to her, one which she was sure would amuse their companions. "Certainly, but may I suggest that we switch roles? That I portray the Beast, if your honour will permit you to be Beauty?"

Jane's mother gaped and said, "Jane! What will our neighbours think? You, a Beast? It will never do. You must suggest sweetness and good temper if you are to find a husband." She continued on in this manner, but was unheeded as Mr. Vincent slowly nodded.

"Yes. Further, I shall portray Beauty as Miss FitzCameron. With amended teeth, of course."

Once agreed upon, they needed only to decide the point in the story to represent and the pose for the tableau. With due consideration, they settled upon the moment when Beauty first sees the Beast as the most dramatic.

Mr. Vincent started by creating the illusion of Miss FitzCameron, but held it for only moments. When he released the folds, even after so short a time, his breath was laboured and his hands shaking. Jane questioned him with a look, but he shook his head.

"I need nothing more than to sit for a moment, if I may."

"Are you certain you are well?"

"Quite." His teeth bared as he snapped his reply. Jane did not feel the urge to query further after his brusque response. Surely he knew his own limits.

Jane pulled the folds around herself, manipulating them until she was satisfied with the arrangement. The cleverness of her plan lay in that, after her audience became accustomed to the face of the Beast, she was certain that her own countenance would appear less severe by comparison.

At one point, Mrs. Ellsworth said, "Oh, I cannot stay in this room for a minute longer. You are too terrible, Jane. Too, too terrible. Some of the weaker ladies might succumb to fright when they view the monster you have created."

Jane laughed at her mother's fears and for a time was able to forget the upset she had experienced earlier.

Mr. Vincent said, "I dream of a day when it is possible to

move images from one location to the next without the human effort of clasping tight to keep the folds from unraveling. Were that possible, then a gallery could be created so that arts such as these were not only the provenance of the wealthy, but that all men might be lifted up by exposure to this, the most ephemeral of arts."

"Is glamour truly the most ephemeral? I would have thought music vied for that place since the notes come into being and are gone as swiftly as they arrive. Each sound exists only in the now, whereas a glamural such as the one you created for Lady FitzCameron will continue on."

"Perhaps, but it is possible to record a piece of music in a fold of glamour. Where is our system for recording the use of folds and threads of glamour? There are papers and treatises on it, but they are as dull and dry as the description of a painting, doing no more to shew the power of a piece or how to re-create it than saying that Sir Joshua painted a sky blue. Someday, mark my words, it will be possible to create a copy of a glamour, and the explosion of possibilities will drive the art to new heights. I imagine a day when it will be possible to create an image in one place and have it be seen instantly in another."

Jane thought of Beth's remarks that Mr. Vincent was passionate only about his art, and reflected that, with such passion, he did not need a human muse to drive him. With these thoughts, she accompanied him and her mother to the drawing room. They presented themselves to Lady FitzCameron, who looked as if she had almost forgotten her request. Jane had a split sensation of relief that she might be released from this burden, and indignation that they had practiced solely for the pleasure of the Viscountess, who did not care. She had no time for more than that, as Lady FitzCameron remarked, "I am most grateful to you."

As Jane and Mr. Vincent took their place in the door of the drawing room, planning to use its great doors as a curtain while they prepared the *tableau vivant*, Jane looked about for Beth and Captain Livingston.

Beth was engaged in conversation with Mr. Dunkirk. On the opposite side of the room, Captain Livingston's attention was captured by a game of cards. Jane pushed their relationship away from her mind as something to concern her later. First she must get through this ordeal of public spectacle.

Jane gathered the folds around herself and created the towering Beast above and around her own form, giving his form all the power of Madame de Beaumont's story. Beside her, Mr. Vincent gave Beauty's dress the style of an older period and put a rose in her hand. When they were ready, a servant flung the doors open and stepped quickly out of the way.

As Mrs. Ellsworth predicted, one or two of the ladies, including Jane's mother herself, screamed at the sight of the Beast. Mr. Ellsworth patted his wife's hand distractedly while she leaned back in her chair fanning herself, even though she, at least, should have been accustomed to the beast by now. Jane blessed the obscuring glamour of the Beast, for it allowed her to smile behind her mask at her mother's silliness.

Then a second shriek, followed by a welter of excitement, echoed through the room. Mr. Dunkirk rushed toward Jane, his face dark with concern and his eyes fixed on the ground beside her. Jane turned and dropped her folds.

Mr. Vincent lay prostrate on the ground, twitching.

Thirteen

The Beast Upset

Mr. Vincent's collapse caused the room to overturn itself in a chaos of emotion. Ladies who had pretended to fright when they saw the Beast conjured from glamour now sank, senseless, under the conviction that Mr. Vincent was dying. Lady FitzCameron fell back in her chair, face as pale as Mr. Vincent's, unable to speak for the horror.

Mr. Dunkirk knelt by the ailing glamourist and held his shoulders firmly against the tremors that quaked through his body. He looked up and his eyes found Jane. "What do we do?"

At his words, those closest turned to her. With horror, Jane realized that she was the most experienced glamourist in the room. "A surgeon. Someone must fetch a surgeon."

Captain Livingston was out of the room in a moment, shouting for his horse.

If Dr. Smythe, the closest surgeon, were out on a call, it could take hours for him to return. Meanwhile, something must be done; but the home remedies were so paltry. "We must cool him." Jane pulled folds of glamour out of the ether and wrapped a cooling charm around Mr. Vincent. She took deep breaths, her ribs pressing against her stays as she worked the folds. Without taking her attention from Mr. Vincent, she asked, "Is there a cold-monger?"

In a house such as this, there must be.

In short order, the cold-monger was summoned. Working together, he and Jane traded the folds of chill between them as Mr. Vincent was carried to a guest room. Once he was established in the bed, Jane passed all control of the folds to the cold-monger and watched as he used his exquisite and specific control over the folds to create a layer of cold air around Mr. Vincent. She placed her hand in the cool air and instructed the cold-monger to bring it to a point that was cold enough to bring the fever raging through Mr. Vincent's body under control, but not so cold as to damage him. That done, the cold-monger tied the folds off. Jane herself took a cloth dipped in water and dribbled it into Mr. Vincent's mouth, knowing that next to overheating, dehydration was the greatest danger.

She had never overexerted herself with glamour this severely, but she well remembered the cautionary tales with which her tutor had frightened her. Like a horse run too long and too hard, Mr. Vincent's heart could burst if they could not cool him down sufficiently.

With the application of the cold-monger's craft, Mr. Vincent's spasming grew less severe, but his breath was still ragged and his pulse too fast. It seemed forever before the surgeon arrived. When he did, he strode straight into the room, without so much as taking off his greatcoat.

Dr. Smythe felt Mr. Vincent's pulse and his face turned grave. Surveying the folds of chill surrounding Mr. Vincent, he said that they had probably saved his life, but whether he would regain his senses was beyond the surgeon's power to judge. Then, Jane was forced to quit the room as the surgeon decided to remove Mr. Vincent's shirt to try him with leeches.

Once outside, beyond the immediate stresses of caring for Mr. Vincent, Jane's own anxiety caught up with her. It was only by placing a hand against the wall to steady herself that she was able to make her way down the hall. She was determined not to faint and add to the doctor's burden. So young a man, struck down in his prime by such a trifle. The illusion should have been well within his grasp, but it was obvious that he had pushed himself too hard finishing the glamural for Lady FitzCameron. Jane should have tried harder to convince him not to do the *tableau vivant* when she saw his hands shaking after holding the illusion for so short a time.

She reached the drawing room, where many of the guests remained, anxious about the fate of Mr. Vincent. By their faces, she could see that some worried for the man himself while others cared only for the gossip. Mr. Dunkirk came to her straightaway and, taking her arm, guided her to a seat. "Your father had to see Mrs. Ellsworth home. He asked me to see you back to Long Parkmead."

Letting Jane regain her equilibrium, he did not ask the question that must surely be on everyone's mind.

Lady FitzCameron was not so patient.

"We saw the surgeon arrive. What has he said about dear Mr. Vincent?" The cold glitter in her eyes belied her words. Jane could almost believe that Lady FitzCameron would be pleased if the man died, for it would increase the value of her glamural.

Jane straightened in the chair and told them all that had passed. When she explained that he might not regain his senses, Beth burst into tears and turned to her brother for comfort. Mr. Dunkirk looked as though strong emotion would overcome him.

Then the party must discuss the shock and horror of the case. Each avowed that they had either known he was too weak and should have advised him not to attempt any more glamour for a fortnight at least, or that they had absolutely no idea anything was wrong with him. Someone—Jane did not remember who—had pressed a glass of cordial into her hand, and she sipped it reflexively as person after person came to ask her to repeat some detail of Mr. Vincent's collapse. At last, Mr. Dunkirk said, "You can do nothing for Mr. Vincent here. Let me take you home, and in the morning we shall inquire."

Though Jane was loath to leave while Mr. Vincent was still so much in danger, she had to concede the intelligence of Mr. Dunkirk's proposal. During the carriage ride home Jane did not have the strength to speak to Beth, who kept repeating a litany of her upset. Her words invoked the horror of the moment when Jane had first seen Mr. Vincent lying on the floor. She replayed it in her mind as surely as if she had caught it in a loop of glamour. His heels drummed endlessly, and he grunted as his breath was forced out of his body each time it arced backwards. Jane pressed her face against the carriage window for the feel of the cool glass, but it did nothing to drive the image from her mind.

Mr. Dunkirk said, "Hush, Beth. We are all of us upset."

Grateful for his intervention, Jane roused herself. "Yes, but you are closer to him than I."

"But the stresses of the event involved you more intimately. I would be astonished if you felt nothing."

His assurance did little to soothe Jane's worn nerves.

Shortly after that, Mr. Ellsworth and Melody met them in the front hall. Melody's pale face shewed her tension. "How is he?"

Mr. Dunkirk said, "According to the surgeon, your sister's efforts may well have saved Mr. Vincent's life. He is less sure if his senses will survive intact."

Melody swayed at these words, and would have fallen if

Mr. Ellsworth had not leaped forward to catch her. Mr. Dunkirk helped him bring Melody up to her room.

What right did Melody have to faint, when Jane had tended the man? If anyone deserved to be overwrought with emotion, it was Jane, but now she had the task of tending to her sister as well. When Mr. Dunkirk had taken his leave, Jane's father asked her to rouse Melody sufficiently to undress her for bed, though Jane was sorely tempted to let her sleep in her gown. Melody had no right to use Mr. Vincent's fate to seek further attentions from Mr. Dunkirk.

With effort, Jane stifled these feelings until she was alone in her room.

There, in the darkness of her bed, Jane surrendered to tears. That such talent, such art, might be unraveled like a skein of glamour tore at her soul. Jane sobbed, muffling her cries in her pillow, until she fell asleep.

In the morning, Captain Livingston brought news that Mr. Vincent had a steadier pulse, but that he had not regained his senses. Jane left him to console Melody while she took the news to her mother, who pressed her hand to her heart and said, "To think that I almost lost you! My darling girl. I always knew you should not practice glamour. Have I not said that you should take care? And to think that you could be lying senseless even now!"

"Mama, I was never in any danger."

"I remember how you fainted when the Dunkirks were

here. If I had known then how close to death you were, I would have been in hysterics. It is not to be borne. You must give up glamour at once. Promise me you will."

"I have never been close to death." Unwilling to continue the subject, Jane picked up the book she had been reading and said, "Shall I resume the story? Sidonia is facing a Laplander with an enchanted drum in the next chapter."

Mrs. Ellsworth cried, "What do I care of Sidonia and drums!" and then lost herself in her ravings.

In some measure, Jane welcomed her mother's overexcited mind, for soothing it kept her own mind off the events of the previous evening. She went down for dinner and learned from her father that Captain Livingston had called again and that Mr. Vincent's condition continued unchanged.

When they went to bed that evening, Mr. Vincent was still unconscious. On the second day, Captain Livingston brought them word that he had opened his eyes once, but had not seemed to see anything, and then closed them again.

That evening, as Jane, Melody, and their father sat in the drawing room, they heard a horse arrive and then a sharp rap at the front door.

They all sat frozen by the same thought: that this could only be news of Mr. Vincent. There were footsteps in the front hall, and then at the door, and then Captain Livingston strode into the room. At the happy expression on his face, Jane pressed her hands to her mouth, still afraid to hope.

"He is awake," Captain Livingston said, without preamble.

Melody squealed and threw her sewing into the air. Mr. Ellsworth closed his eyes and murmured a fervent prayer of thanksgiving.

But Jane waited, knowing that though Mr. Vincent might be awake, his mind might yet be disordered. Her fingers lost their feeling as she clutched the arms of her chair. "Is he—is he alert?"

"Yes. Thanks to you. The surgeon declares that if you had not asked for the cold-monger, Mr. Vincent would not have survived the night. He is weak yet, and must be kept quiet, but he is out of danger."

Jane let out a breath she had not realized she was holding as all the fear of the past two days left her body in a great rush. She pressed her hands over her face and wept with relief.

Mr. Ellsworth patted Jane awkwardly on the back. "Captain Livingston, you have our profound thanks for bringing us the news so faithfully. I believe this calls for a celebratory brandy."

Jane lifted her head, wiping her eyes. "Yes, indeed. Please join us."

"I must decline, as I need to continue on my rounds. Aunt Elise has charged me to deliver the news to all our neighbours, and if I celebrate at each, I shall be unable to complete my rounds."

"Where are you off to next?"

"The Marchands."

Melody laughed. "Then you should fortify your strength beforehand."

"I fear you have the right of it. But after the Marchands, I proceed to the Dunkirks, and I would prefer to have a clear head when I greet them."

Jane looked for some sign of self-consciousness in his manner when he mentioned the family of his secret fiancée, but saw nothing untoward. His ease of carriage gave no hint that Beth had spoken of Jane's unwitting participation in their *tête-à-tête*. Nor was this surprising upon reflection, for when would the couple have had time to meet?

"I hope Miss Dunkirk is well. It must be hard on her to see her instructor struck down thus," Melody said.

"Ah. Well, you know how excitable young girls can be. Miss Dunkirk is not half so steady in her thoughts as I remember you and Miss Ellsworth being when younger yet than she."

Melody nodded judiciously. "It is true that I have often remarked to myself that her interest in the arts was too keen for such a delicate mind. I am surprized that Mr. Dunkirk encourages such fancies as hers."

Jane could not let this betrayal of her friend stand. "I believe that the arts allow one a safe outlet for passions which could not otherwise be borne. We women have no recourse to the distractions available to men. Is it not better to spend one's excess energy in the act of creation than to allow oneself to become overwhelmed?"

Captain Livingston shook his head. "I think, rather, that the steadying influence of discipline does more to build a level mind."

"Such as one finds in the service of His Majesty?" Melody said.

"Just so." Captain Livingston bowed to her.

Jane could hardly credit his behaviour; to shed such disdain on one to whom he was affianced was beyond understanding. She could only suppose that he hid his attachment to Beth behind the mask of he who "doth protest too much."

"Well, regardless of your feelings," Jane said, "may I ask you to convey my regards to the Dunkirks?"

Captain Livingston readily agreed, but for some time after his departure, Jane was troubled by a sense of unease. Now that her concern for Mr. Vincent's health had decreased, the anxiety she had first felt upon overhearing Beth and Captain Livingston was renewed.

She feared what might come from such a secret.

Fourteen

Curiosity Unrequited

With the news of Mr. Vincent's recovery, the neighbourhood had lost a subject upon which to speculate. Now that it appeared as though he would not die, certain parties returned their attentions to their own health. And so, the morning after Captain Livingston brought word of Mr. Vincent's improving health, Mrs. Marchand arrived to compare her declining state with Mrs. Ellsworth's, who received her friend with all the warmth and cordiality which Jane could not. Jane could be civil and pay Mrs. Marchand the attention due to her by position and common courtesy, but knowing that she was about to embark upon a recitation of her ills, Jane could not be warm.

Melody sat in the corner of the room, safely engaged in making a new fringe, the working of which apparently required all of her concentration. That left Jane to be drawn in by the notice of Mrs. Marchand and their mother.

Mrs. Ellsworth started the recitation. "Oh, dear Joy! You would not believe the agony I have suffered. I was very nearly done in by poor Mr. Vincent. I thought my heart would burst. Poor Charles had to take me home straightaway, insensible. Is that not how it was, Jane?"

"Yes, Mama."

"As to that . . ." Mrs. Marchand sniffed. "As to that, I had to tend to all three of my daughters as well as fight off the trauma of the unhappy event, which nearly oppressed me completely. It is only this morning that I was able to venture from bed, and then only by my deep, deep concern for you. I had heard that you were suffering from chronic neuralgia, that you had been unable to bear either light or sound, so of course I came straightaway, though I had to drag myself from my bed to do so. It was only by a steady exertion of will that I was able to carry my arthritic limbs as far as the door to call for our carriage. I am certain that I do not need to speak to *you* of the effort. You understand me perfectly well."

"Oh, yes. The doctor was quite certain that I had suffered an irreparable harm at the fright. I remember quite clearly: he said, 'Madam, your nerves will never be sound, no matter what I do.' My only hope is that I live to see my girls married. Preparing for a wedding will do my poor nerves in, but I would do anything for my girls." She dabbed at her eyes with the tiniest, most delicate scrap of handkerchief. "Only imagine: my nerves will never be sound."

"I am surprized that the doctor said that; to me your nerves have always seemed so strong. But then, to one who suffers as I do, anyone with greater health is to be admired."

Melody set her fringe down suddenly. "I have just remembered that a tonic of rose petals is supposed to provide comfort for injured nerves."

"May I help you with that?" Jane stood at the chance to escape the unvarying conversation which their mother had with Mrs. Marchand, one which revolved only around their various ailments and the marriage prospects for their daughters.

"Thank you, yes. I will definitely need your help, and of course, we would both do anything for our beloved mother." So saying, Melody retreated through the drawing room door with Jane close behind her, neither girl giving either of the older ladies time to voice a word of protestation.

As soon as they were out the front door of the house, Melody lifted her skirts and ran for the Long Walk. Laughing, Jane ran after her, feeling as if their governess were chasing her with a tonic. In truth, the combined forces of her mother and Mrs. Marchand were almost as bad.

Turning into the maze, she chased her sister to the center, where a few blossoms still clung to the rosebushes. Melody collapsed onto the bench, laughing and breathless. Jane tumbled down beside her.

In the blush of their narrow escape, they were only capable of laughter. Anyone passing the maze would have thought a gaggle of schoolgirls had gotten lost in its midst. By gasps and hiccups they caught their breath again, only to look at one another and burst into laughter anew.

Jane knew that only a small part of this was hilarity at the supposed escape. More of it was a release of the tension which both had been under for days.

Throwing her head back and exposing her swanlike neck, Melody laughed anew. "I could not remain there for a moment longer."

"We will have to go back, eventually."

"Then let us delay as long as we might."

"But if we stay too long, Mama will think that we have become lost in the maze, or, worse, that wild beasts have ravaged us."

"Let her!" Melody sprang to her feet and ran to the roses. "Perhaps if I tear my gown on the roses, she will imagine wolves and tigers stalking the maze; then it will always be a place to which we can retreat."

Melody's suggestion of tearing her gown reminded Jane too much of her faking another injury. She lost some of her levity. "I think Mama has quite enough imagination on her own."

"Feh. She only imagines horrible things. I can imagine wonderful things happening in this garden."

"Indeed? Mama imagines wolves; I imagine governesses; Miss Dunkirk imagines lovers. What do you imagine?"

Melody blushed and turned away. "I do not need to imagine lovers between these walls."

"Melody Anne! Is there—oh, but it is too much to expect me to remain incurious with a statement like that. Do tell. Oh, do." She had been so distracted by Beth's engagement that she had paid no attention to Melody's state. Of course, after the incident with her ankle, Mr. Dunkirk had paid Melody every attention, so it was only natural that an attachment had formed. Jane's heart was steadier than she feared it might be at the thought, but she still had to rally herself to be as gracious as a sister ought.

With a flutter of her hands, Melody said, "There is nothing to tell."

"Nothing! If you wish me to believe that, you will have to stop your blushing. I would rather believe that in a week or two I will be offering you sincere felicitations. Surely it will not take more time than that? But I will be patient." Jane bit her lip and then continued. "Only tell me that you are not keeping this a secret from *only* me. Tell me that you are not keeping your silence because you do not trust me."

"I . . . Honest, Jane, there is nothing for me to tell." She bowed her head and stroked the petals of a rose. "I wish that there were, but I am not certain of his regard, and so I will say nothing until I am."

Agitated, Jane stood and paced the perimeter of the garden, thinking. It would be better for her to know than to merely guess and fear. "Has Mr. Dunkirk said nothing?"

"Mr. Dunkirk?" Melody's laugh was sharp. "Yes. He has

said *nothing*, and that is no surprize, in that he cares nothing for me. But there are others who value me for myself, not for my accomplishments. Now I would not have Mr. Dunkirk even if he asked the question tomorrow."

"But you were so—"

"Yes! Yes! I know. But I mistook esteem for love. That his manners are elegant, that his carriage is easy and his understanding superior; these things conspire to make me feel that I ought to love him, and so I imagined that I did. But now, now I know what it is to have that esteem returned. To be regarded—oh, Jane, I would that I could tell you all."

"Why can you not?" Jane shook her head. "I thought you said that you were not certain of the gentleman's regard."

"No. He has given me every assurance, but because he is not at liberty to court me openly, he must spend time in the company of others, which makes me doubt him. I know that he loves me, but then I fear that he does not." Melody plucked the petals from the closest rose, dropping them onto the path, murmuring, "He loves me; he loves me not."

Too shocked to gather her thoughts into words, Jane stared with sightless eyes at the petals tumbling down. The conversation so nearly mirrored that which she had had with Beth that it was only with difficulty that Jane could gather her senses enough to speak. "Am I to understand that you have—that you are seeing this gentleman alone?"

Melody threw the denuded rose stem on the path. "Jane, I have done with answering your questions. They always lead to lectures, and I have no wish to indulge in your careful thoughts. La! From your manner anyone would think you are my mother."

"I do not mean to. I only worry for your happiness. On my honour, I only saw that you were happy and wanted to know why. Nothing more."

Melody broke a rose from its stem and changed the subject baldly. "The danger from Mrs. Marchand should be past now, I think. We should have thought to bring scissors with which to cut the roses."

Though Jane begged and wheedled Melody, she could get no further intelligence from her. Melody would only speak of roses and Mrs. Marchand, demurring from any other inquiries. The camaraderie which had rejoined them on the flight from Mrs. Marchand had fled, and the distance between them grew as they returned to the house. Despite her efforts, Jane was shut as completely out of Melody's thoughts as if she were not there at all. Only when she followed Melody's suggested conversational path and talked of trivial things did her sister engage with her.

Jane struggled with her own feelings of pride, hating herself for playing this game, but afraid that if she did not do so then she would have no contact with Melody at all.

How had their relationship come to this?

Fifteen

A Book and a Gift

A week after the party, Lady FitzCameron decided to remove to Bath, taking Mr. Vincent and the rest of her household with her so that he could better recover in the healing waters. At this announcement, Melody's spirits took a sudden downturn. Could it be—was it possible that Mr. Vincent was Melody's lover? Certainly, with his homage to her in the form of the hidden dryad, it seemed that he harbored some feelings for Melody, and yet Jane could scarcely credit the notion. She could see how his artist's eye would be drawn to her sister's unrivaled form, but Melody had too little love of the arts to be drawn to so rough a man. Jane had only recently begun to see his merits herself. But if not Mr. Vincent, then who?

Melody's spirits brightened only briefly, when the Ellsworths went to pay their respects to the FitzCamerons before their departure. Jane watched her shrewdly for clues. Melody peered around the drawing room as if looking for someone, but then subsided to a bland form of politeness.

Lady FitzCameron received them most graciously, paying special attention to Jane and praising her for saving Mr. Vincent's life.

"My dear, I do not know what we should have done without you. It is unimaginable." She gestured languidly to the table and to a book lying upon it. "I want you to have this as a token of my very real affection for you, and for what you have done for poor Mr. Vincent."

"Lady FitzCameron, no thanks are needed." Jane curtsied, almost thrown off balance by the jab in her back which her mother gave her.

"Please. I insist." The jewels on her fingers sparkled as she waved Jane forward to receive the book.

It was a handsomely bound edition of Gothic tales with illustrations by the famous member of the Society of Lady Etchers, Alethea Harrison. Such a gift was far more beautiful than any book in her father's library, though its subject matter was more to Mrs. Ellsworth's taste than Jane's. Still, she thanked Lady FitzCameron very prettily, and the Viscountess seemed to think that the business was done.

"I am so very, very sorry that Mr. Vincent is not able to

receive you, being still confined to his bed. Of course, he sends his best wishes and fondest thanks."

Jane had wished to see him herself, to ascertain that he was quite well. The last image she had of him was lying insensible on the bed with the cold-monger's weaves shrouding him.

Melody put her worries into words. "How is he? Is he much improved? Captain Livingston has been so good as to bring us tidings daily."

"When I saw him—was that yesterday?—he seemed quite well, though he is not able to rise yet, and bright light pains him. Still, I think that you could not ask for him to be in better condition. I know that he would be terribly disappointed to not greet you himself if he knew you were in the house, but of course he is too, too grateful for your aid."

So they were not to see him. This troubled Jane, who had wanted to drive the horrible image of his collapse out of her head. "I wonder at your moving him to Bath if he is still confined to bed."

"Dr. Smythe thinks it is quite the best thing. The waters, you know, and the air there will be so much better for his recovery. Of course, he will be in my carriage, not one of those horrid post carriages, and we will keep the shades drawn. My nephew will accompany us, and he will help terribly with the journey." She paused, and her eyes briefly rested on Melody before returning her bland gaze to Mr. Ellsworth. "Your family will miss Henry terribly, I am certain. He seems so much more in residence at Long Parkmead than at Banbree

Manor. But he is a young captain, after all, and you know how they like to *wander.* I do *try* to keep him under control, but it is so terribly difficult."

It seemed that Lady FitzCameron had her suspicions that Captain Livingston had formed an attachment, but she chose the wrong target for his affections. Jane refrained from glancing at Melody in an effort to not give Lady FitzCameron a false confirmation.

Mrs. Ellsworth, oblivious to the hints that Lady FitzCameron cast that she did not approve of the possibility of an attachment between her nephew and Melody, said, "Oh, he is such a good young man. It's so kind of you to loan him to us. I'm sure I don't know how we should have gotten along when Melody turned her ankle if not for him. You might almost say that Jane's helping with Mr. Vincent was a repayment for your nephew's aid with our poor Melody." She blinked, clearly pleased with the analogy she had drawn between two vastly different events.

Only with effort did Jane keep the incredulity from her countenance. Even had Melody's injury been real, her life had never been threatened. Jane cleared her throat and sought to change the subject. "And have you found a home in Bath?"

Lady FitzCameron said that they had. They had taken a house on Laurel Place, an establishment which she had occupied in years past and had even thought of purchasing so that they might always have a residence in Bath. "If you ever have reason to be in Bath, you must call on us. I insist."

As they issued promises that they would visit, Banbree

Manor's butler crossed the room and leaned down to murmur in Lady FitzCameron's ear. Her mouth tightened and her gaze flicked to Jane. She nodded once and waved the butler back. "Miss Ellsworth, would you be so good as to oblige Mr. Vincent with a visit?"

The butler must have misunderstood—surely Mr. Vincent had meant to ask for Melody? "I do not wish to trouble him, if his health is too fragile to admit visitors." Jane kept her gaze fixed on Lady FitzCameron. She wanted to look at Melody to see what effect this invitation had on her, but she could not without drawing attention to her sister.

Lady FitzCameron examined a ring on her right hand. "I am informed that he will not rest easy until he has had an opportunity to thank you personally."

With that, there was nothing for it but for Jane to follow the butler abovestairs. The walk down the hall seemed longer than when she had last taken it, and the air grew thick with apprehension as they neared the bedchamber where she had last seen Mr. Vincent.

The curtains within were drawn tight and the lights low, which lent the room a sense of gloom. All glamour had been stripped from the chamber. It was a meaner, less substantially furnished room than Jane had thought. She could not contain her surprize that Banbree Manor needed glamour to maintain an illusion of wealth.

"Perhaps you might guess at the real reason Lady FitzCameron hired me." The dry voice at last brought Jane's attention to the man she had come to see.

Mr. Vincent lay propped in bed. His skin was drawn and waxen with a translucence that almost let her see through his bloodless skin to the skull below. His hair lay lank against his scalp, and a gray coating of stubble masked his cheeks, though not enough to disguise the gauntness beneath. Had his health really been spent on creating the illusion of a profitable estate? "I would not presume to guess at the Viscountess's affairs. I would rather inquire about your health."

He smirked. "Always proper, Miss Ellsworth. My health is as you see it. Bright light pains me, as do harsh sounds and any scrap of glamour." He nodded at the bare walls around them. "That is why I am allowed no visitors: not because of the need to conserve my strength, but because Lady FitzCameron does not want their poverty displayed."

How dare Lady FitzCameron treat him thus. To spend his health and then confine him in order to hide her ill judgment was beyond criminal. "Is that why you are going to Bath?"

"In part. Dr. Smythe does seem to think the waters will do me some good, but I loathe the idea nonetheless. Forgive me; I grow resentful in my confinement. You are my first visitor." He rubbed the bridge of his nose, sighing. "Would you do me the kindness of opening the top right drawer of my bureau and bringing me the book in it?"

"Of course." She rose, grateful for an activity to distract her from his pitiable state. "Am I truly your first visitor?"

"Captain Livingston has stopped in, but I think merely to report to others. We have nothing of moment to say to one another."

Within the bureau, Jane found the notebook in which she had seen Mr. Vincent sketch. At this close range, she could make out the remnants of the initials V. H. embossed upon the worn leather cover. She turned with the volume and held it up for him. "Is this it?"

Mr. Vincent nodded. "I should like for you to have this. As a thank-you for saving my life."

Jane was so shocked that she nearly let the book slip from her grasp; to what purpose did he want her to have his sketches? "No thanks are necessary. Truly, it was nothing but what any person with—"

"Please, Miss Ellsworth, do not torture me with your civil phrases. Or at least use them to accept my gratitude with grace. I should be clear that it is not for preserving my breathing form for which I thank you, but for my art. Dr. Smythe has repeatedly told me that I shall make a full recovery and that I owe that to nothing more than your quick thinking. It is true that I might have lived without your efforts, but as a husk. That would have been a slow death for me. So it is—" He paused and looked at her with such focused intensity that Jane felt his gaze burn through to her spine. "It is for my art, which is my life, that I thank you, and it is my art which I offer as thanks."

Even diminished as he was, the force of his personality dwarfed Jane's. It did not seem any wonder that Melody felt Mr. Vincent's regard when with him, if he looked at her with this directness, which went far beyond what was normally due a lady. In that moment, Jane doubted that Mr. Vincent were capable of regarding *anyone* with less than his whole being.

"Please sit by me and I will explain as best I can."

Jane sat in the rough chair by his bedside as he slid to the edge. He reached for the book and opened to the first page. "This contains my thoughts on glamour and my efforts to codify a system for recording it."

Strong, masculine handwriting strode across the page; the tight script wrapped around an ink sketch in the corner. Despite herself, Jane leaned closer, fragments of sentences leaping off the page at her, fragments like *explore light and ways to transport it. Perhaps storing in glass?* and *Without passion, there is no art, only technique.*

"But this is your life's work! I—"

"Exactly." He pursed his lips and growled low in his throat. "I teach the techniques of glamour to Miss Dunkirk. But techniques are not art. To you, I want to give my art. Whether these writings hold the key, I do not know, but I think they might. You are always so careful, so methodical in your thoughts and actions. I should like to know what levels of art you could reach if you relaxed your guard."

"I am courteous and follow the civilities which are expected of one in polite society."

"And your glamour reflects that. You are one of the finest natural technicians I have seen, and you have a rare eye for form; but for all that your art is lifeless."

"Are these the words of thanks you want me to accept with grace?"

He laughed. "No. Only the book. I would rather have you honestly angry with me than polite."

She took his measure for a moment; though he disdained empty courtesies, his roughness of manner seemed at times to be a shield for a more gentle nature. "It is not so easy to be angry with you."

"You were, though, for a moment. When you are angry, your face stays calm, but your skin flushes. I have had several opportunities to notice this."

Jane felt her skin warm with shame that her feelings had been so transparent. "Are you certain that I was not embarrassed?"

"Quite." He looked away again, returning his gaze to the book in his lap. "I owe you more than my life, and this is the most precious thing I have to offer. Will you let me thank you in this manner?"

Mr. Vincent's face, whether from illness or emotion, shewed a naked need to be clear of the debt he perceived that he owed Jane. She would protest that he owed her nothing, but that would only agitate him further, and were she honest with herself, she would admit that she wanted the knowledge in those pages. She wanted to prove to him that her art was not lifeless.

"Yes. I will accept your thanks in the manner you offer."

Mr. Vincent nodded without looking up, then shut the book and handed it to her. "Thank you."

Jane took the book. "You are welcome." The moment begged for more comment, but no words seemed capable of filling it. She rose then to go, accepting silence as the best option. Only at the door did she remember that he might, yet, have some message for Melody, but could not bring herself to acknowledge a possible attachment directly. "Have you any messages you wish me to carry?"

He shook his head. "May I call when I am well?"

Jane hugged the book to her. "Of course. I look forward to shewing you the fruits of your thanks."

He seemed smaller even than when she had entered the room, but less drawn. Jane did not waste his time with the forms of polite farewell which he so loathed. She left the room quietly and returned to her family.

They were full of questions about Mr. Vincent's health, which Jane did her best to answer. Behind them, eyes glittering, Lady FitzCameron asked a different, silent question. Jane did not answer her, but when they ended the visit, she did not join the vague pleasantries, promises to visit one another, and entreaties that Lady FitzCameron not be too long out of the neighbourhood. Nor did she take Lady FitzCameron's gift; only Mr. Vincent's.

Of the two books, only one had value to Jane.

Sixteen

Change and Fury

Once in the carriage on the way back from Banbree Manor, conversation turned at once to rehashing the visit. Jane suffered her family asking yet more questions than they had before.

"Now you must tell us how dear Mr. Vincent is. I am certain that Lady FitzCameron painted a rosier picture than warranted. Surely the poor man is close to death." Mrs. Ellsworth fanned herself, waiting for Jane to satisfy her curiosity about another's ailments; waiting, no doubt, for a symptom which she could claim as her own.

Jane, for her part, wanted nothing more than to quit the company of her family and explore the world inside the book Mr. Vincent had given her. She turned it over in her lap. "He remains as I described—weak, but shewing every promising sign of a full recovery."

"I am glad to hear that," Mr. Ellsworth said. "He seemed a fine man, and to be struck down so young would be a terrible shame."

Melody suddenly pulled Mr. Vincent's book from Jane's lap. "What is this? Lady FitzCameron gave you an old journal?"

"No!" Jane snatched it back, her voice snapping through the carriage.

Spots of red coloured Melody's cheeks, and she lifted her chin. "Am I not good enough to look at a gift from the Viscountess?"

"Jane, let your sister see." Mrs. Ellsworth rapped Jane's arm with her fan. "You mustn't let Lady FitzCameron's notice go to your head."

"With all due respect, Mama, this is not a gift I am at liberty to share." Jane held the book tightly to her chest, trembling with anger at the unjustness. To be blamed, to be called selfish when Melody took everything that Jane cared about, took precedence because she was beautiful and Jane was not—it was not, had never been, fair.

"Not at liberty! La! As if you had special instructions from the Viscountess. We were all there, Jane; we all saw her presentation. I say, though. That's not the book she gave you at all."

Mr. Ellsworth sat forward. "What is this? Did you take the wrong book?"

"No. No, I left Lady FitzCameron's book there."

At that, Mrs. Ellsworth let out a small shriek of dismay. "Left it there? How could you! Her Ladyship will think you did not want it, and then what will she think, but that you think yourself too good for her gifts? Charles, tell the driver to turn around at once."

"Hush for a moment." Mr. Ellsworth waved his hand at his wife and kept his eyes on Jane. "If that is not the book Lady FitzCameron gave you, where did it come from?"

"Mr. Vincent." Jane's eyes clouded with tears, unaccountably. "He wanted to thank me for saving his life."

"Mr. Vincent?" Melody's voice was full of astonishment. "You traded the favours of Lady FitzCameron for an artist's? Really, Jane, you are too strange."

Jane blinked her eyes clear and stared at her sister. No sign of jealousy clouded Melody's face; no sign, indeed, of anything save bafflement at Jane's behaviour. But Melody had said that she had a lover, and if it was not Mr. Dunkirk, it had seemed so clear that it must surely be Mr. Vincent. If not him, then who?

"I thought you had a fondness for Mr. Vincent, with all your inquiries as to his health."

"Fie, Jane." Mrs. Ellsworth sniffed. "Everyone in the countryside was asking after him. And why should we not be concerned with his health? I only wish that people would take half the interest in mine, for I am sure that I suffer as much as he does. More so, if truth be known, for my ailments have gone on for years and his have only lasted for one week. Charles, you have not turned the carriage around yet."

"Nor shall I. We are nearly home. I will walk over after dinner to fetch the book."

"But we could go back now."

"Yes. Or I can walk back in quiet solitude, which is my preference."

Jane's parents continued their small bickering until the carriage arrived on their own front sweep. As soon as it came to a halt, Jane bolted out of it and straight into the house. She could not bear another minute in her family's company, or anyone else's, for that matter. Racing up the stairs, she locked herself in her room and collapsed on the bed.

There, she gave way to angry sobs. Angry at her parents for noticing so little beyond that which went on in their own house. Angry at Melody for her selfishness, which was only enhanced by the way everyone petted her. And most of all, angry at herself for not being able to govern her own feelings. Nothing today had done her any real harm, yet she felt as though her nerves had been flayed and left out for the tanner.

Was this the state that Mr. Vincent wanted her in to create art? With her emotions so high, Jane could not see to manage glamour, let alone compose a piece of art. She rolled over on her back and stared at one of her watercolours, which hung on the wall next to her clothespress. It shewed the sea from one of their trips to Lyme Regis. The shore had been beautiful morning after morning, so Jane had set up her easel on the ammonite pavement and tried to capture the glory of the sunrise. This one had come closest of all the sketches she had assayed.

But Mr. Vincent was right. Though her colours were correct, and her use of light and shading exacting, the whole of it was lifeless and dull. Jane grabbed the book and almost threw it at the painting, her arm already drawing back to throw before she thought better of her actions, bit the inside of her cheek, and fell back against the bed.

If he wanted to see emotion in her work, she would shew it to him. Jane opened his book and began to read.

When Nancy called Jane to dinner, her head was heavy with new ideas. The book was not laid out in any ordered way; it wandered from subject to subject as Mr. Vincent had thought of them. He sketched out notions for glamurals and spoke of the ideas underlying his plans.

With reluctance, Jane tore herself away and joined her family for dinner, but if anything was said of import, she did not hear it. Her head was too full.

Mr. Ellsworth reached across the table and put his hand on hers. "Where have you been, Jane?"

She started. "I beg your pardon."

"I asked, what do you think about going to Bath?" Seeing Jane's uncomprehending expression, he continued, "Melody has just proposed it for your mother's health. Your mother, naturally, thinks this a splendid idea. What do you think?"

"I had not thought that the waters at Bath were considered a good curative for nervous complaints. I would rather think that the noise and crowding should be too much for Mama." To go to Bath, no, Jane could not tolerate that. Its reputation as a place of healing only existed to justify its status as a retreat for society. One might speak of going to Bath to escape the crush of social obligations, but they were more numerous in Bath than anywhere save London during the social season. Then, too, if Jane were honest, she was worried that a move to Bath would force her into company with Lady FitzCameron and Mr. Vincent, and she needed more time to study before she saw him again.

"Charles, do not listen to that silly girl. Bath is quite the right thing for me, even if my nerves cannot improve, as the doctor says. I have so many other complaints for which it would do a world of good. Ask Melody, she will tell you. Only do ask her."

"I am certain, Papa, that a removal to Bath would be the best. I worry so about Mama."

Trying a new tactic, Jane said, "Perhaps we should ask Dr. Smythe. He knows Mama's needs best, surely. Would it not be best to see if he thinks it will do Mama more harm or good?"

Mr. Ellsworth nodded at the reasonableness of her suggestion. "I shall ask him on his next visit."

"I could perish by then. You know how my nerves are. Really. Charles, I should think that you did not care for me at all the way you are willing to let me suffer."

"I let you suffer precisely as much as you wish."

Jane pressed her hands against her temples. "Perhaps you should all go to Bath and leave me here. I have no stomach for the crowds."

"What a splendid idea!" Mrs. Ellsworth perked up right away. "It is so much easier to manage having one daughter out than two, and the *ton* will be there at this time of year, so Melody will surely catch the eye of a beau in the fashionable set. Only think, Charles, how nice that would be."

He harrumphed. "We cannot leave Jane here by herself. That would not do at all. And no one has asked whether *I* want to go to Bath."

"Papa, do you want to go with us?" Melody laid her hand on his arm. "Say you do, please? It would be so lovely."

He patted her hand. "But think of your sister. I will not leave her alone here. It is not right."

"I do not mind, Papa," Jane said, excited by the notion that she might have the house empty of all her relations. "Nancy would be here to look after me, and I could follow by post chaise if the solitude became too oppressive."

At last Mrs. Ellsworth seemed to awaken to the proprieties of the situation. "No. No, it will not do to have you alone in the house. Unchaperoned! What would the neighbours think? You will have to come with us."

"The neighbours would think that I am safe being left alone because I am an old maid. I am of an age and a character where I can serve as a chaperon more readily than needing one." Jane put her utensils down on the table and turned to her father. "Please, Papa. I do not want to go to Bath. If you feel you must take the family, then that is all well and good, but leave me here."

He leaned back in his chair and laced his hands across his waistcoat, drumming one thumb against his belly. Tucking his chin in, he studied them each in turn. Jane felt his gaze on her as if she had just come in from hiding from her governess; she was not sure what she had done that made her feel vaguely ashamed, but she still flushed under his gaze. After a length, he snorted. "I will stay here with Jane and the two of you can go to Bath. I will contact our solicitor to see you settled there for a visit. Does that suit all?"

Jane shook her head. "You should not miss out on Bath on my account."

"I would not stay home if I did not want to. I am well satisfied to miss Bath." Mr. Ellsworth winked at her.

"I think it is a splendid idea. Don't you, Mama?" Melody clapped her hands. "I can look after Mama in Bath and you can look after Jane here. How perfect."

Jane had her doubts about the advisability of sending her mother and sister to Bath without anyone to check their behaviour. But without agreeing to go to Bath herself she could not see a way to convince her father, who patently did not want to go, to accompany them.

With that decided, the family resumed their evening rituals, finishing dinner and withdrawing to various places in the house. Mr. Ellsworth excused himself to fetch the book from Lady FitzCameron's, but since he took his pipe, it was clear that the errand merely offered him a reason to be out-of-doors.

Only Jane did not go to her accustomed place in the drawing room. As soon as she could, she went back to her room and once more took up the only book which could interest her: Mr. Vincent's journal.

Seventeen

Leaves and Confession

Jane spent the next morning lost in Mr. Vincent's book, ignoring the bustle of activity that passed through the halls as her mother and Melody prepared for their departure on the morrow. They were, both of them, quite determined to travel with Lady FitzCameron to Bath. Jane so could not bear the constant repetitions of her mother's delight at being able to travel in the company of a Viscountess that she hid in her room.

Mr. Vincent's words by turns fascinated and frightened her as he spoke of the intersection between technique and passion. Never before had she had the opportunity to look this deeply into another person's thoughts. While speaking of the importance of expressing feelings without trapping them in societal expectations, he, at the same time, examined his own feelings in minute detail, breaking them down in an almost scientific study. Anger might be channeled into storms, or by contrast, turned to become the intricate detail of bark.

She turned the page. There, in a few exquisite lines, he had rendered Beth, with a note penned below her. "Remember what it was to be young."

Only at the mention of Beth did Jane remember herself. She had not seen the girl since the night of Mr. Vincent's collapse. Her conscience pricked at her now, knowing that Beth must surely be feeling the coming absence of Captain Livingston. It was so tempting to turn one more page, to read just a little farther, but if she did, Jane well knew that she would lose herself for the remainder of the day.

Jane tucked the book under her mattress to protect it from idle eyes while she was away at Robinsford Abbey, then set out. She pulled the pink shawl she had worn to Lady FitzCameron's ball around her for warmth; the day was sunny, but she would not hold hope that it would stay warm all day.

The first signs of autumn were beginning to shew in the hedgerows and in the leaves on the hillside. As she walked to Robinsford Abbey, she collected a bundle of leaves from a field maple turned an early gold. Her eyes seemed to see new detail in everything she touched, such as the dark veins of the leaves standing out in sharp relief against amber. The day was still warm from the sun, but the air carried more than a hint of the coming cool.

Down the lane, Mr. Dunkirk rode toward her, mounted on a black gelding that moved like a shadow under the golden trees. Jane imagined pulling wings out of the ether for the steed. As he neared, Mr. Dunkirk swung down. "Miss Ellsworth. How fortunate. I was on my way to see you."

Jane blinked. "Me, sir? I confess you surprize me."

Though attempting to be at his ease, Mr. Dunkirk's face had a disturbed melancholy look. "Yes, well. May I accompany you for a short time? I would like a moment of your thoughts."

"Of course. Though as I am headed to Robinsford Abbey, you have made a trip to see me in vain."

"To see Beth?" He turned the horse around and began walking with Jane back the way he had come.

"Just so." Jane walked beside him, waiting for him to convey whatever intelligence he had.

The leaves crunched under their feet, sending spicy scents of loam and bracken up to tickle her nose. In her mind, she wove the folds of glamour it would take to re-create such a scent, but even with that distraction, her skin was aware of how close Mr. Dunkirk stood to her.

Finally, he made a soft anguished cry. "I do not know how to broach this. I believe you to be an honourable woman, and so I cannot ask you to betray any confidence that my sister might have given you, and yet—" He broke off and Jane glanced at him. The mask of ease had swept away, and all his worry lay naked on his face. Jane's heart seized in her chest, knowing with a certainty that he would ask her about Captain Livingston. She kept her features calm with effort.

Mr. Dunkirk twisted the reins in his hand and said, "It might be best if you heard Beth's history, so that you would understand why I ask you to—why I ask what I will ask. You might remember that Beth had not learned glamour as part of her studies. It was my parents' intent that she learn that as a matter of course, along with the other finer arts, and so they engaged a tutor. I doubt that you will remember this conversation, given everything else that happened the evening of Mr. Vincent's collapse, but I made reference to Beth's first tutor in glamour."

"I do. Your discomfort made it stand out in my mind."

He nodded and continued. "Mr. Gaffney came to us with excellent letters of reference. Though young, he was a man of great skill. My father had no reason to doubt his skills or his character. Ah! But how I wish he had doubted. Even the most cursory of inquiries . . . But I get ahead of myself."

Mr. Dunkirk paused for a moment of reflection. Sighing a bit, he continued. "I was away at school, as was my brother, Richard. I like to think that I might have noticed if I had been home. She was always a dreamy child, given to romantic fantasies. Once, she sent me a story she had written in which a clockmaker created an automaton of a monkey as a means of winning the love of his fair lady. Such fancy! It was only natural that my father should want to engage an excellent tutor, believing that Beth would shew an aptitude in glamour. Mr. Gaffney settled in our house and was engaged to work with Beth daily to improve her skills beyond the schoolroom glamour which every girl learns. I believe that he did start in this manner. When I came home from Oxford for the holidays, Beth shewed me what she had been learning and I thought, even at the time . . ."

Jane pressed her hand against her lips in complete empathy with his emotions, even without fully knowing the cause.

"Even at the time, I thought that Beth had not learned as much as she ought to have, but was willing to believe that perhaps she did not have as much aptitude as my parents had hoped. No one else said anything, and I, fool that I was, said nothing, not wishing to bring discord where everyone seemed content. I returned to Oxford after the first of the year.

When I came again three months later, Beth put on a very pretty *tableau vivant* for us, and I was relieved that my fears were groundless. Even then, though, I remember noting that he had stood by her, but presumed it was to catch her if she fainted. He was flushed and sweating, but I attributed that to a mixture of pride and nervous energy. Now—oh, now I understand all too well why he was flushed. I also remember the laugh she gave when she finished and how, when I praised her, she said that all the praise belonged to Mr. Gaffney. I should have seen it then. In her manner; in his. But I had been so long away that I thought she was only growing up. And him? What did I know of him? Only what my father told me, which was nothing but praise.

Shortly after, I left the family to go hunting with some fellows of mine. We were gone some days in the country, and only when we returned to my friend's house did I find that I had an urgent post from my father. Beth had run away with Mr. Gaffney."

He paused again to collect himself, the memory even now too raw in its horror for him to continue without effort. Jane could see all too clearly why Beth did not want her brother to know she had a secret engagement; it would only bring this earlier indiscretion to mind.

"You cannot—indeed, I hope that you cannot—imagine the horror this gave me. I had known, you see, that something was not right. But with Gaffney's references, with his manners and bearing, it was impossible to imagine that he had spent his time with Beth, not teaching her, but wooing her. Though the clues were small, they were there for me to see in hindsight. Her poor performance at the holidays, followed by a sudden leap in ability. And then—then I understood why she had given all praise to Mr. Gaffney. She had not performed the *tableau vivant*. He had. To mask the hours spent together and how little they worked on glamour, he had worked the folds of glamour from his place by her side. Had I but looked, I would have seen it.

The scoundrel took her across the border into Scotland,

and after a week, I caught up with them. I met him in the only manner that I could."

Jane, startled, stopped in the lane and said, "What? Did you meet him to—?" Her thoughts went to the box on the mantel in his drawing room, and to the dueling pistols it contained.

"It was unavoidable, after what he did to Beth." He rubbed his palms on his britches, as if trying to wipe off blood. "Beth does not know. She knows only that I arrived and took her home. Her virtue . . . she is so trusting, and has such a very good nature, but she was only fourteen. How we managed, I do not know, but we managed to keep the knowledge within the family."

Jane murmured that she was honoured by Mr. Dunkirk's trust, and would keep it. As they began to walk again, she thought of Beth's desperate plea that she not reveal her engagement. Beth might not know what had happened to Mr. Gaffney, but she must surely suspect.

He smiled wryly. "This, then is my dilemma. If I believe, as I do, that you will not betray a trust, then Beth's story is safe with you; but if you will not betray a trust then you will not be able to answer my question. But I must ask, so please forgive me for the burden I place on you."

He stopped. The air between them was charged with the question they both knew he must ask. Jane trembled, waiting.

"Does Beth have a relationship with Mr. Vincent beyond that of student and teacher?"

The relief. The sudden, palpable relief that flooded Jane's limbs nearly overwhelmed her senses. She laughed outright. "No. I can honestly say that she does not, and have no fear of breaking a trust."

At her words, Mr. Dunkirk heaved a sigh. "Thank you, Jane. I—" He broke off at the shocked expression on her face, only then realizing that he had used her Christian name. "Forgive me! Beth speaks of you so often as Jane that it has become more natural in my thoughts than it ought. Please, please forgive my impropriety."

Jane held up her hand to stop him, though her heart trembled at his words. "I am certain you meant nothing." That he felt it natural to think of her by her given name was so marvelous, so unexpected, that she could barely pay heed to the next moments.

He thanked her, she was certain of that, but the details of his thanks were hidden behind the wonder that he had used her name. The moment passed, faster than she would have liked, and his attention returned once again to Beth. "You have no idea how much more at ease I feel." He looked ahead to where the steps of Robinsford Abbey waited for them. "I am glad you are coming to visit Beth today. She has been melancholy, and you always bring cheer to Robinsford Abbey."

"Do I? I had not thought I brought anything with me today but a bundle of leaves."

"You do." His gaze was steady, and it seemed as if he might say more, but he turned suddenly to attend to some trifle on his horse.

After an awkward series of half-sentences and pauses, he and Jane managed to find a comfortable footing for conversation and finished with the pleasantries that were necessary to satisfy both that nothing untoward had happened.

And yet, Jane could not hear the crunch of gravel underfoot for the echo of her name repeated in his voice. Nor could she see the sun shining on the oak trees for the memory of Mr. Dunkirk's gaze when he assured her that she brought cheer to Robinsford Abbey.

Eighteen

Order and Disarray

When Jane and Mr. Dunkirk arrived at the door to Beth's room, the enormity of the history that Mr. Dunkirk had just revealed to Jane returned and drove out all thoughts of his use of her name. It added to the weight of the knowledge Jane should not have, but now that she knew these elements of Beth's past, she was required to conceal that knowledge within herself.

Jane bid adieu to Mr. Dunkirk as she was admitted to Beth's rooms, and prepared herself to be cheerful and of service to her friend.

The disorder of the room almost undid her resolution, with gowns thrown over chairs, a tray of uneaten food sitting on the writing table, and books on the floor by the chair where their unhappy owner had dropped them. The glamour in the room conspired to shroud it in gloom, with heavy folds of darkness masking the corners. Beth lay in bed, the covers disarrayed around her. Her hair was down, in tangles, and her skin was as pale as fog.

Jane could not restrain a cry of dismay at the sight, which did little to stir the unhappy maiden. Surely Mr. Dunkirk had not been in his sister's rooms, or he should know that there was more wrong with her than simple melancholia. This was depression, black, dark depression.

"Beth?" Jane went to the bed and sat beside her. "Dear Beth, tell me what is the matter."

Beth rolled over and gazed at her listlessly. "Jane."

Her cracked, faded voice pierced Jane's heart, but Jane would not let tears fall. She brushed the hair back from Beth's face. "Will you tell me? Do, please. It worries me to see you so distraught. Perhaps if I knew what the trouble was I might be able to help."

Beth sighed. "Nothing can help. Henry is gone away and I shall never see him again."

She burst into sobs, each cry tearing from her throat as if it would be her last. Jane exclaimed and did her best to console the girl. Gathering her up, Jane rocked her back and forth as she cried, incoherent, on Jane's shoulder. "Hush, hush. It cannot be as bad as all that. The world is too small to never see someone again."

With an inarticulate cry, Beth pulled away and flung

herself back to the bed, hiding her face in the pillows. "You don't know! You don't understand. He's leaving tomorrow. When a man leaves, he never comes back."

Jane chilled. Oh, how wrong Mr. Dunkirk was to think that Beth did not have some guess as to the fate of her tutor. How could she not, and yet feel so sure that she would never see Captain Livingston again? "Forgive me. You are right; I cannot understand. You must tell me."

Beth said some words in response, but her agony was so great that they were unintelligible.

"Beth, you must gather your senses. Were your brother to see you in this state, he would surely guess the cause of your upset. Already he suspects that your affections are aligned with someone. I beg you to restrain your emotion."

Even as the words left her mouth, she could feel Mr. Vincent standing behind her so strongly that she turned to look. He was not there, of course, but his idea was. What need was there to restrain emotion when they might channel it?

As Beth's sobs began to ease, from exhaustion more than control, Jane turned her attention to the heavy folds of glamour that shrouded the room. "You must help me set the room to rights, so that your brother will not see your torment."

Beth rolled over; her face was blotched red and swollen from tears. "I can think of nothing but *him*." It was all too clear that she meant Captain Livingston.

"Nonsense. You were able to think and control yourself well enough to create this glamour." She gestured at the unnatural shadows that hid the corners from view. "Only think, Beth, you must turn those same skills to creating the illusion of a light and carefree mind."

"I tell you, I cannot. All my mind is overrun with darkness, and that is all the glamour I can create."

"Mr. Vincent speaks of channeling anguish into the details of bark or putting it into the bright pain of a spring sunrise. Captain Livingston's departure would not cause you such grief if it were not founded on pleasure, so we may focus on that more pleasant memory to aid as a mask for the current pain."

Beth groaned and hid her eyes with her arm. "You make it sound so easy that I am certain you know nothing of lost love."

"Do I not? Look at my face, Beth, and imagine that I could ever have enjoyed love which was *not* unrequited. Do not tell me that it is impossible to pretend to be content when one is far from it."

Slowly the arm lowered, shewing Beth's eyes, wide and horror-stricken. "Oh, Jane. Forgive me. I did not mean to imply that you were so insensitive as to—"

Jane shook her head, unwilling to continue a conversation which would lead to Beth asking Jane for whom she had unrequited love, which would force Jane to talk of Beth's own brother. That would be an untenable conversation under any circumstances. "Rather, I am flattered that you think I am so easy to love as yourself." To break the spell, Jane cast about until she found a brush on the dressing stand table. Picking up the heavy silver brush, she began to brush Beth's hair out. Starting at the ends, she worked the tangles free. Beth slowly relaxed under her care. "Now, dear, will you undo the glamour you placed?"

Beth sat. Her movements were stiff like an old woman's, and she held her head in her hands before reaching for the nearest fold of glamour. She tugged the knot loose; as it came undone, the folds of glamour reeled back into the ether, pulling the heavy darkness from the corner. With each fold Beth undid, the room brightened, and if Jane were not mistaken, the activity also brought some of the languor out of Beth's limbs.

The change did not last long, however. Sighing with the completion of her activities, Beth sank back onto the bed, listlessness already returning to dull her features. "There."

In this instance, the severeness of Jane's face served her well, for she formed such a picture of determination that Beth sat up again and draped her feet over the edge of the bed. "Forgive me, Jane. I am so tired."

"That is only natural. You are exhausted, poor thing, and your blood is sluggish from being so much abed." Jane saw the necessity for keeping her occupied. "But if we leave the room so untidy, your brother will remark on it."

"Let him remark! Let him know my misery."

"You cannot mean that."

"No." The momentary fire faded. "I do not." Beth looked around the room, and tears sprang to her eyes. "You said that he suspects. . . . Why do you think that?"

Jane bit the inside of her cheek, uncertain if the knowledge would do more harm than good. Slowly, she said, "He asked me."

Beth's eyes widened, and she clutched Jane's hand. "You did not tell him! I am undone if he knows."

"No. No, my dear, of course I did not tell him. But he can tell from your manner that something is wrong."

"Yes, yes. You are right. I see that now." In a frenzy, Beth staggered up from the bed and began picking up clothes with a desperate fever. "He must not know about Henry. I should die—die, I tell you—if he did."

Jane mistrusted Beth's new animation as much as she did the melancholy which had kept her in bed. Watching her friend carefully, Jane picked up the books from the floor and frowned as she read the titles. *The Mysteries of Udolpho*, *Memoirs of Emma Courtney*, *Romeo and Juliet*, and *The Orphan of the Rhine*—all of them titles to excite the greatest emotions. Any one of them would have been enough to give the strongest of intellects a momentary pang of empathy for the fictional characters, but Beth, with her unhappy history, stood no chance against the powers of these combined authors. Jane bundled the books together, intent on trading them for volumes which might arouse feelings of happiness and reminders of the beauty in the world.

Beth tucked the last of her gowns back into the clothespress. Her face had taken on some color, but Jane did not give her time to reflect or for the listlessness to return. She pulled fresh threads out of the ether, weaving them together into skeins of light that she used to brighten the room, then handed them to Beth to tie off.

Jane then began hanging folds about the ceiling, mimicking the sunrises which Beth so loved. Beside her, Beth painstakingly tied the folds with hands that shook from so simple an exertion. Jane's heart ached at her friend's unhappy state.

Would compassion count as a strong emotion in Mr. Vincent's eyes? For it was compassion for her friend which drove Jane to endow the room with life. Though he would not see this simple glamural, Jane felt a new awareness stir within her as she wove the folds around the walls. In the skeins creating an ash tree, Jane put her frustrations with Melody, picking out each small insult in the twisting lines of the branches. A patch of evening primroses held her confusion at Mr. Dunkirk's actions, the petals alternating between pleasure and affront.

The effort soon made the room seem too warm, so Jane folded her pink shawl and laid it across the back of one of the chairs. Its color brought a pleasing glow to the room. Jane caught the hint in its gentle tone and, remembering Beth's fondness for the roses of the maze, she created the faintest hint of rose in the air and created a gentle breeze which fanned the room.

With a flush on her cheeks and her breath quickened by the exertion, Jane surveyed the room with satisfaction. It breathed with a life and vitality beyond the simple lines she had sketched; now it was up to her young companion to rise to meet the new mood in the room. Jane spoke, calmly and almost idly, of simple things, and in the course of her conversation, began to elicit responses from Beth. With all the caution of a hawk trainer she drew Beth out, though it was clear enough that the girl was acting somewhat to please Jane. Still, her manner was not as dark as it had been when Jane first arrived.

After relaying an amusing anecdote from her childhood, involving a pumpkin and her mother's favourite hat, Jane at last provoked a smile. "There. That smile is what I have been missing in these rooms."

"You are too good to me."

"Nonsense. I am only as good as you deserve, no more. I'm certain that Melody would tell you that I am not good at all." Jane tried to laugh, but she had hit too close to her own source of pain. "Did I tell you about running away from Mrs. Marchand with her?"

Beth shook her head, so Jane relayed the tale, provoking another smile. Pleased that she had so much more success with Beth than she ever had with her mother's melancholy, Jane helped her complete her toilet, promising, as Jane's governess had always promised her, "You will feel better if you wash your face."

At that, Beth rewarded her with a small laugh, clearly recognizing it as universal advice from her own governess, but she did as Jane suggested.

When Jane left Beth that afternoon, she had a faint hope that this change in mood might last. Taking the volumes of

Gothic tragedies with her, Jane promised to return the next day with books that she hoped would help fill Beth's mind with more pleasant thoughts than of lost love.

She wished she might find a book that would soothe her own troubled mind as well, but she could think of none that dealt with the matter of secrets and lost loves save for ones which ended in tragedy.

Nineteen

Trust and Distractions

As soon as Jane opened the door, she saw Mr. Dunkirk sitting in a chair opposite it. He started as much as she, and jumped to his feet. Her heart still pounding, Jane placed her finger on her lips and stepped into the hall, pulling the door softly closed behind her.

"How is she?" Mr. Dunkirk's voice was so low that she needed to step close to hear him.

"She is well." Jane's knees trembled from the shock of seeing him.

"I have been replaying our conversation and cannot help but wonder if I heard a 'but—' in your denial of Beth's affections for Mr. Vincent. I must ask: Is there someone that my sister has affection for?"

Jane stared at him, aghast that the very topic which she thought she had so neatly dodged had returned to plague her. "You must understand that my confidence belongs to her in this. Telling you will do more harm than good."

"So there is someone."

"Mr. Dunkirk!" Jane bit off the sentence before she could go farther. She swallowed, pushing down her angry retort until she could trust herself to speak. Mr. Vincent's thoughts on emotion and art did not take into account those feelings that arose from a suppressed secret. Jane turned and began to walk away from Beth's door; whatever else happened, Beth could not be allowed to think that Jane was in collusion with Mr. Dunkirk, or all the girl's trust would be lost. "Mr. Dunkirk, I would suggest to you that Beth's history gives her every reason to keep her interests close to her heart."

She watched as a dawning awareness took place in Mr. Dunkirk. He squeezed his eyes shut and murmured, "May it please God that she never find out the truth."

"Please God indeed! How could you have thought that killing the man would set things right?"

His eyes flew open as if she had slapped him. Mr. Dunkirk stopped for a moment in the hall, with his nostrils flaring like a racehorse. His jaw clenched once; then he said, "I was a younger man then, and full of righteous anger for my sister's honour. Understand that I would not make the same choice today."

"And yet you badger me for confirmation of your suspicions as if you *would* make the same choice."

"What would you have me do? Ignore the change in her manner? Should I have rather let her remain wed to Mr. Gaffney?"

Jane nearly stumbled in her shock. "They were wed?"

"I—Yes. They were. He had seen that as the surest way to secure his fortune." Mr. Dunkirk passed his hand over his face. "You understand why I am so protective of her. She is too trusting and too tender-hearted. You think me too harsh, but what would you have done?"

What indeed? Even now she held to her bosom the knowledge that Beth *did* have a secret engagement. Mr. Dunkirk would be appalled by how much Jane knew and did not tell. And yet, Beth's engagement could do no harm, for it was to a man for whom her family could have no objection. Surely, surely it would be for the best to remove Mr. Dunkirk's fears and tell him.

If it were not for her pledge to Beth, and the certain feeling that Beth would never forgive her for such a betrayal, Jane would relay all that had transpired. But she shook her head. "I cannot say. But you should be aware that she is unlikely to engage you in her confidence, for she is frightened of you."

He started back. "Of me?"

It should not surprize Jane that even with his superior intellect and admiration of taste in a household, that he should not think of things as a woman would. "Of disappointing you."

"Then the man—"

"Stop. Please, stop. I cannot ask your sister to trust me and then breach that trust by relating all of our conversations." Jane held up her hand to stop him from questioning her further on what those conversations were. "Mr. Dunkirk, I will go so far as to promise you that if Beth hints at actions that will lead her to harm, I will let you know. I will not let her go down paths that are unsafe. You must trust me that far, at least."

"I do."

She saw that he understood her, and her anger softened. She looked down at the books in her hands. "If you want to do your sister some good, then offer her distractions. She is young, and her history gives her much reason for melancholy. Books such as these would make any girl sigh as if her heart were being broken, and Beth is too tender-hearted to resist them."

She held out the books to Mr. Dunkirk. As he reached for them, their fingers brushed, sending a sudden wave of heat through Jane's breast. She flushed, and fumbled with the books, dropping two on the floor. Mr. Dunkirk stooped to retrieve them, giving Jane a bare moment to master herself.

When he stood, she was able to apologize gracefully and say, "I will come tomorrow with some books more suited to a cheerful temperament."

Mr. Dunkirk smiled with such warmth that Jane was forced to look away. It was too easy to imagine more than grateful relief in his expression. She had done nothing to draw Mr. Dunkirk's attention to herself other than visiting her friend. That look of approbation in his eyes, which she had so long sought, discomfited her more than gave her satisfaction.

Though it was not without some satisfaction, perhaps, for as she retraced her steps back to Long Parkmead, her mind returned to the conversation which had happened on this very path, and to his momentary indiscretion. Jane repeated his accidental familiarity in her mind, thinking over how she should respond next time, if he happened to slip again. If he said, "Jane," she could laugh and suggest that since he had used her name twice, perhaps it might be easier to continue its use. No, that would be a good deal too forward. Better if she simply did not acknowledge the intimacy, as it would neither give him permission nor tell him that she resented it.

This marked a rare instance where ambiguity would be much the best thing.

Twenty

Packing and Discovery

At home, Mrs. Ellsworth descended the stairs as Jane entered the house. "Where have you been all morning? Your father is no help. No help. And Nancy! Oh, I am at a loss for what to do. My dresses are in a complete disarray. You must help me, Jane. No one else is as tidy as you. I must be packed tonight if we are to go with Lady FitzCameron tomorrow morning."

Jane glanced into the parlour, where Melody sat curled with a book, undoubtedly already packed, but unwilling to assist their mother. With a sigh, Jane followed her mother upstairs. "Perhaps you should delay your trip so that you have more time to prepare."

"Oh no. It is such an honour to travel with

Lady FitzCameron, such an honour. And to be known in Bath as the acquaintances of a Viscountess—and not merely acquaintances, but traveling companions—will be such the thing." Mrs. Ellsworth stopped in the doorway of her room. "There. You see. I simply must take these gowns, but Nancy wrinkles them when she tries to put them in my trunk."

The room seemed a mirror of Beth's chamber, with dresses strewn about and disorder hanging in the air like glamour. Jane took a breath to gird herself and stepped in to tidy another room. It would do her good to keep busy, though Jane wanted nothing more than for the day to pass so that the morrow might return and she could go back to Robinsford Abbey. She was certain that she had not imagined Mr. Dunkirk's increasing regard for her, but she could not be certain how much of that was because of her friendship with his sister.

As she assisted her mother, the time passed so slowly that Jane twice picked up the mantel clock to make certain that she could hear it ticking. During the space of the afternoon, Jane packed the trunk three times, and then had to unpack it as her mother changed her mind, yet again, about which of her dresses she must have with her in Bath. Only when Nancy called for dinner was Jane able to convince her mother that the last selection of dresses was the one she should chuse, else she would not be able to travel tomorrow. "Lady FitzCameron plans to leave at dawn, Mama. We do not want to still be packing then. Besides, if you find that you need something else, I am certain that there are modistes of quality in Bath."

"Oh! Yes. You are quite right, Jane. And I have been needing new dresses, you know. That is why I could not settle on any of these, because none of them suit."

"Of course, Mama." Mr. Ellsworth would not be well pleased at the thought of his wife spending money on the high-priced fashions in Bath, but at the moment, Jane was willing to sacrifice some of her inheritance for a bit of peace. She tucked one last ribbon into its spot and followed her mother to dinner.

As Mrs. Ellsworth passed Jane's room, Melody slipped out the door. She spied Jane and visibly flinched.

A red flush extended from her face to the neckline of her dress, but she managed to affect an easy manner "Oh, Jane. There you are."

"I was helping Mama pack. Was there something you wanted?"

"No. I mean, yes." Melody looked at the door. "I—I was wondering if I could borrow one of your bonnets for Bath."

"Of course." Jane put her hand on the door, feeling that something was not right. "Which one did you want?"

"The—the one with the cherries. If you can spare it. I do not want to trouble you if you cannot. I am sure I could do quite well without it, only that it seems as if it would . . ." Her voice trailed off as Jane opened the door to her room.

It seemed no different than she had left it, save that Nancy had made the bed. Her bonnets were untouched and her dresses were in the wardrobe. Her paints were in their place. Mr. Vincent's book lay on the table by her bedside. Nothing seemed out of place, yet something nagged at her. She tried to pay it no heed as she pulled the cherried bonnet down from its place.

"I am certain you will wear it more fetchingly than ever I have." Jane handed the bonnet to Melody.

"Thank you, Jane. That is very kind of you." Melody turned the bonnet in her hands. "We should go down for dinner, I suppose."

"Yes. We had better."

Jane let Melody precede her out of the room. As her hand closed on the doorknob, Jane suddenly remembered tucking Mr. Vincent's book under her mattress with a memory so strong that she had to turn to see it lying on the bedside table to verify that it was out of place. It was possible that Nancy had found it while making the bed, but Jane's memory offered her yet another picture, this of Melody reading as Jane entered the house. The book in Melody's hands had been small and leather bound.

Before Jane could stop herself, she said, "And how did you enjoy Mr. Vincent's book?"

Melody halted on the stair, the bonnet still in her hand. "What do you mean?"

"I left Mr. Vincent's book under my mattress."

"No, it was on the—" Melody broke off, seeming to realize what she had implied with her denial. She did not turn around, but the very line of her back and the way her shoulders drew up around her neck gave every indication of guilt. She started down the stairs again.

Jane hurried after her. "Melody, that book was private. You had no right to read it."

At that Melody turned, using the foyer as her stage. "Oh, to be sure. Though why you should be ashamed to have such a lover as Mr. Vincent, I can scarcely fathom. What maiden would not crave a wild artist of low birth for her groom?"

"I do not understand you. Be that as it may, it was wrong of you to read something that was in my room, something which you knew that I did not want read."

"Oh, lecture me about proprieties, Jane. Do. The hypocrisy is so very clever of you, to pretend to such maidenly reserve and then to carry on with your artist."

"What are you on about? That book contains only his thoughts on the nature of art, but those are thoughts he entrusted to my care and are not intended for general consumption."

"Have you not read it all, then?" Melody threw her head back and laughed the same laugh that called beaus to her side. "My poor, dear sister. I do look forward to Mama's reaction when he comes to declare for you."

A rap sounded on the front door, and Jane leapt half into the air. Melody cut off her remarks as Mr. Dunkirk was let in.

Jane's heart spasmed. Beth must have taken a turn for the worse after she left. Before she had time to compose herself, Mr. Dunkirk bowed to Jane, then Melody. He held her pink shawl over his arm.

"Forgive my calling so close to the dinner hour. You left your shawl this afternoon, Miss Ellsworth, and Beth was concerned that you might miss it."

"Thank you, Mr. Dunkirk. You need not have troubled yourself on my account, but your effort is much appreciated nonetheless. I had planned on calling tomorrow and could have fetched it home then."

"Ah, but then you would have had two wraps, and that would have been awkward. Besides, it made my sister happy to think of doing good for someone else, even by my proxy." His tone indicated to Jane that he would do anything to keep his sister's spirits high.

Melody shook her head, smiling and artless. "That is splendid of you, Mr. Dunkirk. This is Jane's favourite, you know, so you have done more good than you might realize. I gather your day was an eventful one, if it caused Jane to go about leaving her favourite shawl places?" Her tone, the way she tilted her head coquettishly to the side, all indicated that Melody had her opinion on what those events were and thought the shawl was the proof she needed. She could have no idea of the turmoil that teasing must produce in Mr. Dunkirk, or even in Jane. To Melody it must seem that the shades of red and white which Jane and Mr. Dunkirk turned could only mean that he had asked her that intimate question which every woman most wants to hear.

Jane rose to the occasion first, finding that there was a truth she could say without betraying the trust which both Mr. Dunkirk and Beth had placed in her. "It was eventful indeed, Melody. Beth and I redecorated her room, and it was too hot to wear the shawl during our efforts. I quite forgot it."

"I should have recalled it," Mr. Dunkirk said, "but their improvements were so charming that I was distracted."

"I would find many things easy to forget in your presence, Mr. Dunkirk; I am surprized that Jane only left her shawl."

Mr. Dunkirk cleared his throat. "I—I should return to my sister and leave you—I mean not overstay my welcome here."

"Nonsense, you must stay for dinner." Melody took his arm. "Mama will be devastated if you do not."

"I should not like Beth to worry about me."

"That is understandable," Jane said. "Perhaps you both could join us tomorrow?"

"Oh, but Jane, Mama and I will be gone then. You would not want to deprive us of Mr. Dunkirk's company, would you?" She turned back to Mr. Dunkirk and looked at him through her long lashes. "Do say you will stay for dinner."

"I—" He glanced at Jane, as if pleading with her for aid. "I really must not stay."

Jane said, "We shall have you over when Mama and Melody return from Bath. At the moment, though, I am certain that your thoughts are with your sister, who is not well."

"Yes. Yes. That is exactly it. My sister, who is not well. I need to return to Beth, my sister, who is not well. Yes." He had begun backing slowly to the door.

Melody let go of his arm, seeming to realize that she was fighting a losing battle. "I am so sorry to hear that Miss Dunkirk is ill. Do give her my regards."

"Thank you, I shall." He bowed, said his good-byes, and exited.

"Jane, you surprize me. Two suitors, when I thought you had none!" Melody tossed the cherried bonnet to Jane. "You had best keep this. It will go so well with your favourite pink shawl."

Jane reached to catch the bonnet, but it tumbled to the floor. The delicate Venetian glass cherries cracked against the hard marble floor. Trembling with outrage, she stooped to pick it up, turning it so that the fractured glass caught the light. "What have I done to inspire such ill feelings? Tell me now so that I may apologize or make amends, but do not keep punishing me for an offense which, if given, was unconscious on my part. You have said that Mr. Dunkirk and Mr. Vincent hold no interest for you, and yet it seems that you resent their attentions to me."

Melody's face, unexpectedly, softened and saddened. "Jane; oh, Jane. You understand nothing. I resent the fates that gave you all the tools to interest them and left me with nothing."

"What? Gave me the tools?" Jane laughed, half sobbing. "Have you not seen how I stand against the wall at a dance, wanting to dance but having no suitors? Or the way the gentlemen come to your side when you hint at wanting them to appear? Should I thank the fates for giving me an overlong nose? Or shall I thank them for my sharp chin? My sallow complexion, rather?"

"Thank them for your arts and talents." Melody lifted her perfect chin. "I have nothing to offer them but my pretty face, and once they have seen that, what reason can I give them to remain by my side?"

There were Melody's jealously claims again! Jane understood them no more than she did at any point. She had been given the same advantages and opportunities as Jane, with the added gift of beauty. If she had not learned music or painting, it was because she had taken no interest in either, not because the opportunity had not presented itself. "They must surely see your merits when they talk with you."

"I have found only one man who is able to see past my face, past my deficit of talent, and see me within. I should not be jealous of you, but it is hard to break a long habit."

"How long a habit?"

"Since I first realized that you were talented and I was not." She sighed. "Indeed, though you will not believe it, I am sorry that I read Mr. Vincent's book. I should not have done it. I am sorry." Melody's eyes were round and glistening with tears. "Forgive me, Jane, but even if you do not, read the rest of the book, or at least look at the pictures. That's all I really did."

Before Jane could respond to Melody's claims, the dining room door opened. "Jane? Melody? Are you coming to dinner?" Mr. Ellsworth peered down the hall to them.

"Yes, Papa. La! You would not believe who stopped in, but Mr. Dunkirk! Jane left her shawl and he returned it."

"Did he, now?" Mr. Ellsworth beamed. "You must tell us all about it, only do come. Your mother is fretting because the soup is getting cold."

Though Jane's body rebelled at the thought of sitting through dinner, she recognized that her mother, at least, would be hurt beyond measure if Jane did not attend dinner the night before they left. And as they were to leave at dawn, it would not be too much longer before there was peace in the household for reflection. "Coming, Papa."

She set the bonnet aside on a table in the hall. There would be time enough to repair it after Melody left.

Twenty-one

Wolves and Muses

Exhausted, Jane went to bed as soon as she could slip away after dinner and settled in a chair by the small grate in her room with Mr. Vincent's book. A slight apprehension kept her from at once opening the book to look for that at which Melody had hinted, though she could not have said whether she was more afraid that the pages held something other than ruminations on art or it was simply one of Melody's inventions. Jane ran her finger over the embossed V. H. on the cover with no notion of what name the *H* might represent, nor why the initials were different from his name. It occurred to her that she had no notion what Mr. Vincent's given name might be.

Jane opened the book to the page she had last been reading.

I have been experimenting of late with the effect of combining a wilder underlayment of paint with a very precise, thread-specific, top coat of glamour. On the whole . . .

Jane left the page marked and skipped forward, looking for the pictures. She paused at a series of pages detailing a glamural he had done at a home in London, then skipped ahead to a sketch of a single fern frond. Though the writing below it tempted Jane, with its discussion of how energy could be saved by duplicating the threads for the larger frond on smaller and smaller levels, she turned the page, skipping through the text beyond to a series of pages shewing the plans for Lady FitzCameron's dining room. Jane scanned the delicate lines of his sketches for hints of the nymph, but did not see any, nor anything else to excite remark beyond Mr. Vincent's skill.

Past this she found a hasty sketch of the view from the top of the hill overlooking her father's strawberry patch. She almost turned the page before she saw the words, "the Ellsworth woman."

> *. . . damned if the Ellsworth woman did not see my* Sphère Obscurci *and re-create what took me weeks of trial and error with as little thought as climbing the hill. I am angry, but also filled with excitement, as this is the first opportunity I have had to see someone else create an* Obscurcie, *and it gave me an idea to try for my* lointaine vision.

When the Ellsworth woman worked the folds, she did it with a slight variation. I believe I can use the same aspect of the light folds' properties to lift an image from one place to another. My concern at this point is that the folds must be constantly managed, as one would with a recording of music, so it cannot be worked for much more than ten minutes without fatigue. Still, this is more success than I have had on my own.

She is clever, I'll grant her that. I've not seen anyone use a slipknot to change a figure, as she changed her Daphne to a laurel tree. I should thank her, if my pride were not so affronted.

Jane let the book drop for a moment, remembering their confrontation on the hill; his conduct became more accountable in the light cast by his words. She turned the page looking for the next image, and saw one of Melody, with the single word "Nymph" penned under it. No other text marred the page, only her face, tilted slightly back with laughter; and yet, Jane saw the downturned lines in the form, so that though her sister laughed, she seemed unbearably sad.

Compressing her lips, Jane turned the pages, skimming past the tempting instructional text and pausing on sketches of the doves which appeared in Lady FitzCameron's dining hall, again on an achingly beautiful sketch of the apple tree, and then on herself.

The image of herself lay in the corner of a margin, scribbled as a doodle. He had caught her exactly in a moment of intense concentration. The text around her image dealt with the similarities between the textures of cloth and of blossoms, but she could see no link from them to her image save that she had stood near that apple tree on the day he had drawn it. She lingered there for minutes longer than such a tiny drawing warranted, but her attention was all aroused by curiosity—what had possessed him to draw her?

Had he been drawing her during their conversation on the nature of perfection in art? When had he left off the apple tree and turned to her, even for the brief span it took to draw the tiny image?

Jane turned the page, and her breath left her body.

In unskimping detail, the lines of Mr. Vincent's pen rendered Jane, faithfully following the path of her overlong nose, not shying from the sharpness of her features, and yet—and yet, through the grace of his lines, the drawing attained a level of beauty, not by altering Jane's features, but through the caress of the pen itself. Jane trembled in her chair as if his pen traced across her skin.

And then she saw the single word he had written below the portrait: *Muse*.

With a cry, Jane threw the book from her and jumped to her feet. Muse? He could not mean that except in irony. She paced the confines of her room, agitated beyond expression. Beth's words came back to Jane unbidden: " . . . *he had no room in his life for anyone other than his muse.*"

No. Impossible. He must not mean that *Jane* was his muse. In those pages, there must be an explanation of his meaning. Jane dropped to her knees where she had flung the book and turned it over, flipping the pages forward to the drawing of her. Beyond it must lie the key to his thoughts, and so Jane turned the page.

Only words met her gaze. She sighed with relief to see that the text dealt with the nature of light and shadow. Surely the caption had meant nothing, or he would have expounded on it. Jane turned the page again.

Her portrait lay in the margin again, small, without connection to the surrounding text. And again, on the next page. Jane flipped through the pages faster now, finding small illustrations of herself in the margins in more frequent intervals, as though his thoughts had turned to her whenever idle.

Then came the illustration for the nymph in the dining room.

On the verso page, the illustration was of Jane, not of Melody, as the final figure appeared. On the recto, the illustration had Melody's face. Between them, Mr. Vincent had written, "*I shall employ a slipknot, such as I saw Miss Ellsworth use, so the figure can blend from one to the next as I wish. Others can only see the one nymph, but I know my muse is trapped in the tree. Would that I could release her so easily! The wishing almost makes me chuse to drop my masquerade.*"

This, then, was what drove Melody's anger tonight: that her worth was compared in illustration, and Jane deemed higher. But, oh! That Mr. Vincent saw her as a muse! And how then to account for his words to her at Lady FitzCameron's when he said that her art was without life?

How could he find someone a muse whose work he found less than inspiring, whose work he found lifeless?

Thoughts and emotions fought within the confines of Jane's skull. She wanted at once to run to Lady FitzCameron's to confront Mr. Vincent before his departure at dawn, and also to go to Melody and confide in her. Though much trust was lost between them, there was no one else to whom Jane could turn without betraying the trust Mr. Vincent had placed in her by giving her his book.

She must also consider the fact that he had given the book to her knowing what lay at the end, knowing—yes, knowing—that his affections were laid bare in its pages. She could not think. The room pressed in on her. She should go to him and confront him. But that was not possible, and so she must wait in this tiny room, confined and pinched, until morning.

If Jane could only sleep, then her senses might be more ordered and she would know how to respond; but slumber seemed as impossible as the idea that Mr. Vincent thought of her as his muse. Jane stifled a cry and snagged a fold of glamour out of the ether.

Perhaps if she exhausted herself, she might find sleep. She pushed her agitation into the lines of a birch tree, finding structure in its straight trunk and letting her trembling nerves express themselves in the delicate vibrations of the leaves. Her breath quickened, and Jane turned to giving the birch tree a sister. Reaching for the edges of exhaustion, Jane sketched a grove of trees in the corner. Her blood pounded in her veins, shaking her knees with its pulsing. She wanted to fly from the room, so a flock of doves soared above her birch trees, making her head spin with their flight.

Jane heard a door open in the hall, coming from what could only be Melody's room.

Footfalls passed her room. What could her sister be doing up when dawn and her departure were yet hours away? Jane thought for a moment of following her sister and confessing her unease, but the fatigue she had so longed for tugged at her bones. Sleep was not far away. Jane reached for another fold of glamour and heard the front door open and shut.

That sound in the dead of night disquieted her and tore the veil from her grasp. She looked out the window and beheld Melody, with a shielded lantern, creeping into the maze; the thin beam of light from the lantern cut through the dark in front of her sister. Of course, with her departure to Bath she must take her leave from her secret lover. Jane stood irresolute for only a moment before she, too, crept out the door, intent on following her sister.

If she could let Melody know that her nighttime excursion was noticed, perhaps she would forgo it, and then Jane would have no qualms about either her own or Melody's behaviour. In truth, though, she knew that Melody would merely slip out another way and make her appointment in a yet more furtive manner. It was perhaps better to preserve secrecy until the revelation of her presence might truly accomplish something.

Jane slipped down to the ground floor and then out the kitchen door to the garden. Eschewing the Long Walk, Jane made for the side of the hedge. Her breath sounded unnaturally loud in her own ears.

Her memories of fleeing her governess led her to a place where the yew boughs gave every appearance of thick, verdant growth, but had been trained past a missing shrub. It was easy to push them aside and slip through the wall of the maze, entering it at a deeper point than Melody. In this way, using a very different map of the maze than its designer had intended, Jane reached the center of the maze before her sister. She paused before walking to the entrance of the center, listening for any noises within. Footsteps, pacing on the gravel, betrayed an anxious gentleman. Jane could not enter the heart of the maze without his awareness.

The walls in this portion of the maze were too tightly woven for her to slide through without noise. If only there were a way to see what was happening inside without entering the center of the maze.

The cool night breeze carried with it the sound of lighter footsteps approaching from the true entrance, which could only be Melody. By their sound, Jane judged that Melody had entered the Spider's Colonnade. Jane had perhaps two minutes before her sister gained the center.

She wished for nothing more than to be able to see through the wall. It struck her, then, that Mr. Vincent had offered her a solution with his explanation of *lointaine vision*. She need only work the light folds with care, bending them over the hedge to carry the scene within to her. Jane sank to the ground, knowing that this would take more energy in her exhausted state than she could maintain while standing. She reached out for the folds and began to weave them together.

Throwing the skein of glamour over the hedge, she saw the image of rose blossoms at her end of the folds. Carefully, she cast about like a fisherman until the end of the skeins found a man whom Jane had no expectation of seeing. Waiting in the center of the maze stood Captain Livingston.

A sweat stood out on Jane's brow that even the night air could not cool.

Livingston paced across the garden such that Jane had to push the folds of the *lontaine vision* after him to keep him in her sight. Her breath came yet more rapidly. Jane wiped her brow with the back of her hand.

Then Melody entered the image.

"Henry!"

Captain Livingston embraced her—embraced her!—as if he did not have an engagement with Beth. "Dearest, forgive me for not coming sooner." He bent to kiss her.

Melody pushed away from him. "You might have at least sent a note."

"Please, you must forgive me. Banbree Manor is full of servants who want nothing more than to carry word of my actions back to my aunt. She holds the keys to any inheritance I am to receive."

"My father will settle us with a handsome sum."

"So you have said, but is it not more prudent to delay but a little while longer, so that we might live in a lifestyle more suited to your beauty?"

"Oh, stop. What do I care for such things?"

He laughed and drew her close. "You might care very little now, but I would not want to see you in a cottage without a maid to do the work for you. I have a plan, my love, and it will only take but a little while longer. I beg you not to betray me with your looks or your actions in the next days. In Bath, my aunt will expect me to flirt with every pretty bonnet that walks past, and so I shall, but I love only you."

Melody sighed. "Henry, I do not like the deception."

"These are only words, love, and words shall never harm thee. Words mean nothing. Are we not engaged?"

Jane could hardly hear Melody's response for the buzzing in her ears. She realized that the fatigue she had so sought was close to overwhelming her, so she tied off the skein and lost sight of them.

"I sometimes wonder if your proposal was nothing more than pretty words."

"Then let me shew you that I love only you."

Jane could not let this stand. If there were a time to reveal herself, it was now, before her sister's honour was completely lost. She clambered to her feet, and the maze reeled about her. Clinging to the shrubs for support, Jane fought to stay conscious.

At the first rustle of branches, the voices in the maze stopped. “Who’s there?” Captain Livingston cried.

Melody gasped. “Mama said there were wolves in the forest. What if they’ve found their way into the maze?”

“There are no wolves in Engl—”

Jane stumbled against the hedge and dropped to her knees in the path.

“Henry! Draw your pistol!”

Jane opened her mouth to call out, but the world tipped sideways, and the ground slammed against her.

Twenty-two

Leaving the Maze

Jane heard the sounds of wolves around her and Melody's voice crying for help in the distance. Trapped in the branches between hedges, Jane struggled to reach her sister, but the branches dug deeper into her, weaving through her flesh like folds of glamour.

Cracking her eyes, Jane left the dream maze and woke with her face pressed against the gravel of the path. She had not left the maze at all. Her mouth felt stuffed with cotton batting, and her temples throbbed with the lingering effects of her overexertion.

She stiffened. How long had she lain in the path? Her nerves tied themselves into tangled skeins as she realized that gentle light suffused the maze. Beyond the maze, no sounds disturbed the morning, save for the gentle chirp of birds and the rustle of the wind through the shrubbery.

The damp and chill, combined with her own exhaustion, would certainly lead to a fever, and yet Jane wanted nothing more than to lie in the path rather than confront Melody.

The situation was far worse than she had expected. Melody was not merely in a secret engagement, she was engaged to a man who had already engaged himself to another. How was Jane to tell her father? And once he knew, what action could he take? To forbid their engagement, surely. To deny Captain Livingston admittance to their company, of a certainty. But how to do so in such a manner that it would not bring dishonour on their family, or the Dunkirk's or Lady FitzCameron's? The Viscountess would certainly not take kindly to the insinuation that her favourite nephew had been making advances that went so far past improper as these. Jane's stomach twisted.

And what of her promise to Mr. Dunkirk? If ever there were a condition which placed Beth at risk, then her engagement to Captain Livingston was surely it. And yet Jane felt a cutting certainty that Mr. Dunkirk would feel compelled to seek satisfaction from Captain Livingston if he knew.

That, Jane could not condone. No matter the captain's offense, taking his life would not set things right. Nor could Mr. Dunkirk be so easily assured to win, if a duel were in the offing. To face a glamourist such as Mr. Gaffney was a far different thing than facing a captain in His Majesty's service.

She must try her level best to dissuade him, if he seemed set on pursuing that course.

Slowly, so as not to risk another faint, Jane pulled herself to her feet. She followed the curving paths of the maze back out by the regular route, one hand always upon the yew to aid in her balance. As she walked, she felt somewhat steadier, but nausea still gripped her middle.

Though the light shewed that it was somewhat past dawn, she saw no sign of her family's carriage on the front sweep. Jane made her way up the Long Walk. She tried to believe that the lack of a carriage was because her mother had delayed travel due to health, yet dread slowly filled her with conviction that her mother and sister had already departed.

Her stride quickened as she neared the house and saw no signs of the bustle that must precede a departure. Bursting into the house, Jane hurried for the stairs and nearly collided with Nancy as she came down.

"Lord, miss. You gave me a start. Your ma was looking for you, and here I thought you were still in bed."

Thank heavens; they had not gone. Jane slowed her headlong rush. "Thank you, Nancy. I will attend her at once."

Confusion creased the maid's face. "But she's been gone this hour or more, miss. She was right put out that you weren't there to see her off, she was. They tried to wake you before they set out, but Miss Melody told me to let you sleep. She said you were feeling poorly when you went to bed."

Jane gripped the banister to keep from falling. Gone, with Melody in the company of Captain Livingston. Oh! What mischief would occur while they were in Bath.

"Are you well, miss?" Nancy seemed only now to see Jane's disheveled appearance. What a state she must look, from having slept the night in the shrubbery.

"Yes, thank you, Nancy." Jane must apply at once to her father to bring Melody and their mother back to Long Parkmead. She took her leave of Nancy and descended to the ground floor to seek her father out in his study.

"Papa, may I have a word with you?"

"Eh? Of course, come in, come in. Good heavens! Jane, are you quite well?" Mr. Ellsworth pulled a chair out for her with a haste that alarmed Jane.

"I am troubled, Papa."

"That I can well see." He pulled a twig of yew from her hair before settling behind his desk. "What is troubling you, my dear? Your mother was half beside herself with worry when you did not descend to see them off. I assured her that you were in good health, but now I wonder if I was quite right to do so. Am I mistaken that this is the gown you wore yesterday?"

Jane glanced down at the damp and dirty fabric. "It is, sir."

"And did you spend the night out-of-doors, as it appears?"

"I—I did." Jane twisted her hands in her lap. "It is because of this that I need to speak with you on a subject of some delicacy."

"Hm." A vein pulsed in her father's forehead, and he rose to his feet, turning around the room. "I must say that I thought better of him than this. And of you, for that matter."

"I beg your pardon?"

"Well, what is a father to think? You were absent for nearly all of dinner, though you sat with us. There was a look in your eye which I have not seen before. I wondered—and you might think that I am too old to notice such things—but I wondered if a certain gentleman would be calling on me soon. I thought I should be delighted if he did, but then to have you appear before me as if you had spent the night out-of-doors, and with a delicate subject to discuss? What would you have me think?"

Jane blushed and stammered. "No, sir. You are mistaken, though I apologize for concerning you thus. I assure you it is not on my account that I come to you."

"Well then, what troubles you?" He hooked his fingers in his waistcoat and peered down his nose at her.

Now, faced with the prospect of explaining her fears about Melody, Jane felt all the apprehension that came with imparting unhappy news to one's parent. Her throat tightened against the words that she must say. She wished that she had ordered her thoughts before seeking her father in the study.

"I am worried about Melody," she said, starting with the

simplest of the facts, knowing that she would have to proceed to overheard conversations and speculation before long.

"Melody?" That checked his pacing. He sat. "She has been somewhat downcast in the past weeks, as have we all, but I had reason to hope that the removal to Bath would do much to restore her spirits. Indeed, I think I have seen a brightening over the past days."

"It is precisely the removal to Bath which concerns me." Avoiding her father's gaze, Jane continued. "Some weeks ago Melody intimated that she had an attachment to a gentleman, which I now know to be Captain Livingston."

"He has paid her attentions while at the house, but I was not certain. Well, their time in Bath will do nothing but cement the bond."

Of course, without the conversation that Jane had overheard, Captain Livingston's behaviour would seem the model of propriety. She sighed and forced herself to continue, hoping that it would not damage her father's good opinion of her. "I would that I could share your happiness even in that measure. There are two things you must know, and it grieves me to relate them. The first is that Captain Livingston has said that his aunt would not approve of their attachment. The second is that I know him to be engaged to another woman."

Mr. Ellsworth's breath came very quick. He looked over her disheveled state once more. "How do you come to have this knowledge?"

"I—I followed Melody last night. I know I ought not

have eavesdropped, but I saw her slip out of the house and realized that she must have scheduled a rendezvous with her beau. I had thought to follow in case anything untoward occurred."

"Did it not occur to you to awaken me? That I might have been more aptly suited to this task?"

Jane faltered, faced with an inner understanding that her actions had been based on spite and not sisterly regard. She hung her head. "I was angry at her, Papa. I should have woken you, but she had pried into my own affairs—"

"Ah ha! So I was right that there is a gentleman in your heart." He waved his hand to brush that issue away. "We will not distract ourselves with that. Tell me about your statement that Captain Livingston is already engaged? This brooks a certain amount of disbelief, I must admit, as his behaviour has always been the model of propriety."

"I cannot tell you any details, as the knowledge was given to me in confidence." Jane would not betray Beth's faith in her, at least not to her father, though the very real possibility existed that she would have to tell Mr. Dunkirk, based on her promise to him. "I ask that you accept my word that it is true."

Rubbing his mouth, Mr. Ellsworth leaned back in his chair and stared at the ceiling. After a moment, he glanced sharply at her. "This, then, is what I propose. I will follow your mother and sister and engage them to return home."

"They will not want to return."

"True." He grunted and resumed his study of the ceiling.

"The most expedient course is to tell your mother that you are ill; she will fret and return home at once. I will not offer Melody the choice of continuing on with the FitzCameron party, though you and I both know she will request it."

The relief that Jane had hoped would come of telling her father had not arrived. Instead, a sickness turned in her stomach, knowing that Melody's faith in her would be forever broken. It made her feel an even more conscious betrayer of her sister's trust than when she had followed her into the night, but despite her anger at Melody, she could not tolerate the thought of letting her sister ruin herself.

Her father saw some of this conflict in her face and said, "You have done right to tell me."

Jane nodded. Though she knew he was correct, her heart remained unconvinced.

Her father pushed back his chair. "I must be on my way if I am to catch them before Shaftesbury. You would do well to be on your way as well, if you want to be back from Robinsford Abbey before we return." At the surprize evident in Jane's features, he said, "I will not press you for confirmation, but I may have my guesses as to the young lady who has taken you into her confidence." Mr. Ellsworth pressed his hand against Jane's cheek. "My dear, I do not envy you. This cannot please her family."

"No, sir. It cannot."

"Still. Take a moment to mend your toilet." He shook his head and smiled fondly at her. "You look half a madwoman."

Mr. Ellsworth went his way, leaving Jane to climb the

stairs to her room. She opened the door and stopped, struck dumb by the glamural covering one corner of the room.

She had forgotten her efforts to exhaust herself the night prior. The wood she had made waved in the breeze, with more vitality than she could have imagined emerging from her hands. The level of detail she had employed was not what made the difference; it was the tension underlying the straight graceful boughs, as if they yearned to uproot themselves and move, giving the whole scene life. Jane laughed.

She had created a glamural of which Mr. Vincent might approve, but in the one place in the house that he could not go. The mirth nearly overwhelmed her, then mixed with sobs and panic and turned into a panting fit that caused Jane to press her hand over her mouth. She shut the door and leaned against it, with her eyes screwed tight. *Oh, Mr. Vincent, how should I transform this terror into art?* Perhaps it could become its opposite in a row of perfectly ordered tulips. Another bubble of laughter almost overwhelmed her, but Jane caught her breath. Whatever Mr. Vincent might think, there was a time to govern one's emotions, and this was that time. Jane needed all of her rational thought about her.

Twenty-three

The Box on the Mantel

By the time Jane had made herself presentable enough to call on the Dunkirks, she was somewhat steadier in her sensibilities. She would need some excuse to visit, so she thanked providence that she had promised to bring happier books for Beth. Jane took a quick detour to the family's small library and picked a handful of books which might suit.

Her hands shook, realizing the greater need that Beth would have for these when Captain Livingston's treachery was exposed. Jane swallowed the bile rising in her throat, tucked the books under her arm, and set out for Robinsford Abbey.

Had it been only the day before that she had

walked this path with Mr. Dunkirk? She passed the spot where he had begun to relate Beth's history, and then the place where she had learned of his duel with Mr. Gaffney, and then the oak tree by which he had said her name. There was the path which led to the apple tree where she had discussed the nature of perfection with Mr. Vincent. Had it been there that he had begun to think of her?

Jane shook such fancies from her head. It did not signify that Mr. Dunkirk had called her by name or that Mr. Vincent thought her his muse; what mattered in this moment was that Beth stood to be injured by Captain Livingston.

In short order, Jane was admitted to Robinsford Abbey's drawing room, there to await the pleasure of the mistress of the house. Unable to sit and pretend that there was no urgency to her call, she paced instead. The glamour that she had shewn Beth how to work on the bookshelf clawed at her senses; stiff and unyielding and yet perfectly executed. Jane wanted to rip the offending work from the ether and redo the whole of it.

Mr. Dunkirk entered in a riding habit. "Miss Ellsworth, what a pleasure. We had not looked for you until later this afternoon."

"Please forgive the earliness of my call."

"Not at all." He looked at the volumes in her hands. "I appreciate your devotion to my sister more than I can tell. Beth will join us shortly; we were set to go for a ride, but she is delighted that you have come."

Jane glanced at the books which she had forgotten she

was carrying. None of these would provide comfort to Beth once Jane had related the particulars of Captain Livingston's betrayal. For that Beth would need the support of her brother, and yet, could Jane rely on him to react with a steady mind? But she could not see her way clear to another course. He must be told. "I am afraid, Mr. Dunkirk, that I have brought these books merely as an excuse to call."

His manner changed at once. "What is the matter?"

"You recall that I promised that I would let you know if Beth was in any way endangered?"

He became quite still.

"I must ask for a similar promise from you; I must ask that you not settle on a course of action without consulting me, for it turns out that the matter affects my family as well."

"I see." He gestured to a chair. "Please."

Though her joints ached with an urge to flee, Jane sat, still clutching the books as if they could shield her with their happy endings. "Will you promise me to consult me?"

He shifted uncomfortably in his seat. "I do not know if I can, in good conscience. I must guard my sister's safety to the best of my abilities."

Jane nodded, biting her lip. She took a breath and continued. "As I must guard my sister's."

"Pardon?"

"I have only just learned that the same man courts them both."

Mr. Dunkirk pushed himself out of his chair and strode

to the window. Even the morning light did nothing to soften the tension in his form as he stood with his back to her. "Will you tell me who this man is?" His voice was so even and so level that Jane felt a chill.

"I ask you to promise me that you will do nothing rash."

He took in a breath, still staring out the window. "*That* I can promise you. Who is he?"

Even with his promise, Jane felt such foreboding that she needed to swallow before speaking. "Captain Livingston."

A shriek sounded from the door to the drawing room. "No!"

Beth flew across the room, eyes wild. Jane shrank back in her chair as Beth set upon her, hands slapping at Jane's ears and face. "I hate you! I hate you!"

"Beth!" Mr. Dunkirk seized his sister from behind in an attempt to wrest her away from Jane, but her hands sought purchase in Jane's hair. The force yanked Jane's head painfully forward. He twisted Beth's hands, prying them out of Jane's hair. When she pulled away, strands of lank brown hair hung from her grip. She screamed and sobbed as he dragged her, writhing, away from Jane. Mr. Dunkirk held onto her and said, "You must listen. You must be calm."

"She promised."

"And she has kept her promise to both of us. I knew you had formed an attachment; do you hear me? I already knew. I only asked Miss Ellsworth to tell me if it was a dangerous one."

Jane sat trembling in the chair, unable to breathe. Now, when a swoon would be most welcome, all of her faculties spun with keen awareness of the betrayal, however justified, that she had inflicted on her friend.

"She's lying. He would not—he loves me."

Rousing herself, Jane said, "Beth, I saw them—"

"You are not helping." Mr. Dunkirk shot a look at Jane so sharp that she shrank back into her chair. He tilted his head down so his mouth was by his sister's ear. "Now listen, dear heart, you must be calm or you will alarm the servants. We do not want them carrying tales. No harm has been done so long as this remains between the three of us. Do you hear me?"

Beth moaned. "She's lying. Make her admit that she's lying."

"What has she to gain by lying? Hm?" He waited for a response, but Beth lay limp in his grasp. "May I trust you to be calm?"

She nodded, though her breath shuddered through her body like a storm.

"I am going to let you go. Please do not embarrass us with a further scene." He let go of his hold on Beth. Where he had held her wrists, vivid red marks shewed the shape of his fingers.

She stood for a bare moment before running out of the door, the sound of her feet pounding down the hall, no doubt headed to her room. Mr. Dunkirk watched her go, his face a terrible mask of rationality.

Jane closed her eyes to block the sight of the perfect calm that masked the bright anger which burned in his gaze. How would Mr. Vincent draw that face? The lines etched themselves across her inner vision. Jane shuddered.

She heard Mr. Dunkirk cross the room, and the clink of glass as a decanter was opened. Jane opened her eyes. He held a glass of brandy, which he drank from hastily before pouring a second glass and handing it to her. "My apologies."

She sipped the brandy, and the fire burned straight into her stomach, mixing with the bile in bitter upset. "I am sorry—"

Mr. Dunkirk held up his hand to stop her and shook his head in silence. Sinking into the nearest chair, he covered his eyes with his free hand. They sat in silence a while longer, until at last he lifted his head, shewing his red-rimmed eyes. "It was not my intent to place you in this position. Nor Beth's, for that matter. Your friendship has meant so much to her."

"It is only natural that she blame me for betraying her trust. Even if she did not overhear me telling you about Captain Livingston, she surely must have suspected from his unwillingness to approach you." Knowing this to be true did nothing to ease the pain in Jane's middle.

He nodded. The only sound in the room was the mantel clock and Jane's own breath, which tore against the sides of her throat. Mr. Dunkirk studied his brandy, turning the glass in his hands. At last he cleared his throat. "What will your family do?"

"My father has gone to fetch Melody and my mother home. Beyond that I do not know."

Mr. Dunkirk pursed his lips. "Do you expect them soon?"

"I am not certain. I do not know how far they will have gone before my father catches them, nor how much difficulty he will have in persuading them to turn back."

"He will not relay the tale there, I hope." Mr. Dunkirk looked up quickly, his gaze narrowing again.

"He plans to tell them I am ill. Which is not far from the truth."

"Let me see you home."

"Surely you need to be with Beth."

He snorted and set the glass down. "She will not tolerate my presence for hours yet. I have opportunity and a carriage; it is a small enough thing to make amends. Will you—" His face whitened suddenly, staring at the window, even as Jane heard the sound of hoofbeats.

She turned, rising out of her chair as if somehow that would transform the view from the window. Clear enough in the morning sun, Beth leaned close over her mare's neck, riding away from Robinsford Abbey.

Mr. Dunkirk cursed and dashed to the door of the drawing room, then halted suddenly. "She has gone to him." Breathing hard, he turned on his heel, strode across the room to the mantel, and snatched the inlaid box of dueling pistols.

"Mr. Dunkirk!" Jane held out her hand, as if that would stop him.

He bowed grimly to her. "It seems that none of us are keeping our promises today." With that, he sprinted from the room, his face set and hard as stone.

Jane gathered her skirts and raced after him. Mr. Dunkirk shouted for his horse, cursing as he went. Though Jane called after him, pleading with him to do nothing rash, he paid her no more heed than if she were a terrier yapping at his heels. Her only confirmation that he was aware of her presence was when he snapped at a footman, "See to it that Miss Ellsworth is safely home."

Then, he was on his dark gelding and away, riding with the tails of his coat streaming behind him like the wings of the dark beast.

Jane stood at the door, hand pressed against her breast to stop the pounding of her heart. He would kill Captain Livingston, or die trying; she was quite certain of that. Jane turned to the footman to whom Mr. Dunkirk had given his order regarding her. "Will you saddle a horse for me?"

He bowed correctly, asking no questions, and within a span of ten minutes, Jane was faced with the Dunkirk's grey mare. The hostler had evidently taken measure of her and known she was no horsewoman.

Another time she would have blessed him, but now she

craved speed, not a nursemaid. She urged the horse down the sweep in the wake of Mr. Dunkirk, with no more notion of how she would catch him than of what she would do when she caught up.

Twenty-four

Duels and Deals

Jane bounced in the saddle, slamming against the hard leather and driving home every ache, every fatigue she had gained from her night out-of-doors. The mare could not sustain a gallop for long, so Jane was forced to endure walking her in the midst of her urgency. The countryside rolled past with all the haste of a Saturday picnic.

When Jane judged it safe, she pressed the horse to a gallop again. Noon passed, and she had seen no sign of any of her family, only a farmer on his way to town.

Then, a lone rider rode toward her. Jane's heart rose, hoping that it was Mr. Dunkirk and that he had changed his mind, but the man had neither the coloring nor the bearing.

"Why, Miss Ellsworth, is it?" As he neared her, she recognized Mr. Buffington, the loathed man from Lady FitzCameron's party. He doffed his hat on seeing her and turned his horse to accompany hers. "This is a surprize. I had understood that you were unwell."

"No. As you see, I am not." She gave him a moment of courtesy, though she paid no heed to her own words. When the barest minimum of forms were observed, Jane said, "Did you perchance pass Lady FitzCameron on the road?"

"I did at that. I must say, I question my decision to quit Bath for the idle pleasures of Dorset. Quite the parade of notables has passed me by."

"Whom else have you seen?" Jane asked, though she knew the answer. She wanted to know how far behind them she was.

"First the Viscountess, and then not half an hour after that, I crossed paths with Miss Dunkirk, then Mr. Dunkirk. And I have just passed your family, who alone among the folks I have seen today seem intent on returning from Bath. Who is behind you?"

"The devil, I'm afraid, Mr. Buffington." She pressed the mare forward. That her father had succeeded in turning her mother back from Bath was a small blessing. She had no notion of what would happen when she passed them, given what Mr. Ellsworth must have said about her illness. "If you will excuse me."

"What is happening, if I may ask? The Dunkirks passed me, but neither would give me the time of day."

Jane tried to urge the mare to a gallop, but she merely trotted a few paces and settled back into an amble. "Murder, I'm afraid, if someone does not intervene."

He laughed. "Oh, you women are so melodramatic. Do not expect me to catch you when you faint."

"I would rather hit the ground. Good day, sir." She kicked the mare, hard, and succeeded in making the animal start forward. Doing the numbers in her head, she tried calculating how far she had yet to go. She had no hope of overtaking Mr. Dunkirk, but if she could arrive before any mischief occurred, then she might hope to influence the outcome.

"Stay a minute!" He brought his horse up beside her. "You are quite serious, aren't you? Who murdered? How?"

Odious man! Her foolish outburst had done nothing but intrigue him. Buffington followed her now, his horse keeping pace easily with hers. He reached out and snared her horse's reins from her hand.

Jane gasped and tried to wrest them back, nearly unseating herself in the process. Buffington pulled both horses to a halt; Jane's nursemaid of a steed did little to fight him.

"Are you mad?" Jane tugged ineffectually at the reins in his grasp.

"No, not I." He sat with easy nonchalance in his saddle, smiling at her with condescension in every pore. "I think it best that we pause here until your family arrives."

"I do not have time to wait for them." Jane did not like

to think on what would happen when Mr. Dunkirk overtook Captain Livingston.

"Yes. You had mentioned that you were being chased by the devil. Do tell me more about that. I have always wondered what he would look like."

"You are sure to find out if you do not unhand me."

He laughed. "Oh, yes. I am certain he will be along the road at any moment, also intent on going to Bath. The waters are fine this season, I understand. It is unfortunate that your family must forgo them for your sake."

At last Jane's mind awoke to the fact that Buffington had the excuse that she was unwell as the Ellsworths' reason for returning to Long Parkmead. A reason that was sound enough—until Jane came thundering down the road babbling of murders and devils.

He must think her mad.

"I was speaking metaphorically, Mr. Buffington." Jane straightened her back, feeling for the first time the stray locks of hair which tumbled around her face. She must look the very picture of madness. "I thank you for your courtesy, but I must insist that you release my horse."

"No, Miss Ellsworth. I'm afraid I cannot in good conscience do anything of the sort."

Jane uttered a cry of exasperation and rage. To Buffington's dismay, Jane dismounted and began walking down the road toward Bath, hoping to meet her father the sooner. Though her hope of catching up with Mr. Dunkirk was now shattered, she could not sit here idly while he rode on, intent on murder.

"Miss Ellsworth! There is no call for this. Your family will arrive soon enough."

Jane did not trust herself to speak. She continued to stride down the road as quickly as her skirts would let her. Even with the advance of autumn, the day seemed overwarm, and her chemise stuck to her skin with the clinging heat of summer.

To her right, Buffington rode after her, leading her horse and entreating her to stop. "You should not be walking if you are unwell."

"Then return my horse to me."

"Only if you promise not to ride off."

"Sir, you have stolen my horse. You have no right to make demands on me."

At last Jane saw her father's carriage on the road before her. He rode beside the carriage at an easy pace. As she drew near enough to be recognized, he took on a startled look.

"Jane?" He spurred his horse forward to meet them, dismounting at her side. "What are you doing here?"

Buffington shook his head sadly. "Perhaps you can get an answer from her, for I cannot. She's raving of murder and devils. I fear your daughter's reason is unhinged."

"Murder!" Mr. Ellsworth's customary ruddiness fled. "Who?"

"No one as of yet." Jane, with a glance at Buffington, prayed that her father might understand her desire to preserve what little discretion was left. "My conference did not go as well as we might have hoped. I am afraid the other parties were quite disturbed. Mr. Buffington has kindly taken it upon himself to halt me here rather than allowing me to continue on my errand."

"It was no trouble at all." Buffington waved her words away as if she had praised him.

"Mama wants to know why we are stopped." Melody, as light and fresh as a new day, stepped out of the carriage. "Jane?"

"What?" Her mother poked her head out of the carriage. "Jane! What are you doing out of bed? Your father said you were overcome from use of glamour, after I warned you not to use it and now, to find you here. It is too much. You are too cruel to your mother. Oh! Mr. Buffington; so good to see you again."

Buffington swung down from his saddle and bowed to Melody and Mrs. Ellsworth. In a confidential tone, which did nothing to prevent Jane from hearing him, he said, "I'm afraid the glamour has been too much for her reason, madam, but I assure you that I have done my best to care for her since finding her riding headlong down the road."

"Oh!" Mrs. Ellsworth fell back into the carriage, fanning herself.

Mr. Buffington dashed forward to catch her, though Jane could have told him that it would do no good. Her mother would be overcome for some time regardless of the nature of the offense to her senses. A stubbed toe would be quite as debilitating as a concussion. Her father, long used to these displays, took no notice and turned instead to Jane, leaving Mr. Buffington and Melody to deal with Mrs. Ellsworth.

"Why did you say murder, Jane?"

"Mr. Dunkirk. He left Robinsford Abbey with dueling pistols."

Mr. Ellsworth straightened at that, his jaw setting. "And you tried to stop him?"

"I had no time." Had Mr. Dunkirk more regard for her opinions he would have paused. She could only hope that his ride might have given his heart time to cool from the rage and that her words might this time win their way with reason. Jane looked away from her father, down the road toward Bath, as if she might yet be able to spy Lady FitzCameron's carriage and Mr. Dunkirk. But nothing lay in view but her family's own carriage and the cluster of people tending her mother. The horses, untended, cropped the grass by the side of the road, utterly oblivious to the humans' turmoil.

Mr. Buffington's horse was a fine stallion, rangy, with bunched energy shewing in his every motion. Without being fully conscious of forming a plan, Jane walked to the stallion, took up his reins, and reached for the stirrup. Her father was by her side, helping her up. "I doubt he would listen to me, or I would go in your place. We will follow you, but be careful."

Jane then faced Mr. Buffington's saddle, and quailed as she realized she would need to ride *astride* the horse. Her dress, unsuited to the task, rode up to her knees, leaving her calves strangely exposed. If Mr. Buffington thought her a madwoman before, his opinion would be confirmed by the sight of her now.

Jane pressed her heels to the horse, and he surged forward, making her glad she was not seated sidesaddle. Mr. Buffington shouted as she rode past. She heard another shriek from her mother, which quickly faded under the sound of the horse's hooves.

Faster than she thought possible, she galloped down the road toward Bath. She turned once in the saddle to look back, but a bend in the road hid her family from view.

Jane had barely had time to get used to the sensation of being astride a horse when she topped a rise in the road and spotted the FitzCameron carriage ahead of her. She could tell no more than that it was stopped before the horse plunged down the next slope and it passed from view.

Jane prayed fervently as she pushed the horse forward, and at last thundered around the final bit of landscape that masked her from the scene. The carriage stood in the road by a field, with Lady FitzCameron leaning out of it. Across the field from her, Mr. Vincent held Beth, who struggled in his arms. Between them, Mr. Dunkirk and Captain Livingston paced away from one another, holding pistols in their hands.

She was too late. She had arrived too late.

Not until Jane actually pulled her horse up on the scene did anyone register her presence; the two duelists were focused on their task, and Beth's attention was fixed upon them.

But Mr. Vincent saw her.

Jane could feel Mr. Vincent trace the lines of her face, sketching her with his eyes. She looked down, blushing, all the confusion raised by his book welling up again to fill her senses. In her haste, she had forgotten that he would be here—she would not have chosen to meet him next in this manner. Though it could not have changed her course had she remembered; she still would have been bound to stop Mr. Dunkirk.

But what recourse was left to her? Jane turned the horse from the road and rode it between the duelists. "Stop! I beg you."

At her voice, they turned, their purpose broken for the moment.

Captain Livingston saw her first. His face warred between recognition and baffled frustration. "Miss Ellsworth! Have you come to see the results of your gossip mongering?" A smile pasted itself upon his face with no hint of gladness. "You will forgive me if I am not pleased to see you."

Jane paid him no heed, intent only on speaking with Mr. Dunkirk. She swung herself off the horse and nearly fell to the ground. She felt stiff and heavy, the sound of her heartbeat ringing in her ears. "Mr. Dunkirk! You promised you would do nothing rash."

"This is not rash, I assure you. I have considered my path most clearly. This is the only way to prevent him from harming other young women as he has injured my sister."

Jane clutched his arm, though she had no hope of restraining him. "You cannot think that witnessing a duel can do your sister any good."

Mr. Dunkirk turned his head to where Beth stood, pinned by Mr. Vincent. "I hope that this will prove instructional to my sister, so that she will better consider her actions in the future."

Hoofbeats sounded in the distance, and Mr. Buffington rounded the bend in the road riding Jane's borrowed mare. He rode half falling from the sidesaddle, but he applied his crop brutally to keep the mare charging forward. He pulled up in a billow of dust next to his own horse.

Captain Livingston smiled bitterly at his friend. "Buffington, just the chap I needed. Could you restrain Miss Ellsworth—unless you object, Dunkirk?"

"Not at all. I think it advisable."

"It seems that I am doing nothing else today." Buffington leapt down and eyed the pistols that Mr. Dunkirk and Captain Livingston held. "Are you in need of a second?"

"As much as ever." Captain Livingston smirked and regripped the pistol.

"Ah. Then I shan't worry about you."

Jane backed away from Buffington as he advanced across the field. The open space left nowhere for her to hide, nowhere to flee. If he held her, she could do nothing to stop either man. In desperation, Jane wove a *Sphère Obscurci* about herself. Mr. Buffington drew up short for a moment, then shook his head, advancing to where she had last stood. Jane pushed the weave, drawing it to the side as she backed silently away from where she had stood. Her breath came rapidly, but the anxiety pulsing in her veins lent her nervous energy.

Buffington reached the spot where she had stood and spun in puzzlement.

In that moment, Jane saw her course. If she could but keep the two men from seeing one another, then perhaps she might delay the duel until they saw some sense. Breathing deeply, she formed two more *Sphères Obscurcie* and pushed them around each of the participants. It taxed her to form the *Sphères* so far from her, but the sudden curses each man emitted as the other vanished were enough reward for her effort. She tied them off and the strain eased immediately.

Until Captain Livingston stepped out of his. "Clever idea, but it does demonstrate why we do not use such things in the field."

She moved the *Obscurcie* to engulf him again, aware as she did so that all he had to do to overcome her was to continue moving about. Tied off as it was, her own *Obscurcie* would remain intact, even if she fainted, but it took too much effort to keep Livingston masked; and the farther he roamed from her, the harder it was for her to control the threads. She must think of another course.

There was another way to hide them from view, even if it lacked subtlety. Jane reached for the darkest, heaviest folds she could. Weaving them densely, she made a patch of night and placed it like a wall between Mr. Dunkirk and

Captain Livingston. She blew it larger, like the bubble of light which made a *Sphère Obscurci*, but this bubble absorbed the sun and hid it away, casting everything within it into deepest shadow. It passed over her, hiding the field in utter dark.

She gasped with the effort, trying to breathe in the entire world, but kept pushing the walls of the darkness past where the duelists had stood.

Mr. Dunkirk cried out in frustration and rage. As the unnatural night swept over the field, one of the horses screamed in panic. Hoofbeats stampeded across the field as the beasts tried to find their way out of the dark.

Reeling with dizziness, Jane tied the threads off as a horse snorted and drove past her. She staggered on the uneven ground and fell to her knees. For a moment, Jane rested her hands in the dry, invisible grass, trying to gather enough of her remaining energy to reason with the men. "Please, Mr. Dunkirk, let the matter drop. You will do no good to anyone by this route."

From the darkness to her right, Captain Livingston barked a laugh. "It has gone too far for that, Miss Ellsworth. He has insulted my honour with his accusations."

"Your honour!" Mr. Dunkirk shouted. "Is it honourable to compromise a young woman's integrity as you have done?"

Though Jane could not see her, Lady FitzCameron's cultured voice was unmistakable. "I regret the pain that your sister has suffered, Mr. Dunkirk, but I must protest on my nephew's behalf. Henry is too kind in his attentions, and Miss Dunkirk is not the first young woman to mistake that for an especial regard."

"With all due respect, Lady FitzCameron," Jane said, "your nephew has been more than merely kind. He has promised to marry Miss Dunkirk."

Captain Livingston's voice came from a different spot, footsteps crunching in the dry grass. "Is that what she told you?"

"No, Captain Livingston. That is what I heard you say to her. Or have you forgotten your congress with her in your aunt's dining room?"

Silence filled the darkness, and then, "I'm afraid that I do not know of what you speak."

"I was in the room, Captain Livingston. I heard everything. Just as I heard you make the same promise last night to Melody."

He laughed then, closer to her than before. His voice was a mix of desperation and mirth. "Your sister? And who else am I to have courted? As I am engaged to my cousin, Livia, it is difficult to imagine why I would pay court to one, let alone two other women. How do you account for it?"

"I cannot." Jane's memory returned to the maze, the words she had heard him exchange with Melody, and then to the means by which she had heard them. "But I would be happy to replay your conversation with Melody for you, if your memory needs refreshing."

Lady FitzCameron inhaled sharply. "What do you mean by this?"

Jane turned toward the sound of the Viscountess's voice. "I used a weave of Mr. Vincent's design to listen to Melody and Captain Livingston; this weave records the conversation that occurs while it is active. It is tied off in our shrubbery at Long Parkmead."

Captain Livingston suddenly seemed to have difficulty breathing. "That—that is not possible."

Mr. Vincent spoke for the first time, his gruff voice shivering through the dark and down Jane's spine. "I assure you that Miss Ellsworth is fully capable of doing just as she has claimed."

"How do you answer now, Captain Livingston?" Hesitant footsteps sounded to Jane's left as Mr. Dunkirk felt his way forward.

"I am curious when Miss Ellsworth had time to shew you this piece of glamour, as you have overtaken us so early in our journey."

"There was no need to question Miss Ellsworth's report of it," Mr. Dunkirk said.

"I see. Has *anyone* seen it, or are you solely taking the word of Miss Ellsworth in these slanders?"

"Miss Ellsworth is entirely honourable. I trust her implicitly."

"Indeed. Have you asked yourself what Miss Ellsworth believes she will accomplish by making these accusations on my character?"

Jane added her voice to the invisible conversation. "I hoped to convince Mr. Dunkirk to restrain himself from challenging you."

"By laying out a case against me? I think it rather more likely that you have concocted this tale out of jealousy that I have never given you the notice you craved." His angry voice sounded as if he were mere paces from her. "Shall I tell the people assembled here how you have pursued me? Shall I recount how you accosted me the very night Mr. Vincent succumbed?"

Jane gasped at his effrontery. "I have done nothing of the sort."

"Buffington? You saw her press herself against me that night, did you not?"

Buffington sighed. "I do not like to say it, but yes. I came upon you in the dining room before she and Mr. Vincent performed their *tableau vivant*. Miss Ellsworth was behaving in a most unmaidenly manner."

Beth cried from the sidelines. "Jane! Is that why you were in the dining room when I saw you?"

"No!" Jane clenched the dry grass she knelt on. "I told you then why I was there."

"You add slander of this most meritorious of women to your crimes, Captain Livingston!" Mr. Dunkirk's feet crunched upon the straw, moving toward the sound of Captain Livingston's voice. Then a dull thud indicated that he had fallen. He cursed.

"Slander? I?" Captain Livingston laughed. "You accuse

me, taking the word of two silly women above mine? How could you think that I would have feelings for your sister? When have I ever shown her more regard than was due the sister of my aunt's neighbour? Miss Ellsworth states her case as a desire to prevent you from harming me, but her actions have led you to do exactly the opposite of what she claims. If the situation were as she presents it, would not a better course have been to confront me directly with her proof and ask me to make amends? What reason could she possibly have for making so very public this story of hers, save for jealousy?"

From the ground Mr. Dunkirk said, "How do you account for the glamour recording?" But Jane could hear a doubt creep into his voice.

"I do not need to. No one has seen it, save her." Captain Livingston's voice sounded above her; then a hard hand brushed against her shoulder.

Jane shrieked. The hand grabbed her arm firmly, hauling her to her feet. The cold muzzle of a pistol pressed against her jaw.

Twenty-five

Snake in the Grass

"Miss Ellsworth!" In the darkness to Jane's left, Mr. Dunkirk scrambled to his feet.

"Tell them a mouse ran over your hand." Captain Livingston's hot breath hissed in her ear. It stank of brandy.

Around them cries of alarm filled the dark, calling for Jane to reassure them that she was well. Captain Livingston shook her. "Do it. This pistol has but a hair trigger, and my anger alone is enough to make it fire."

Jane did not doubt him. Voice trembling, she said, "A snake. I was surprized by a snake in the grass."

He jabbed the pistol harder against her, reminding her of his threat. Louder then, his words serving as a warning to her and as theater for the others, he said, "Perhaps the snake is a reminder to you of your treachery. I suggest you withdraw your tale."

Jane's tongue dried in her mouth. "And if I did so, who would you marry?"

His hand dug into the soft flesh of her arm. "My cousin, of course, as I am betrothed to her."

Beth's anguished cry cut through the dark. "You said you loved me!"

"I do not know what I said to make you misunderstand so, but I am profoundly sorry for it." Captain Livingston sounded so genuinely regretful that he made a mockery of sincerity.

"Scoundrel. Knave!" The hard metal of the pistol pressed against Jane's jaw with each syllable she spat out. She hardly cared now what he did to her, so angry was she at his lies.

"Have a care, Miss Ellsworth. I should advise you not to engage in any more slander. Think carefully before you speak again."

Of a sudden, the darkness around them vanished and the day spasmed back into being. Jane flinched from the light burning into her wide eyes. The pistol pulled away from her face as Captain Livingston, cursing, tried to shield his eyes from the sudden assault of light.

Jane twisted away from him, taking advantage of that momentary lapse of his attention. She grabbed at the pistol, clutching his hands in an effort to stop him from using it.

His handsome face twisted into a sneer, and he almost lifted her off the ground in the struggle.

"Where are they?" Mr. Dunkirk turned on his heel, looking around the field.

Mr. Buffington shouted, "Livingston?"

Yanking her close, so that her arm contorted painfully behind her, Captain Livingston chuckled as he realized the same thing as Jane; her *Sphère Obscurcie* was still intact, though the darkness she had made had come unraveled by some means. Jane squirmed, trying to escape his vicious grip.

He squeezed her hand painfully, and the gun went off.

The sound echoed through the field, so loud that it came from everywhere at once. Behind her, Beth screamed. Jane waited for the pain which must surely come, but gradually realized that the gun had not been aimed at her.

Captain Livingston released her suddenly and pressed the pistol, its single shot expended, firmly into her hand.

Mr. Dunkirk ran past Jane. "Beth!"

Following Mr. Dunkirk, Captain Livingston dashed past her and out of the *Sphère Obscurcie*. He shouted as he ran, "My God! Miss Ellsworth, what have you done?"

Jane turned. Mr. Vincent had dropped his hold on Beth, and was crumpled in the grass. Blood spattered Beth's dress. Mr. Dunkirk took his sister by the shoulders, looked her over for signs of injury, and then swept her into an embrace.

Tremors of anguish shook Jane; that Mr. Vincent should

be struck down by the errant bullet undid her. Had she made no effort to escape, the gun would not have fired.

Livingston stopped short of the group. At his feet, Buffington clutched his middle and writhed. Blood stained his middle. Jane did not understand. There had been only one shot; was it possible that it had hit both men? She staggered forward, trying to understand what she had done.

Beth's scream grew louder. Jane looked at the pistol still in her hand. Madwoman indeed! But Beth was staring over her brother's shoulder at the captain, not at her. A knife flashed in Captain Livingston's hand, where he held it against Mr. Buffington's throat. Jane ran forward and brought the butt of the pistol down on Captain Livingston's head, as she had used to do with thimbles in their youth.

This had a very satisfying result. He moaned once and pitched forward.

"Miss Ellsworth! Move away from my nephew!" Lady FitzCameron's commanding voice rolled across the field.

Mr. Dunkirk turned and saw Jane standing over the captain and Mr. Buffington, holding the pistol in her hand. His face grew sad. "He told the truth, then! . . . Did you need revenge so much?"

Lady FitzCameron's footman grabbed Jane by the arms, holding her tightly. Jane dropped the pistol on the grass and sagged into the footman's grip. She shook her head, too aware of how damaging the appearance must look. "Captain Livingston fired the gun. Not me."

But Dunkirk was already being won over. "Please, let us

be done with these tales. Why would Captain Livingston threaten his friend?"

Buffington coughed on the grass. "He owes me money. Lots. He is likely trying to pin it on Miss Ellsworth. Discredit her. Marry a rich girl." He looked down at the blood pooling about his hands. "May not last long enough to care."

His words galvanized Mr. Dunkirk to action. Shouting, he called for the footmen to carry Mr. Buffington to Lady FitzCameron's carriage. After a moment of hesitation, the footman holding Jane released her and helped his fellows carry Captain Livingston and Mr. Buffington to the carriage. Beth called for them to aid Mr. Vincent.

His gruff voice rebuffed her. "I am not in need of aid."

The sudden relief that flooded through Jane swept her legs out from under her. She dropped to her knees in the grass. Mr. Vincent sat up, staring at Beth's bloody dress, and asked, "Miss Dunkirk! What has happened? Are you injured?"

Half laughing and half sobbing, Beth explained to him what had occurred since the darkness lifted. Jane, feeling as if she were in a cocoon far removed from the action around her, watched his rugged face bleach paler than she thought possible. Mr. Vincent turned his head sharply and saw Jane kneeling in the grass.

Surging to his feet, Mr. Vincent crossed the grass and dropped to his knees in front of Jane, pulling her into an embrace. Stroking her hair and rocking her in his arms, he murmured, "You are safe. Praise God, you are safe."

Jane clung to him, weeping.

"Forgive me," he said. "I thought to lift the darkness only long enough to see if you were safe; your voice sounded wrong. But I underestimated my fatigue and lost control of the threads."

Jane shook her head, which was buried in his coat. "My fault."

"No." He lifted her head and tilted it back, wiping the tears from her cheeks. "You know full well that of all the participants, you are the least to blame."

Under his gaze, which seemed to see through every layer to her soul, Jane's heartbeat thundered through her and grew louder, until it merged with the sound of her family's carriage. As her father rode across the grass towards them, Mr. Vincent released her. Jane wanted nothing more than to sink back into his embrace, but he helped her to rise, then stood at a proper distance from her. He became the model of propriety when she least wanted it.

Mr. Ellsworth swung down from his horse. "Jane!"

In the distance, Mrs. Ellsworth cried aloud, declaiming the horror of the scene, though she could not properly know what had happened. Melody caught sight of Captain Livingston as his prone body was lifted into Lady FitzCameron's carriage. Screaming in terror, she ran toward him.

Mr. Vincent grimaced. "I believe Miss Melody needs your attention, sir."

In unison, Jane and her father ran across the field to

restrain Melody. Jane looked back once. Mr. Vincent stood where she had left him, his gaze still fastened on her.

She fondly wished to turn back, but Melody needed all her attention. Incoherent with grief and rage, her sister flung herself at the Viscountess's carriage. "Henry!"

Mr. Ellsworth, running ahead of Jane, caught Melody by the waist and turned her about. She screamed, "He's dead! My love is dead!"

Jane led them toward their carriage as Melody craned her neck, trying to see behind her. "Calm yourself, Melody. He is not dead. It is only a blow to the head."

Not heeding her sister, Melody continued trying to get out of Mr. Ellsworth's arms, but he held fast. Together, he and Jane managed to get her back into their carriage.

Jane's mother, to Jane's great surprize, calmed herself and set about tending Melody.

She patted Melody's wrists and temples with rosewater, her movements surer and more capable than Jane could remember. Mrs. Ellsworth only spared Jane a glance. "Tell your father to take us home."

Jane did not need a second urging.

For the ride back to Long Parkmead, Melody filled the carriage with her upset, declaring her wrongs to all who listened. Jane spoke only once, when Melody said, "This is your fault!"

Jane did not turn her gaze from the countryside that passed them by, but said simply, "I know."

Met by this acceptance, rather than the confrontation

she sought, Melody subsided into silence for a moment, until her mother demanded her attention again.

Despite Mr. Vincent absolving her of blame, Jane could not shake the sensation that she should have done something differently. Though she loathed Mr. Buffington, she had no wish to see him dead, nor could she forgive herself for the very real upset felt by Melody and Beth and Miss FitzCameron. Even Lady FitzCameron was touched by this torrid affair, as her favourite nephew's treachery was revealed.

Too late to change her course now, Jane's mind nonetheless filled itself with what-ifs and played the events over and again with different choices.

When they arrived home, Jane excused herself and went straight to her room. The glamour trees stood where she had left them. Mr. Vincent's book lay open on the floor. She stood, breathless on the room's threshold, all the emotion accompanying thoughts of *him* nearly suffocating her.

Jane shut the door behind her, closed the book and set it on the shelf. Without undressing, she crawled into bed and shut her eyes, praying for the forgetfulness of sleep.

Twenty-six

Solicitations

During the week that followed, Jane stayed in her room, unwilling to confront the results of her actions, but small touches of the outside world crept in to trouble her attempts to regain her calm as the motives of Captain Livingston became clearer. From Nancy, she heard that his hopes of paying off the gambling debts he had accrued had been dashed when he learned, after his betrothal to Miss FitzCameron, that her estate was nearly bankrupt. His desperation was so great that he had wooed two women at once, planning on wedding whichever had the largest dowry. The neighbourhood gossip had it that he had eluded justice and fled to America.

From her father, she learned that Mr. Dunkirk had called and asked for her, but what conversation could they have had that was not filled with pain? Nothing would be served by speaking of events past. Her opinion of him could not be repaired, nor was she willing to listen to the empty apologies which his *honour* would demand.

Her mother told her that Mr. Vincent had parted from Lady FitzCameron's company the afternoon of the duel and that none had seen him since. Dr. Smythe visited once, at her mother's insistence, and told Jane that she was in good health, but needed sunlight. He also said that Mr. Buffington would live. That gave Jane her only measure of relief.

And then a knock sounded on her door. Jane roused herself enough to say, "Enter."

Her astonishment was almost overwhelmed by her fear when Melody slipped through the door. Her sister, eyes dark and haunted, looked as if she wanted to flee, despite her recent arrival. "I will understand if you would rather not see me."

"No, please." Jane stood, and gestured for a chair, too surprized to do more.

Melody sat at the edge of her seat and held out a small packet of paper. Jane stared at it for some moments before understanding that Melody intended her to take it.

The packet was so light as to feel almost empty. She folded back the paper to reveal a stem of delicate currants cunningly wrought in glass.

"I know they aren't cherries, but I thought you might like them."

"Thank you."

A silence filled the room between them for some time before either ventured to speak again. Jane considered several of the usual conversational openings, but all seemed too banal to overcome the events that had passed between them. Wetting her lips, she finally said, "I am sorry I followed you."

"Oh! Do not apologize! Not to me. Oh, Jane. I thought of nothing this past week but of how I was wronged. But then—la! you will think it so silly!—then I was in the drawing room and was caught by one of your paintings. The one of me at Lyme Regis, do you remember? I cannot tell you what it was that I saw there, but it reminded me how you have always treated me with such devotion, and I realized that all my anger at you was misplaced, because I *knew*. I must have known that Hen—Captain Livingston was engaged to Miss FitzCameron, and yet I was too foolish to admit it." She stopped and looked at the handkerchief in her lap, wringing it into a tight cord. "So I have come, though I have no right, to beg your forgiveness for being selfish and awful and—"

She got no further, for Jane flew across the room and hugged her sister, weeping with her. We shall leave them there as they exchange many heartfelt words, intermingled with tears and laughter.

That afternoon, Jane let Melody coax her down to the drawing room. Though it was not as easy as before, the old routine gave her enough measure of comfort that after dinner, when her father said, "Jane, will you favour us with some music?" she was willing to comply.

Rising from her seat by the fire, Jane said, "What would you have, Papa?"

From the sofa, her mother said, "Something cheerful. None of these newfangled songs of doom and gloom. A nice gavotte or a rondo would suit. There has been entirely too much moping, if you ask me, which of course none of you have, and yet, I will tell you that it is not good for you to be so much absorbed with yourself. You must think of others and not dwell so much on past injuries."

Melody and Jane exchanged glances at this sudden reversal of their mother's opinions. Melody hid a smile behind the fringe she was making. "Play what you like, Jane."

The keyboard felt strange under her fingers. Had only a week passed since she had last played? It seemed like a lifetime. Jane began by sketching idle notes upon the keys, accustoming herself to music once more. She pulled glamour out to match the notes she played, but the dark purples and twilight colours gave too large a hint of the turmoil still buried in her heart.

Of all the things she did not understand, she did not know why Mr. Vincent had left. It gnawed at her, and the uncertainties shewed in her art.

Mindful of her mother's request for something cheerful, Jane began Beethoven's latest sonata. The ache in her breast played underneath the happy refrain. Jane let her feelings bleed out under the cover of this joyous song and into the glamour, so that as the colours frolicked over the pianoforte, a yearning lurked between them.

The sound of a carriage rolled up the sweep.

"Who is it?" Mrs. Ellsworth said, peering fretfully at the windows from the sofa.

Jane continued to play as Melody peeked out, frowning. "I do not recognize the equipage."

Moments later, Nancy appeared at the door of the drawing room. Jane let her song end and waited to hear who had come to call. Nancy's face was red, and she kept looking over her shoulder. "Mr. Ellsworth, there's a solicitor here who wants a few moments of your time."

"A solicitor?" Mr. Ellsworth folded his paper. "Certainly, shew him in."

"He would like to see you privately in your study, if he may." Nancy curtsied, waiting for an answer.

The family exchanged glances, and Mr. Ellsworth harrumphed. "Well. I'll see what the fellow has to say." He tossed his paper on the side table, leaving them to wonder what a solicitor would be doing at Long Parkmead. Their curiosity was further raised when their father barked with laughter upon exiting the drawing room. He shut the door behind himself so they could only discern sounds of great cordiality receding into the distance, until at last the voices vanished into the study.

At a loss for what to do, Jane began playing again. Her mother pretended to read, and Melody made a few half-hearted adjustments to the thread of her fringe. Jane had barely begun the second movement when her father flung open the doors of the drawing room with such suddenness that she jerked her hands from the keys in surprize.

He was accompanied by a tall man with a crop of curly brown hair, who carried a leather binder tucked under his arm. "Mr. Sewell, this is my wife, Mrs. Ellsworth, and our daughters Jane and Melody."

Mr. Sewell bowed appropriately to each of them, but his eyes lingered on Jane. The hair on the nape of her neck stood quite on end.

"What is it? What's the matter?" Mrs. Ellsworth pressed her hand against her chest. "Lady FitzCameron is suing us for defaming Captain Livingston—I knew it. Jane, this is your fault."

Melody stood abruptly. "Leave Jane alone! You know I would have run off with him if she had not stopped me."

"Well, I never!" Tilting her small nose up in a sniff, Mrs. Ellsworth dabbed at her eyes with a square of lace. "We did not raise you to speak so to me."

Mr. Ellsworth cleared his throat. "Be that as it may, Mr. Sewell has some things to discuss with us. Jane, may I ask you to wait in my study? This will be but a moment."

Clammy dread gripped her. "Of course, Papa." Her eyes stung with suppressed tears as she left the room, berating herself for bringing such trouble on her family.

Nancy stood in the hall, watching her with wondering eyes. Jane was determined not to crumble here. She entered her father's study, grateful for the brief sanctuary she would be granted to gather herself.

Mr. Vincent stood at the window.

At her startled cry, he spun. "Miss Ellsworth. Forgive me, I did not mean to startle you."

In the week since she had last seen him, a remarkable transformation had occurred. His features had lost some of their gauntness and once again had a healthy colour. His cheeks were smoothly shaven; his hair clipped neatly. Every aspect of him spoke of ease, and yet there was a hesitancy in his manner.

Jane spoke first. "I—I did not know you were here."

"Did your father not tell you?"

She shook her head. "I only saw the solicitor."

He grimaced. "I apologize for that. It may not have been necessary, but I wished to take no chances on my errand."

"What errand is that?"

"You may recall that I lack the gift of words." He rubbed the back of his neck. "Did you finish my book?"

"Yes." She put her hand on the doorknob. "I shall fetch it for you."

Mr. Vincent held his hand out, with a deep entreaty written on his face. "No. No, it is for you. Did you—did you understand it?"

No longer trusting her legs to support her, Jane sank into the nearest chair. "I think I did."

Steepling his fingers together, Mr. Vincent pressed them against his lips and nodded. He studied her, looking for an answer in her form. Then, as if he could not stand the pain of wondering, he turned from her to the globe on her father's desk. Spinning it idly, he said, "Perhaps then, you understand—no. I will not play at guessing games." Stopping the globe, he turned back to her. "I have given you no reason . . . and yet. Miss Ellsworth, I have come here tonight to ask for your hand in marriage. Will you—will you say yes?" His voice cracked on the last word.

Jane opened her mouth, but the joy, where she had expected nothing but fear, stopped her breath with a single sob.

Mr. Vincent's face dropped. In that moment of vulnerability, she realized that he was younger than she had taken him for.

He nodded and stepped back, his mask of gruff distance returning. "Of course. My apologies. I will not trouble you further."

"Wait!" Jane stood, realizing that he had mistaken her pause for a refusal. "Yes! Oh, please, yes."

Slowly, as if glamour were being stripped away to reveal a true dawn, his face brightened. "Do you mean it?"

Jane nodded. She reached out, wanting to enfold this gruff bear of a man in her arms and comfort him, to make magic together, and to watch the world grow old with him. He met her halfway, and the last reservations fell away as they embraced.

Though he denied a skill at words, everything Mr. Vincent said in that tender moment brought Jane unbearable joy. She sighed and pressed her head against his broad chest. He tucked his chin over her head, and they fit together as neatly as a puzzle. "There is one more thing you should know." His words rumbled and vibrated through her being.

"Yes?"

She could feel the tension come back into his frame. "Vincent is not my surname."

"I know."

"You do?" He held her at arm's length, all astonishment.

"Beth told me."

He frowned. "What did she say?"

"That Mr. Dunkirk had investigated you and that Vincent was not your real name. Nothing more." Jane cocked her head. "Is that why your journal has the initials V. H.?"

"Indeed. Does that bother you? That I have lied about who I am?"

"No. Your art tells me everything I need to know." Her mind went to the glamural in her room. She itched to shew it to him.

He smiled and kissed her on the forehead. "You should know that Vincent is my given name. My surname is Hamilton; I brought Mr. Sewell to verify that I am who I say so that your father might have no reservations about the match."

"It would not matter if he did."

"It flatters me that you say so." Mr. Vinc—No, Mr. Hamilton led her back to her chair and seated her in it. "I changed my name because my family was embarrassed by my artistic interests. I promised them that I would work in anonymity to protect their honour, such that it is. My father is Frederick Hamilton, the Count of Verbury. I am his third son. There is no fear of having to suffer the intricacies of court life, as my brothers are both in good health, but it does mean that we can live in comfort, without having to suffer the pains of an itinerant glamourist's life."

Jane heard only one thing in his explanation. "You will not give up your art to return to them!"

"I already have." He kissed her hand. "I found something more important."

"No!" Jane stood, and took him by the hand. She could not explain her own thoughts as she ran up the stairs to her room, Vincent close behind her. Jane flung open her door and pushed him through. He stopped at the sight of the glamural.

He was silent for a long moment.

She waited, not afraid of his judgment, because she knew well that the glamural was better than anything she had ever attempted, but for him to understand what she meant by shewing it to him. In the lines of the trees there was a surety that she had not known she possessed. The leaves trembled with her as if attuned to the passion she felt for Vincent. A breeze caressed them, and through the glamour she could imagine his touch on the wind.

"Jane . . ." He trailed off, lost in the forest she had created.

"You gave me this." Pressing his hand between her palms, Jane willed him to understand. "It belongs to both of us now, and I will never forgive myself if you give up art. Not for me."

Vincent laid his free hand against her cheek. "Promise me that you will always be my muse."

"I will."

His eyes creased in a smile, and he bent down to kiss her with gentle lips.

In the hall below them, Mr. Ellsworth cleared his throat.

Vincent straightened, turning a remarkable red. "Ah." He almost levitated out of her bedchamber with embarrassment. "Mr. Ellsworth. Your daughter was just shewing me her glamural."

"Yes . . . I see that. We were wondering if there were any answers to any questions?" Mr. Ellsworth had his thumbs tucked into his waistcoat, and looked far too innocent for his own good.

"Yes, sir." Vincent took Jane's hand and led her down the stairs. Mr. Ellsworth beamed when he saw them holding hands. Suddenly, Vincent stopped on the stairs. "Wait. I forgot this." He fumbled in his pocket and produced a ring set with a sapphire and ringed with black pearls. The dainty thing looked lost in his strong hands.

Jane trembled as he slipped it on her finger. His face was bright with unspoken sentiment, and Jane lost herself in his gaze. He raised his eyebrows, sighed, and nodded his head toward where her father waited at the foot of the stairs.

She laughed and followed Vincent down the stairs.

Mr. Ellsworth stood with his back carefully to them until they arrived. "Well? Where will you be living?"

Jane squeezed her betrothed's hand and lifted her chin. "We shall be traveling where his work calls him."

Mr. Ellsworth laughed and punched Vincent on the arm. "See, I told you she would not let you give it up. My daughter is too clever to stop a talent such as yours." He turned to the drawing room. "Come. Melody and Virginia are standing at the door listening. I do not want to strain their ears."

The evening passed in merriment, though Mrs. Ellsworth could not stop proclaiming her astonishment. When the lovers parted for the night, Jane's heart left Long Parkmead with Mr. Vincent Hamilton, but she was not separated from it for long.

Denying her mother the excitement of a lavish wedding, Jane prevailed on her father to grant her a small private one. She and Vincent were married by Mr. Prater on the Friday after his proposal.

Jane packed her trousseau and traveled with Vincent, working at his side to create glamurals. Such were their combined abilities that they came to the notice of the Prince Regent and worked a commission for him which inextricably linked the Vincents' name to good taste.

In turn, their frequent visits to the great houses led to Melody finding a love as true as the Vincents' was for each other. With this marriage, all of Mrs. Ellsworth's desires for spectacle were met as Jane and Vincent created the wedding glamour for Melody.

And Mr. Ellsworth, who desired nothing more than to see his two daughters happily wed, lived to enjoy his grandchildren, whom he took on rambles through the maze at Long Parkmead and fed strawberries and spoiled as much as he was allowed.

Though the Vincents' latter career might seem strange for a pair of glamourists, its path led them always in pursuit of perfection. In that way, they created their own paradise through their works of artistry and passion. But those details belong in other volumes. All that is required for an understanding of their love is this small scene from their declining years.

When asked by a young glamourist for advice, Jane looked at the now white-haired Vincent and smiled. "Find your muse. After that, all else will follow. Meanwhile, your technique on weaving folds could use some refinement."

Vincent looked up. His eyes twinkled in their map of lines. He mouthed, "Muse."

Jane pursed her lips to hide her smile. She was content with her role; she had a muse of her own.

Acknowledgments

Allow me first to acknowledge the enormous debt I owe to Jane Austen, who not only inspired this novel but has taught me much about the importance of small details. My husband, Robert Kowal, deserves much praise for his patience and encouragement. He is my Mr. Vincent.

I would be remiss if I did not thank my first readers: Michael Livingston (yes, that's where Captain Livingston got his name), Emily De Cola, Jenny Rae Rappaport, Federica Regec, Mary Claire Brooks, Eve Celsi, Elizabeth McCoy, Julie Wright, and Julia Thorne.

Special thanks to Aliette de Bodard, who came up with the French terms for the various glamours. Laura Boyle from Austentation.com, as well as Keith Dansey of the Hat Works Museum, who patiently helped me with Regency hat questions.

Then there are the friends and family who have supported me and whose names might seem familiar to you: Spencer *Ellsworth*, Suzanne *Vincent*, *Edmund* Schubert, Ken *Scholes*, *Joy Marchand*, *Nancy* Fulda, Will *McIntosh*, Brad *Beaulieu*, *Livia* Llewellyn, Lon *Prater*, *Beth* Wodzinski, *Elise* Tobler, *Laurel* Amberdine, George *Sewell*, and *Alethea* Kontis.

I shall close by thanking the wonderful people most directly responsible for this book's presence in your hands: my agent, Jennifer Jackson; my editor, Liz Gorinsky; my copy editor, Deanna Hoak; the book designer, Nicola Ferguson; and the jacket designer, Terry Rohrbach of Base Art Co.

Thank you for your time and attention. May you find your muse.

Glamour Glossary

Glamour: This basically means magic. According to the Oxford English Dictionary, the original meaning was "Magic, enchantment, spell" or "A magical or fictitious beauty attaching to any person or object; a delusive or alluring charm." It was strongly associated with fairies in early England. In this alternate history of the Regency, glamour is a magic that can be worked by either men or women. It allows them to create illusions of light, scent, and sound. Glamour requires physical energy in much the same way running up a hill does.

Glamural: A mural that is created using magic.

Ether: Where the magic comes from. Early physicists believed that the world was broken into elements with ether being the highest element. Although this theory is discredited now, the original definition meant "A substance of great elasticity and subtlety, formerly believed to permeate the whole of planetary and stellar space, not only filling the interplanetary spaces, but also the interstices between the particles of air and other matter on the earth; the medium through which the waves of light are propagated. Formerly also thought to be the medium through which radio waves and electromagnetic radiations generally are propagated" (OED). Today you'll more commonly see it as the root of "ethereal," and its meaning is similar.

Folds: The bits of magic pulled out of the ether. Because this is a woman's art, the metaphors to describe it reflect other womanly arts, such as the textiles.

Sphere obscurci: French for "invisible bubble." It is literally a bubble of magic to make the person inside it invisible.

Lointaine vision: French for "distance seeing." It is a tube of glamour that allows one to see things at a distance. The threads must be constantly managed or the image becomes static.

Turn the page for an advance taste of the continuing adventures of Jane and Vincent, in Mary Robinette Kowal's

GLAMOUR IN GLASS

forthcoming from Tor Books in Winter 2012

One

Dinner Conversation

There are few things in this world which can simultaneously delight and dismay to the same extent as a formal dinner party. Finding oneself a guest of honour only increases the presentiment of unease, should one be disposed to such feelings. Jane Vincent could not help but feel some measure of alarm upon hearing her name called by the prince regent, for though she fully expected to be escorted into dinner by someone other than her husband, she had not expected to accompany his royal highness and to be seated at his right hand. Though this was but an intimate dinner party of eighteen, by the order of precedence her place should be at the rear of the line. Yet one could hardly express such doubts to His Royal Highness the Prince of Wales, Regent of the United Kingdom of Great Britain, Faerie, and Ireland.

The only honorific Jane could claim on her own was that of Mrs. David Vincent, and her entire claim for being invited at all lay in her marriage to the prince regent's favourite glamourist. As the prince regent led her out of the Red Room, Jane felt all the eyes of those assembled fall upon her, and under their gaze the inadequacies of her station magnified. The dove silk which had seemed so fine when she had commissioned it last summer now seemed drab and shabby by comparison to gowns such as Lady Hertford's rich claret velvet, which had long sleeves slashed to allow peeks at a cloth of silver. Her mother had wanted to buy her a new gown, but Jane had resisted. She was an artisan now, and had no intention of pretending to be high society. . . . And yet, being escorted by the prince regent made that choice seem less easy now.

But all that worry dropped away as she entered the dining hall, which glittered and dripped with diaphanous folds of glamour hung to create the illusion of a water folly filled with mermaids and sea horses. She and Vincent had laboured for the past three months on the spectacle and they could justly be proud of the effect, though she would have to retouch the anemones when she had a chance. The colour was off when compared to the palette of this winter's fashions.

The prince regent stopped with her on the threshold and inhaled in pleasure.

They had taken the octagonal ballroom designed by Mr. John Nash for the fête honouring the defeat of Napoleon and transformed it for the coming New Year's Eve celebration by remodelling it as the home of a sea king. Elaborate swathes of glamour masked the walls so that they appeared to be in the midst of a coral palace with views onto an undersea world. Past the crenellations of the illusionary walls, brilliant tropical fish schooled in waves of shimmering colour. Light seemed to filter down through clear blue water to lay dappled on the crisp white tablecloths.

The prince regent smiled and patted her hand where it lay on the dark blue cloth of his arm. "My dear Mrs. Vincent. I have long been an admirer of your husband's work, but you have led him to new heights of glory."

"You honour me, your highness, far more than I think I deserve."

"I honour you as much as *I* think you deserve, and you must grant that my wishes are the law in this land."

Jane let him lead her swiftly across the vast ballroom to the head of the table and place her by the chair on his right hand. Only then did Jane understand the true gift the prince regent offered her. They had far outpaced the guests immediately behind them, who paused on the threshold, apparently overcome by the room. As the line forced them forward, they proceeded towards the table, but slowly, with eyes fixed in wonder on the illusion. Positioned as she was, Jane stood in a perfect place to witness the the guests' approbation over and over again as even the most jaded of them halted to gasp upon the threshold.

Their faces shone with wonder at the work she and Vincent had created.

As the last couple approached, his royal highness leaned over and whispered in her ear, "Now watch."

Her husband stood on the threshold, escorting in Lady Hertford. The prince regent began to applaud, and, as one, his guests joined him in saluting Mr. Vincent. Jane did not know whether to applaud with them out of her own deep admiration for her husband, or if she should remain silent, since she had borne half the burden of the work about them. She settled for clasping her hands at her breast and letting forth an unfettered smile.

Vincent paused, clearly taken aback by this overt shew of acclaim. He inclined his head gravely, then, straightening, led Lady Hertford to the foot of the table and her place at his right hand. Never comfortable in company, the sternness of his face masked what Jane knew to be very real feeling.

The prince regent reached for his glass and raised it. "To Mr. Vincent and to his bride, who shews us that he is no longer a glamourist without peer."

Jane blushed at the attention as every head swivelled to her. She could see them recalculating her worth and now understanding why the prince regent had led such an unprepossessing woman into dinner. Under the weight of their stares, her gaze fell to the table, taking refuge among the plate and crystal assembled there. Her relief when the prince pulled her chair out and seated her could scarcely be imagined.

Accustomed as she was to the more retiring life on her father's country estate, Jane had not looked for any honours when she married Mr. Vincent. The few scant months of their marriage had been filled with work and the joy of learning to shape their lives together. This commission had seemed honour enough when it had come, almost as if it were a wedding gift from the prince regent.

Around them, the footmen began bringing out the first course, a turtle soup. Jane was glad to have the activity distract attention from her. She took advantage of the respite to gather herself so that when the prince regent next addressed her, she would be better prepared for conversation.

The initial topics were of such amicable and unstrenuous weight as the weather, and if she thought it might snow on the morrow. She did not and said so.

This relieved his royal highness, as the press of carriages expected for the New Year's Eve festivities would be immense. By the time the soup was cleared, Jane felt somewhat more at ease and was able to engage the prince regent in a conversation about music, a topic on which they shared some common ground.

"You must allow that Rossini is far superior to the fluff that Spohr is passing off as composition. It staggers me that the Italian fellow is not better known." The prince regent placed his spoon in his soup bowl, signalling to the footmen that it was time to clear the table and move on to the next course.

"I have not had the privilege of hearing his music performed in earnest, so I am not a good judge, I am afraid."

He snorted. "You only have to examine the page to see the difference between them. One's music flows with the inevitability of a stream, the other staggers from theme to theme like a drunken beggar." He lifted his glass and nodded over it to the gentleman on her left. "Am I not right, Skiffy?"

On her left, Sir Lumley St. George Skeffington abandoned the conversation with his dinner partner to answer. "Of course you are right. When are you ever not? But what is it that you are right about this time?"

"I suggest that Rossini is superior to Spohr."

"Oh." Sir Lumley waved his hand dismissively. "I do not follow such things. Ask me about a tailor and I might honour you with an opinion."

The prince regent smiled, and glanced sidewise at Jane. "Then pray, tell me what you think of Monsieur Lecomte?"

"Oh! Horrid. Horrid, I tell you. I have never seen a man with less understanding of the nature of cloth than he displays. Why, did you know that I went in on the recommendation of a friend, whose advice I shall not favour henceforth, and Monsieur Lecomte had the temerity to suggest superfine cloth? To me?" He took out a perfumed handkerchief and dabbed at his forehead. "I spun on my heel and left without another sign. It was clear he was not *current*."

Smiling, the prince regent adjusted the sleeve of his coat, which was, Jane was startled to note, cut from superfine cloth. "So, you see, Mrs. Vincent, he does not always agree with me."

Sir Lumley leaned back in his chair in a shew of mock horror. "Now, Prinny, you do not mean to tell me that you have graced M. Lecomte with your business?"

"I was, I confess, curious to see how a man who claimed to have worked for Napoleon might measure against our good English tailors."

Jane smiled in polite interest. When the silence seemed to indicate that it was her turn to speak, she ventured to ask, "How did you find him, your highness?"

The prince considered for a moment and then offered a single word: "Posturing."

"And yet you wear the coat he made for you?" Jane studied the coat. It was cut along French lines, but she had begun to grow used to that as the fashionable set raced to catch up with the other side of the Channel. "Might I inquire as to why?"

"It amuses me."

Jane was uncertain if that amusement stemmed from the tailor or from the near apoplexy he had brought on in Sir Lumley. Her attention was distracted from this question, for, in examining the prince's coat, she happened to spy the glamural beyond him. She could barely stifle an "Oh!" at what she beheld and kept her demeanour placid only with some difficulty.

Behind a window in the coral, they had placed a school of iridescent fish, swimming past at intervals. The effect had been achieved by measuring out a long spool of thin glamour which contained no illusion save for occasional bubbles, and then looping it around to tie to the fish. Though Jane had used such threads of empty space before, she had worked with none so long as this. It had required her to stand in one place to manipulate the thread for exactly as long as she had wanted the interval to be. Her husband had but recently shewed her his technique of braiding seemingly like threads together at somewhat different lengths to create the appearance of random intervals. Jane had created the fish thrice, one that came at three minutes, one at five, and one at eight. It created the illusion of but one school of fish, swimming past at random moments.

And yet, as she watched, two schools of fish went by hard on the tails of one another.

"Do you not think so, Mrs. Vincent?" His royal highness leaned close to her, smiling.

Jane blinked, alarmed that she had lost all trace of the conversation. "I could hardly dare to venture an opinion."

"You do your husband wrong, if you should not vouch for him."

She would do her husband more wrong if her fears about the fish were correct, and yet to admit that she had been ignoring the prince would not do. Jane sought for some answer that would serve. "But you see, your highness, as his wife I am over-partial to him and cannot be trusted to give an unbiased opinion. I must bow to yours."

"Then I will make it so, and trust that it give you some pleasure as well." The prince regent lifted the asparagus tongs and offered her a few delicate spears.

Jane nodded her assent, without having the least idea of what he would make so, while darting glances at the window where the fish appeared. If she unfocused her attention on the tangible world and let her vision slip into that realm of ether where the folds of glamour lay, she could study the thread as it flowed past. From watching others, she knew that such distraction gave her countenance a somewhat vacuous expression which might be appealing on certain beauties, but not on her own unassuming plainness. It was too at odds with the sharpness of her features to be pleasing.

The knot went past. It had, as Jane suspected, slipped. What alarmed her more was that it shewed every sign that it was on the verge of coming untied altogether. She tried to remember what she had anchored that thread of glamour around.

"And have you been to the continent before, Mrs. Vincent?"

The question brought Jane's attention back to the table. "I have not, your highness."

"Then I suggest avoiding the north of France when you go, though I cannot remember where Mr. Vincent said his colleague lived. Still, I counsel against it, as well as parts of Spain and Italy. While Napoleon has abdicated, there are still factions that would seek to put his son on the throne. I think it shall be calmed by the time you travel, but you must let me make some arrangements for your tour."

Jane was all astonishment. To the best of her knowledge, neither she nor Vincent had spoken of going abroad, and yet the prince regent spoke as if it were a surety that they would go. "Your highness—"

He held up his hand. "Mrs. Vincent, you must do me the favour of not using my title with every sentence. It does wear on one. In an intimate setting such as this, I would rather be reminded that I dine with friends than that I am prince. I shall have enough of that tomorrow, and while it does have its merits, one enjoys it only for a time."

He referred, of course, to the grand opening of the ballroom to the public, in which he would dine in great state. Once the ballroom was open, there would be no opportunity for repairs. Jane would have to attend to the fish as soon as dinner had completed, lest they unravel further.

"Of course . . . and yet, one must call you something."

"Oh, as to that"—Sir Lumley again disregarded his duties to his dinner partner to drawl—"we all call him 'Prinny.' I dare say he would like you to do the same."

"Oh yes, would you do me that kindness?"

"And you shall call me Skiffy." Sir Lumley leaned in close. "We are all terribly fond of you, for your husband's sake."

Not for her own, but this could hardly surprize Jane. She assayed a smile while trying to recall where the thread of glamour went. "Thank you for the honour. And have you known each other long?" In this manner, she hoped to distract the gentlemen to talk between themselves. No matter how rude that might make Sir Lum—Skiffy to his dinner partner, it would grant her some brief span in which to puzzle out the fish. While Vincent had created glamurals this elaborate before, if perhaps on a smaller scale, it was the most intricate work which Jane had yet attempted, and the sheer number of threads, folds, weaves, and braids of glamour overwhelmed her memory.

"Prinny had come down to Eaton for a fête back when your husband was still a Hamil—" Skiffy cleared his throat, just avoiding pronouncing the name that Vincent had renounced. "Even in those days Vincent had the reputation of being a curmudgeon. Though we were all terribly fond of him."

Jane's attention was now split in two. On the one hand, she worried about the fish, for, if on their first commission together, she introduced a flaw into their work, it would not bode well for their future projects. And yet, Vincent so rarely talked about his life before giving up his family name to pursue his art that her curiosity was piqued beyond all else.

"Your husband had glamoured the clock tower so it shewed the time backwards!" The prince—Prinny—threw his head back and laughed.

Skiffy picked up the tale again. "Oh, the deans were furious at that one, because he had managed to tie the glamour off so it did not shew in the least. In any case, they could not conceive of how someone might have gotten up the clock tower to weave one. Which shewed your husband's cleverness, for he did not climb the tower at all."

"No? How did he do it then?" Jane's interest in her question faltered almost at once as she finally traced the thread of glamour to its source. The fish's trailing line was wrapped around the support for the coral reef comprising the wall opposite her. She had thought herself frightfully clever for finding a way to contain it thus without having to loop the thread into the earth for stability, but the trouble she now faced was that if the knot came undone all at once, it might snag and cause an unravelling in the wall as well.

Prinny chuckled again. "Your husband created it from the base of the tower."

Jane choked on her turbot at this and had to hold her serviette to her lips to stifle her coughing. The prince patted her on the back and passed her a glass of water.

"Thank you." She cleared her throat, conscious of once again attracting more attention from the table than she might have wished.

At the foot of the table, Vincent studied her, his brows raised in concern. She gave him the smallest shake of her head, to let him know that she did not require his aid, though she desperately wished that she were near him. One of the distinct disadvantages of being married was that one never sat with one's spouse when dining in company.

Giving the prince regent her attention, Jane kept her composure smooth. "Though I above all should be partial to my husband's talents, still I find my credulity stretched by this."

Even with her deep admiration for her husband's skills, Jane could scarcely imagine the sheer strength it would take to work glamour from such a distance. As with a small stone, in the hand it might seem to weigh nothing, but if one held it at the end of a rod, it became increasingly difficult to manage. Though glamour borrowed the language of textiles to describe it, there were ways in which the manipulation of glamour also resembled water. One might direct a jet across a fountain, but it always wanted to return to the ground, widening into a mist as it arced downward. So too, with glamour: a glamourist could hold a strand of light pulled from the ether and direct it across a room, only to see it bend and lose its resolution. A skilled glamourist learned to adjust the ways in which the strand left his hands to compensate for its propensity to return to the ether, but it took much greater effort than producing a glamour at close range. To create a glamour from the base of a clock tower would have required great strength and steadiness of hand.

"Oh, it is quite true." Skiffy leaned in again, so that she could see the powder on his cheeks. "They all thought that something had gone wrong with the mechanism, and were after the clock-keeper's head. The poor fellow was up to his arms in the gears when Hami—when Vincent relented and undid the glamour. It happened right as the fellow pulled out a gear that truly broke the clock. Do you know what your husband did then? The great curmudgeon proved that it was all an act, for he stood beneath the clock tower and retied his glamour so that it shewed the clock running the correct direction. He saved the clock-keeper's job by that, and I think it very handsome of him."

Jane could not be surprized by the generosity her husband had shewn, but her attention was drawn again to that detail of distance in Skiffy's telling. If Vincent were able to manipulate a glamour to create a clock illusion from so great a distance, perhaps he could retie the knot in the fish without drawing unwelcome attention to himself. Jane would have to stand and walk over to the section of the wall, which, besides the attention it would draw to her, would be rude to his royal highness . . . *Prinny*, that is.

At the foot of the table, Vincent was now engaged in conversation with Lady Hertford. He did not spare a glance in her direction. Her attempt to reassure him had, it seemed, been too successful.

Perhaps her fears were amplified by the company she kept, and yet Jane could not help thinking of the courses yet to come and estimating the time which remained for the dinner. Would the knot continue to slip, or might it hold through the meal? She pushed the asparagus on her plate, unable to think of anything else. While the question of a few fish might seem but a trifle, to Jane, placed as she was in a position above her rank merely on the merits of the work around them, the thought of having the glamour *fail* at this moment was a thing of horror. To be sure, knots did sometimes come undone, but the prince regent, for all that he styled himself Prinny, had not paid them for inferior work. Left to its own, it would come undone before the end of dinner, and it would likely damage the coral with it. The work they would have before them to have it repaired in time for the official opening of the ballroom tomorrow would be immense.

Jane bit the inside of her mouth. No. No matter how honoured they were by this small dinner, the simple fact was that her role in life had shifted from guest to artisan, and, as such, her duties were clear. She set her knife and fork on the table and lifted the serviette out of her lap.

The prince stopped in mid-sentence, and Jane realized that she had again lost track of his conversation. "Are you unwell, Mrs. Vincent?"

"I am quite well, thank you." She could not bring herself to call him Prinny. "Only I have noticed a spot in the glamour which I must attend to."

"Now? During dinner? Surely you have worked hard enough to have some rest." The prince shook his head in wonder. "I see why Mr. Vincent finds you so appealing. You have the same focus on work that he does."

"And yet, not his skills. I am afraid that if the knot I have noticed comes undone it will require more effort to fix later. It will be but a moment, and then I shall be better able to focus on enjoying the evening."

Scooting his chair back, the prince regent said, "I know the artist's temperament too well to attempt to dissuade you again."

For that, at least, Jane was grateful. But when he arose to pull out her chair, conversation in the room stopped and all the guests attempted to rise themselves, unable to remain seated while their prince stood. Vincent rose as well, his face filled with alarm. The prince regent waved them back to their seats before retaking his own seat.

Jane smiled with as little concern as she could muster, though her heart raced as if she had already begun to work the glamour. "Please ignore me. I do not wish to disturb."

Keeping her head down, Jane walked across the ballroom floor as quickly as she could.

In moments, Vincent was by her side. "Jane, are you well?" His low voice grumbled in his chest, but the hand he pressed against her elbow spoke of deep concern.

"Embarrassed, rather. This school of fish is coming untied." She stopped in front of the window in the coral and reached out to grasp the line of glamour that the fish looped round on. "Please sit down. There is no sense in both of us standing here. It will be some moments before it comes around again, and as this is one of my illusions, the error is entirely my fault." Letting the thread trail loosely in her fingers, she waited for the knot to come around again.

Vincent did not move from her side, and she could feel the warmth of him even through the heavy material of his coat. It was Bath coating, not the superfine which "Skiffy" so abhorred. Jane took a strange and momentary pleasure in that before she chided herself. They were not fashionable members of society who had to worry about such things, and being in such people's company would seduce her into wanting pretty things which she did not need. Still, she thought that her husband cut a fine picture, and that there was no harm in thinking so.

"Will you not sit?" She turned to find him staring at her with a disarming smile.

"Because you ask, I shall. Muse." He leaned forward as if to kiss her, and then glanced sidewise at the company, who had *all* turned in their seats to watch them. Straightening, he offered her the most correct of courtesies from husband to wife, and returned to his seat.

Jane set her back to the rest of the ballroom, grateful for that pretence of privacy. When the knot came under her fingers, she tightened her grasp to stop the fish. Carefully, she inched the two schools towards the proper relation to one another and then tied the knot with a triple hitch. It was less elegant than the cloverdale special she had used before, but it was unlikely to come undone.

Letting her attention return to the room, she stepped back from her work and was pleased to note that the diners had stopped paying her any heed. In truth, even the most astute observer would have noted only a woman standing with her back to the room, because the adjustments she had to make to the glamour were too subtle to be noticed. Only Vincent watched her, and offered her one of his rare and radiant smiles. Flushed more than the small amount of glamour merited, Jane returned to her seat, managing to slip into it with the aid of a footman before the prince regent noticed that she had rejoined the table.

She was thus prepared to enjoy the rest of the meal . . . until the table turned, of course.